Such Stuff

First published 2016 by Walker Books Ltd
87 Vauxhall Walk, London SE11 5HJ

This edition published 2017

2 4 6 8 10 9 7 5 3 1

Text © 2016 Michael Morpurgo, Clare Morpurgo and Mark Morpurgo
Illustrations © 2016 Michael Foreman

The right of Michael Morpurgo, Clare Morpurgo, Mark Morpurgo and
Michael Foreman to be identified as the authors and illustrator respectively
of this work has been asserted by them in accordance with the Copyright,
Designs and Patents Act 1988

This book has been typeset in Optima and Sabon

Printed in Great Britain by Clays Ltd, St Ives plc

British Library Cataloguing in Publication Data:
a catalogue record for this book is available from the British Library

ISBN 978-1-4063-7367-7

www.walker.co.uk

MICHAEL MORPURGO

Such Stuff

a story-maker's inspiration

Clare Morpurgo & Mark Morpurgo

Illustrated by Michael Foreman

WALKER BOOKS

For Kippe and Jack, and Tony
M.M.

Contents

Introduction

I don't go looking for ideas for my stories. They just seem to come to me. I've always been very lucky that way. Of course, like any writer or artist, I keep eyes and ears and heart and mind open and alert; my feelers, my antennae always out. That is how all of us catch our dreams. Much of *Such Stuff* explains how I have done this with my books, which of course is why it is called "Such Stuff as dreams are made on". Not my words of course, but William Shakespeare's, from *The Tempest*. Reassuring to know that Shakespeare used the same source material for his dreams as I do: memories, history, war and peace, the lives of others, the times we live in, the people and places we know and care about.

I am also very receptive to the ideas of others for my books. So many have been suggested in the first place by friends and family, by publishers and illustrators (particularly Michael Foreman, the instigator of a dozen or more of my stories, and the illustrator of this book too). In this case, though, it was my younger brother Mark who came up with the idea. Mark has very kindly often come along with his wife Linda to talks I have given at festivals, particularly in Scotland where they live. He had noticed that by far the most common question asked at these events was: "How do you come up with your ideas?". Sometimes it was a general question about inspiration, Mark said, but more often it was specific to one book. And over the years he had heard me tell the story behind just about every single one of my stories, heard me talk often of the seed of a story and the growing of it in my mind, in my research, in my dreamtime. And, Mark kindly pointed out, "because the question is so often asked, you do rather too often, repeat yourself. Then of course I have to sit there and listen to it all over again. Not that I am complaining, much. In fact not at all. It is really interesting for a reader to know what gives rise to a story in the first place, the history, the anecdotal background, the cause. So, why don't you write a book that definitively answers this question?"

So that is what we have done. In this book I have revealed the memories, stories and history, the people and the places, that weave themselves, dream themselves into many of my stories. Mark has researched the historical roots, the facts and figures of the historical truths and myths that do often run through my books. And Clare, chief collaborator on all my books over the last forty or more years, and my wife too, has picked out an excerpt from each book, to encourage you to read the rest! Well, she is the daughter of a publisher. And Rosalind Morpurgo took on the huge task of reading all our scribbles and getting the manuscript typed and into good shape. So this is very much a family book, made together, by all four of us. We hope you enjoy reading it as much as we loved making it.

Michael Morpurgo.

PS If you allowed a PS to an introduction, I want to thank Michael Foreman, Gill Evans and everyone at the wonderful Walker Books for taking on this unlikely book and enabling it to happen. Thanks to William Shakespeare too who helped with the title.

War Horse

THE DREAM

For all sorts of reasons, when the time came in 1980, at thirty-seven years of age, I was ready to write *War Horse*, and later *Farm Boy*, too, which is almost a sequel, but not quite. To begin with, I was a child of war. I grew up in London just after the Second World War. Next door to us, in Philbeach Gardens, was a bombsite, where we played – no one ever invented a better or more sinister adventure playground. Right by my school, St Matthias in the Warwick Road, there was another bombsite, a forbidden and therefore fascinating place. You got the ruler on the back of your hand if you crawled in there. I got the ruler on the back of my hand a lot. We had rationing. Sometimes I was allowed to carry the ration book for my mother when we went shopping – maybe the first proper responsibility I ever had. One-legged soldiers sat on street corners, wearing their medals, begging. We played war in the streets and bombsites, in the school playground, us against the Germans. If you were picked as a German, you had to die and lose in the end. We learnt *Achtung!* and *Heil Hitler!* from the war comics we read. We sang songs about Hitler, and learnt that Himmler was very "sim'lar".

Then there were the tears, my mother's tears on the anniversary of my Uncle Pieter's death in the RAF. His photo was always there on the mantelpiece, a young man in his RAF uniform, looking right at me, I thought; I noticed later he was actually gazing into space. But I felt then he was looking into my eyes. I revered him, though I never knew him. He was the hero of the family, and in a way, still is, for me, anyway. I am seventy-one. He died aged twenty-one. He had been an actor, a promising one by all accounts. He only had two years on the stage. He never had a family, never had the chance of peace, never knew the contentment that the years can bring. I learnt very young that the grieving never dies, that the loss lingers.

As a schoolboy I read the poems of Siegfried Sassoon and Wilfred Owen and Edward Thomas, who had fought in an earlier war, the one that was supposed to end all other wars, the First World War. When I was older, I saw the musical *Oh! What a Lovely War*, the play *Journey's End*, read *All Quiet on the Western Front*, witnessed in all this the courage and camaraderie, the killing, the grieving that so many had lived through. For a brief year I went into the army, in part at least because I was in awe of those generations. Maybe I was testing myself, I don't know. But a taste of preparing for war, training for it, taught me rather quickly that I wanted to live my life in a world of peace, that peace was what these generations had been fighting for, peace and freedom, not simply a continuation of war.

Many, many years later, after years of teaching in junior schools, I found myself moving to Devon, with Clare and the family, to help with Clare's great project of bringing city children into the countryside and giving them an experience of farming life they would never forget. She called it "Farms for City Children". We set up the charity at Nethercott House near the village of Iddesleigh, a place as deep in the Devon countryside as you could find. I was already writing, and had been for a while. *Friend or Foe*, my Second World War evacuee story was just out, and there were one or two others as well. But so far I had written well within myself; my readers, very often the children I was teaching, rather more important to me than the stories themselves. It had been a means to an end: to get children enjoying stories, and writing their own stories too. So, as I was already a bit of a writer, I used to go one evening a week up the lane to Nethercott, and read to the city children by the log fire. Sometimes half of them were asleep by the time I had finished. Country air, I kidded myself.

We were new in the village, still finding our feet, getting to know people. We joined in the community. I rang the bells in the church; Clare helped with the flowers. Everyone made us feel very welcome and we soon got to know who everyone was. There were three old men in the village who particularly interested me. They had been living there at the time of the First World War, I was told. Two of them had been soldiers, and gone to the war. I went up to the pub one day, and there was one of them, sitting by a fire: Wilf Ellis, in his eighties by then, an antique dealer in those days. We had bought only one thing from him, an oil painting of a fine racehorse called Topthorn, and thereby hangs a tale too! We got talking. All I said was: "I heard you went to the First World War, Wilf. That right?"

"I did," he said.

I thought that was it, that he would say nothing more. I could feel it was a question I should never have asked. But then, after a while, Wilf spoke up again. I don't think he stopped for an hour. It was an outpouring, to a comparative stranger, of all that had happened to him in the trenches. He had been gassed, hospitalized, wounded, his life spared by a German soldier. He talked of how they longed only to be warm, dry, not hungry, free of lice, how they longed above all for it to be done with, just to go home and see the ones they loved. They wanted the agony to be over. He took me down to his cottage later and showed me his trenching tool, his photos, his medals. As he was talking, two things occurred to me: that he was passing his story on to me, a young man (then), a

4

writer, and that for the first time in my life I was hearing about war not through a film, a play, a poem, a comic, nor a novel. I was hearing it straight from someone who had been there, lived through it.

Within a day or two, my interest quickened further. I went to see the other old soldier in the village who, I had been told, had fought in the war. He fished in the river and he had been Master of Foxhounds – that's all I knew of him. Captain Budgett, he was called. He lived down the end of my lane and seemed only too willing to talk. "I was there with horses," he said. He had been to Palestine, the desert, been captured and imprisoned by the Turks. It was obvious he wanted to talk more about the horses than the Turks. I let him talk. This was not a sentimental man, that was clear. But he spoke movingly about how much man and horse relied upon each other for survival. "My horse, he was my best friend," he told me. "And I'm telling you, he listened, really listened."

I think it was as he was talking that I first conceived the notion about writing a story about a horse in that war. This way, if the war could be seen and told through the horse's eyes, I could follow a horse's journey through the war as it was first used as a British cavalry horse, then captured by the Germans, then as it wintered on a French farm. This way, I thought, I could tell a story of that war from all sides – friend and foe, and civilian too – and this way, witness the universality of the suffering of war, of the pity, of the killing and the dying, and of the longing and hope too.

One phone call to the Imperial War Museum the next day helped hugely. "How many horses went to that war?" I asked.

"About a million," came the reply.

"And how many returned home afterwards?"

"About sixty-five thousand."

So then I thought: the horses died in about the same numbers as the men, and in the same ways too, shot, blown-up, on the wire, in the mud. They died of exhaustion and disease. Now I didn't just want to tell the story, I had to tell it, needed to tell it. But there was a problem that could not be solved, that seemed insurmountable. To tell the story, as I now knew I had to tell it, from the perspective of the horse, I was going to have to write it in the first person. The horse would be telling it, writing it. There is, of course, a rather famous book where this happens, but which was written a long time ago, when such a device might have been acceptable, *Black Beauty*. So iconic is this classic story that any book using the same technique might seem to be some sort of pale imitation. And then, of course, told in a horse's voice, it could so easily become mawkish and sentimental. The more I thought about it, the more I worried about the voice. This was to be a serious book – yes, certainly at its heart a story about a boy and a horse and their love for each other, but also a story about the suffering of war and the longing for peace. Above all, it had to be credible, and certainly not ridiculous.

Could I do this the way I wanted to do it? Could I risk using the horse's voice? Would even *I* believe in it as I was writing it? Could I become horse? Faced with this difficulty, I very nearly gave up altogether. But so much else was in place. I would set the story on the farm where I live, in the cottage where I live. I knew by now who had lived where at the time of the war. I had researched the lives of the working people, stood by their graves in the churchyard. I walked where they walked, was familiar with the fields they tilled, the ditches they dug, the streams and rivers where they fished; I knew the bluebell woods where the badgers roamed and where the swallows nested in the barns. I had even chosen the name of my horse – Joey, after a roguish, strong-willed foal we had on the farm. I had watched him growing, helped train him to a halter, lunged him. So much was ready, and I so much wanted to get on and write it. But I simply could not find the confidence to do it. I could not believe in the voice.

One small incident gave me the spur I needed. As I have said, I used to go up to read to the city children who came to stay at Nethercott. I would go up to do this, usually on their last night, before they returned to London or Birmingham or Bristol or Plymouth. So one dark November evening, after milking, I found myself walking through the fine drizzle up the lane and into the stable yard at the back of this large Victorian house, their home for a week. There was one light on over a stable door. I saw a small boy standing there stroking the horse's head – Hebe, she was called, a Haflinger pony, and a great favourite with us and with the children. The boy was in his dressing gown and slippers. He was called Billy. I was about to call out to him to go indoors out of the rain, when I heard him talking to the horse.

Now Billy should not have been talking, because Billy didn't talk. Everyone knew that. I had been told by the teacher the first day the school arrived, almost a week before. "Michael," she said, "best not to ask Billy any questions because he won't answer, and if you try to encourage him to answer, he is liable to run off home. He's done this at school. We just leave him be. That's how he likes it. We think he must have a terrible stutter or something. He's been with us two years and he never speaks, not to us, not to the other children." But here was Billy talking to this horse, the words simply flowing from him, all about his day on the farm and what he'd done and how he was going home the next morning, and how he'd miss her.

I went to fetch the teachers. They had to witness this miracle, I thought. So I did, and we all stood there in the darkness, and watched and listened, in disbelief, in wonder. It was in those few brief moments that I realized something else. This wasn't just a miracle because Billy was talking. There was another one going on that I had not taken in until now. Hebe was listening. Captain

Budgett had been right: horses listen, really listen. Hebe was standing there because she knew at that moment she was loved and needed. Horses are sentient, feeling creatures. They have great need for affection, as we do. No, it is not sentimental. Of course it isn't, I thought. And if I can write it right, then my story might just work. I could try the voice. I could do it.

I made one concession though: I decided not to let Joey tell his story right away. I would set the scene, introduce Joey to the reader, and ask the reader without really asking, to make that leap of imagination, tell them that this was a story written for all the men and horses who went to that war, and especially for those who did not come home. In the little introduction set in the village hall in Iddesleigh, I wrote that there is still hanging today a painting of Joey on the wall, under a clock that stands always at five to ten. There is, in fact, no painting, but there is a clock. So the painting is a pure invention, a device.

For two decades this book of *War Horse* was hardly read – it barely sold a thousand copies a year. We tried to get a film going, wrote several scripts for it. No one was interested. Then Michael Foreman suggested I write a sequel, the story of Joey when he comes home after the war, when tractors were taking over from horses on the farm. Great idea, I thought. So I wrote *Farm Boy*, and Michael illustrated it beautifully. But *War Horse* was still hardly being read. So no one discovered there was no painting in the village hall, because no one was interested enough to come and look.

Then the National Theatre decided to make a play of *War Horse* – with life-sized puppets. Ridiculous idea, I thought. Well, I was wrong. In over seven years, more

YOU ARE CORDIALLY INVITED TO ATTEND THE POST PREMIERE RECEPTION OF

A STEVEN SPIELBERG FILM

WAR HORSE

AT THE QUEEN'S GALLERY
BUCKINGHAM PALACE, BUCKINGHAM PALACE ROAD, LONDON, SW1A 1AA

IMMEDIATELY FOLLOWING THE UK PREMIERE SCREENING

THERE WILL BE AN OPPORTUNITY TO VIEW THE EXHIBITION
The Heart of the Great Alone: Scott, Shackleton & Antarctic Photography

CARRIAGES 11.30PM
DRESS CODE: BLACK TIE

PLEASE BRING THIS INVITATION WITH YOU
STRICTLY NO ADMITTANCE WITHOUT PHOTO ID

It was grand, but there were no carriages waiting at 11.30!

than seven million people have seen it globally.

The National Theatre has never had such a hit. Steven Spielberg came to see it and made a movie of it, seen worldwide. Soon dozens of people were visiting our little village to find out where Joey was born, to see the village green where he was sold off as a cavalry horse to the army in 1914; and of course they would turn up at the village hall asking to see the picture of Joey on the wall, and the clock. There was a clock. But there was no painting.

Local people became a little tired of making lame excuses for the absence of the picture to these *War Horse* tourists. "Sorry, we can't find the key to the village hall door." "Sorry, the picture has been sent away to be cleaned." Something had to be done, they said. So in the end, we did something, something very naughty.

By great good chance, on the film set of *War Horse* we met the artist Ali Bannister who had been commissioned by Steven Spielberg to make the drawings of Joey for the film. Clare had a sudden brilliant idea. She asked her if she would do a portrait of Joey in oils, in the manner of the time, around 1914, as described in the book, sign it underneath as it is so signed in the book.

So that's what Ali did. She painted a portrait of Joey in the style of our Topthorn picture that we had bought from Wilf Ellis some time before, and painted it exactly as I had described it in the book. It was perfect. No one would know the difference!

We even had an unveiling ceremony in the village hall to celebrate. And now when visitors come and ask to see the picture of Joey, and they do, he is there looking down on them, ears pricked forward as if he has just noticed them standing there. "He's just like I imagined him in the book," one visitor from Canada was heard to say. Happy ending then!

Ali Bannister's painting of Joey,
now in ~~Iddesleigh~~ village hall

WAR HORSE

Author's Note
In the old school they now use for the village hall, below the
clock that has stood always at one minute past ten, hangs a
small dusty painting of a horse. He stands, a splendid red
bay with a remarkable white cross emblazoned on his fore-
head and with four perfectly matched white socks. He looks
wistfully out of the picture, his ears pricked forward, his
head turned as if he has just noticed us standing there.

To many who glance up at it casually, as they might do
when the hall is opened up for parish meetings, for harvest
suppers or evening socials, it is merely a tarnished old oil
painting of some unknown horse by a competent but an-
onymous artist. To them the picture is so familiar that it
commands little attention. But those who look more closely
will see, written in fading block copperplate writing across
the bottom of the bronze frame:

Joey, by Captain James Nicholls, Autumn 1914

Some in the village, only a very few now and fewer as each year goes by, remember Joey as he was. His story is written so that neither he nor those who knew him, nor the war they lived and died in, will be forgotten.

My earliest memories are a confusion of hilly fields and dark, damp stables, and rats that scampered along the beams above my head. But I remember well enough the day of the horse sale. The terror of it stayed with me all my life.

I was not yet six months old, a gangling, leggy colt who had never been further than a few feet from his mother. We were parted that day in the terrible hubbub of the auction ring and I was never to see her again. She was a fine working farm horse, getting on in years but with all the strength and stamina of an Irish draught horse quite evident in her fore and hind quarters. She was sold within minutes, and before I could follow her through the gates, she was whisked out of the ring and away. But somehow I was more difficult to dispose of. Perhaps it was the wild look in my eye as I circled the ring in a desperate search for my mother, or perhaps it was that none of the farmers and gypsies there were looking for a spindly-looking half-thoroughbred colt. But whatever the reason they were a long time haggling over how little I was worth before I heard the hammer go down and I was driven out through the gates and into a pen outside.

"Not bad for three guineas, is he? Are you, my little fire-brand? Not bad at all." The voice was harsh and thick with

Chapter 1

My earliest memories are a confusion of hilly fields and dark, damp stables,   But I remember well enough the day of the horse sale. The terror of it stayed with me all my life.   I was not yet six months old, a leggy colt who had never been further than a few feet from my mother.   We were parted that day in the terrible hubbub of the auction ring and I was never to see her again.   She was a fine working farm horse, getting on in years but with a strength and stamina of an Irish draft horse quite evident in her fore and hind quarters.   She was sold within minutes, and before I could follow was whisked out of the ring.   I was more difficult to dispose of. Perhaps it was the wild look in my eye as I circled the ring in a desperate search for my mother, or perhaps it was that none of the farmers where were looking for a splindly-looking half-thoroughbred, but whatever the reason I was in the ring for endless minutes before I heard the hammer go down and I was driven out through the gates and into a pen outside.

"Not bad for three guineas, is he?   Are you my little firebrand? Not bad at all."   The voice was harsh and thick with drink, and it belonged quite evidently to my owner.   I shall not call him my master, for only one man was ever my master.   My owner had a rope in his hand and was clambering into the pen followed by three or four

Here's how I got started

drink, and it belonged quite evidently to my owner. I shall not call him my master, for only one man was ever my master. My owner had a rope in his hand and was clambering into the pen followed by three or four of his red-faced friends. Each one carried a rope. They had taken off their hats and jackets and rolled up their sleeves; and they were all laughing as they came towards me. I had as yet been touched by no man and backed away from them until I felt the bars of the pen behind me and could go no further. They seemed to lunge at me all at once, but they were slow and I managed to slip past them and into the middle of the pen where I turned to face them again. They had stopped laughing now. I screamed for my mother and heard her reply echoing in the far distance. It was towards that cry that I bolted, half charging, half jumping the rails so that I caught my off foreleg as I tried to clamber over and was stranded there. I was grabbed roughly by the mane and tail and felt a rope tighten around my neck before I was thrown to the ground and held there with a man sitting it seemed on every part of me. I struggled until I was weak, kicking out violently every time I felt them relax, but they were too many and too strong for me. I felt the halter slip over my head and tighten around my neck and face.

"So you're a fighter, are you?" said my owner, tightening the rope and smiling through gritted teeth. "I like a fighter. But I'll break you one way or the other. Quite the little fighting cock you are, but you'll be eating out of my hand quick as a twick."

I was dragged along the lanes tied on a short rope to the tailboard of a farm cart so that every twist and turn wrenched at my neck. By the time we reached the farm land and rumbled over the bridge into the stable yard that was to become my home, I was soaked with exhaustion and the halter had rubbed my face raw. My one consolation as I was hauled into the stables that first evening was the knowledge that I was not alone. The old horse that had been pulling the cart all the way back from market was led into the stable next to mine. As she went in she stopped to look over my door and nickered gently. I was about to venture away from the back of my stable when my new owner brought his crop down on her side with such a vicious blow that I recoiled once again and huddled into the corner against the wall.

"Get in there you old ratbag," he bellowed. "Proper nuisance you are Zoey, and I don't want you teaching this young 'un your old tricks." But in that short moment I had caught a glimpse of kindness and sympathy from that old mare that cooled my panic and soothed my spirit.

I was left there with no water and no food while he stumbled off across the cobbles and up into the farmhouse beyond. There was the sound of slamming doors and raised voices before I heard footsteps running back across the yard and excited voices coming closer. Two heads appeared at my door. One was that of a young boy who looked at me for a long time, considering me carefully before his face broke into a beaming smile. "Mother," he said deliberately. "That will be a wonderful and brave horse. Look how he holds his

17

head." And then, "Look at him, Mother, he's wet through to the skin. I'll have to rub him down."

"But your father said to leave him, Albert," said the boy's mother. "Said it'll do him good to be left alone. He told you not to touch him."

"Mother," said Albert, slipping back the bolts on the stable door. "When Father's drunk he doesn't know what he's saying or what he's doing. He's always drunk on market days. You've told me often enough not to pay him any account when he's like that. You feed up old Zoey, Mother, while I see to him. Oh, isn't he grand, Mother? He's red almost, red-bay you'd call him, wouldn't you? And that cross down his nose is perfect. Have you ever seen a horse with a white cross like that? Have you ever seen such a thing? I shall ride this horse when he's ready. I shall ride him everywhere and there won't be a horse to touch him, not in the whole parish, not in the whole county."

"You're barely past thirteen, Albert," said his mother from the next stable. "He's too young and you're too young, and anyway Father says you're not to touch him, so don't come crying to me if he catches you in there."

"But why the divil did he buy him, Mother?" Albert asked. "It was a calf we wanted, wasn't it? That's what he went in to market for, wasn't it? A calf to suckle old Celandine?"

"I know dear, your father's not himself when he's like that," his mother said softly. "He says that Farmer Easton was bidding for the horse, and you know what he thinks of

that man after that barney over the fencing. I should imagine he bought it just to deny him. Well that's what it looks
like to me."

"Well I'm glad he did, Mother," said Albert, walking
slowly towards me, pulling off his jacket. "Drunk or not,
it's the best thing he ever did."

"Don't speak like that about your father, Albert. He's
been through a lot. It's not right," said his mother. But her
words lacked conviction.

Albert was about the same height as me and talked so
gently as he approached that I was immediately calmed and
not a little intrigued, and so stood where I was against the
wall. I jumped at first when he touched me but could see at
once that he meant me no harm. He smoothed my back first
and then my neck, talking all the while about what a fine
time we would have together, how I would grow up to be
the smartest horse in the whole wide world, and how we
would go out hunting together. After a bit he began to rub
me gently with his coat. He rubbed me until I was dry and
then dabbed salt water onto my face where the skin had
been rubbed raw. He brought in some sweet hay and a
bucket of cool, deep water. I do not believe he stopped talking all the time. As he turned to go out of the stable I called
out to him to thank him and he seemed to understand for he
smiled broadly and stroked my nose.

"We'll get along, you and I," he said kindly. "I shall call
you Joey, only because it rhymes with Zoey, and then
maybe, yes maybe because it suits you. I'll be out again in

the morning – and don't worry, I'll look after you. I promise you that. Sweet dreams, Joey."

"You should never talk to horses, Albert," said his mother from outside. "They never understand you. They're stupid creatures. Obstinate and stupid, that's what your father says, and he's known horses all his life."

"Father just doesn't understand them," said Albert. "I think he's frightened of them."

I went over to the door and watched Albert and his mother walking away and up into the darkness. I knew then that I had found a friend for life, that there was an instinctive and immediate bond of trust and affection between us. Next to me old Zoey leant over her door to try to touch me, but our noses would not quite meet.

The real war horses

Of all animals, the horse is one of the shyest, least aggressive and most highly strung. Yet for thousands of years horses have been coerced into participation in wars.

In 1914, the British Army had around 25,000 horses. They only had eighty armoured vehicles, relatively new inventions and prone to mechanical breakdown. In contrast, horses and mules were thought to be reliable forms of transport. The army depended on them for transporting goods, ammunition and the wounded.

As the war continued, 15,000 new horses and mules had to be found each month to replace those killed or injured.

Battle conditions represent everything that horses dislike and fear. General Jack Seely remembered: "He had to endure everything most hateful to him – violent noise, the bursting of great shells and bright flashes at night, when the white light of bursting shells must have caused violent pain to his sensitive eyes. Above all, the smell of blood. Many people do not realize how acute is his sense of smell, but most will have read his terror when he smells blood."

For many horses it was the weather and the

mud, rather than the bullets and bombardment, that was the final straw. Roads were broken up, and the poor animals would sink deep into the mud. Sometimes they could not get out, and died where they fell.

Additionally, a horse's daily grain ration was just 9 kilos. This was 25 per cent less than recommended in England in peacetime, where the work would have been much easier. Hunger became a constant problem, particularly in the bitter winters. Horses tried to eat the wheels from wagons, and were sometimes fed sawdust. Besides being injured or killed in battle, thousands of animals died from stress, disease and malnourishment.

Particularly strong and fit horses were sent to the cavalry. Although these horses were not hauling heavy loads, a cavalryman and his equipment weighed about 150 kilos, and cavalrymen were instructed to dismount and walk their horses at every opportunity. In 1914, generals and decision-makers on both sides still used nineteenth-century warfare strategies and assumed that the cavalry would play a pivotal role. At the outbreak of war, Britain and Germany each had a cavalry force of 100,000 men. However, on the Western Front, men and horses came up against barbed wire, machine guns and tanks for the first time. The horrific slaughter that ensued

persuaded many that the traditional cavalry charge was obsolete. Yet, even by the end of the war, there were some who still did not accept this. For example, General Douglas Haig wrote: "I believe that the value of the horse ... is likely to be as great as ever. Aeroplanes and tanks are only accessories to the men and the horse ... As time goes on you will find just as much use for the horse - the well-bred horse - as you have ever done in the past."

Many letters and memoirs touchingly show the effect on soldiers of the slaughter of the animals. Lieutenant Dennis Wheatley described what happened one night: "There were dead ones lying all over the place and scores of others were floundering ... broken legs ... terrible neck wounds... We went back for our pistols and spent the next hour putting the poor, seriously injured brutes out of their misery. We lost over 100 horses."

At the end of the war, a scheme was established to enable officers who had sold their horses to the army to buy back survivors. This was extended so that soldiers who had worked with an animal in the war would be told when it came up for auction. Trooper Huggins bought his "Billy", and wrote: "we had him for years and years on the farm ... he ended his days in clover."

Sadly, happy endings like Billy's, and Joey's in *War Horse*, were all too rare. By 1917, the British Army had over 760,000 horses and mules overseas, but only 65,000 horses returned to Britain after the war. Charities like the RSPCA highlighted the plight of the abandoned animals. The horses were starving, being worked to death, or being sold to French and German abattoirs. In Cairo, the first Brooke Hospital was eventually set up by Dorothy Brooke - the Old War Horse Memorial Hospital.

The removal of horses from Britain had a profound effect on home society. Farming and transport, which had depended on horsepower, had to find mechanized alternatives and by 1918, there was no going back to using horses as before. Today, with fewer than a million horses in the UK, it is difficult for us to understand just how integral to everyday life they used to be. Up to eight million horses from all sides died in the First World War.

Why the Whales Came & The Wreck of the Zanzibar

THE DREAM

Most of my stories take a while to dream themselves up, some take years to gestate. Some lie like dormant seed for decades, before they find the nourishment to enable them to grow. But *Why the Whales Came* was that rare story that was handed to me on a plate. So much was in place, it needed little invention on my part. I found I could sit on my writing bed, pick up my exercise book and simply tell it down.

In a way, I began the whole adventure, was the cause of it happening in the first place, and it was this adventure that provoked the telling of the tale, part truth, part fantastical, that was to become my story. Let me first of all tell you the adventure, and this part is true, absolutely true. I know, because I was there. It happened to me.

This was my very first visit to the Isles of Scilly, nearly forty years ago now. To be honest I didn't want to go at all. But my wife Clare insisted. She had been there as a small child, had loved it, the wildness of it, the beaches, the bird-life, the peace and quiet. One of my sons had discovered it too. So we went, not to France where I wanted to go but to Scilly.

Happy days on Scilly

We found a bed and breakfast on Bryher Island, the smallest of the inhabited islands. The island was quiet, which suited me fine, but the cottage was small and crowded. I was trying to finish a book and needed to be on my own a bit. I asked our landlady, Marion Bennett, where was the quietest place she knew of on the islands. "Samson," she said. "Just half a mile away across the water. Uninhabited. A few ruined cottages, lots of rabbits, black rabbits. And birds. You go there, you'll like as not be quite alone. Very few people go there. Keith, my husband will take you over there, if you like. No trouble. It's a nice calm sea." So off I went in Keith's boat with my writing book and a picnic. I planned to sit on a sheltered rock somewhere and try to write. He dropped me off on the beach and said he'd pick me up around teatime that afternoon and off he went. There I was on a desert island all on my own, but now I was there I didn't really feel like writing at all. I looked around me. I could see the ruined cottages, and the narrow tracks heading along through the bracken. I would explore, do the writing later. That's what I told myself.

I never did do any writing that day. I became completely absorbed in my exploration. I followed the narrow peaty-black tracks through the bracken and discovered six or seven ruined cottages, middens of limpet shells outside each one. Clearly limpets were important to the diet of those people who had lived there. But who were they? Why had they left? I kept finding traces of those long-gone inhabitants: bits of old clay pipes, a rusty knife, the sole of an old shoe. In each cottage there was an open fireplace, and gaps where the windows had been. Some were more dilapidated than others. None had a roof, but the one I had not yet visited at the top of the hill had a chimney, with a gull perched on top, as if he was waiting for me. He was certainly watching me. I followed the track up towards the cottage, passing a well on the way. There was no water in it.

By midday I was sitting in this cottage, happily eating my picnic when I looked up and noticed the weather had changed. Great grey clouds were skidding in from the Atlantic. A wind was getting up, and rain began to fall, a few drops at first, then heavier. I retreated to the only cover I could find, the open fireplace. I sat there in the fireplace and watched the rain come down. The wind was whistling around me, and I began to feel the cottage itself was speaking to me, punctuated by the crying of the gulls above. I felt suddenly I was an intruder, that both the cottage and the gulls wanted me gone. I wanted to go but it was now raining quite hard and I thought I would wait until it died down, until the wind dropped. The wind was whining about the chimney now, but was it the wind? It sounded so like a human voice! I heard rustlings outside the cottage. Just the wind, I thought, or maybe those black rabbits I had been told about. But it sounded more like footsteps to me. There was someone out there. I called. No reply. I called again. No reply. I found myself looking from gaping window to gaping window, sure now I was being watched, certain someone was out there.

I ran out, down the track to the beach and waited there to be picked up. Keith didn't come and he didn't come. It was past four o'clock, five o'clock. Six. All I wanted was to get off this island. I was not wanted there, and I most certainly did not want to be there.

Keith came at long last, apologizing. He had forgotten me, until Clare had reminded him that he had dropped me off that morning. When I got back I had a long hot shower to warm myself through, then came down for supper. There was much merriment about the whole incident. Marion chirped up, saying, "Oh, don't worry, we wouldn't have left you there overnight. We wouldn't do that. There are ghosts over on Samson." The others laughed. I did not. "No, really," she said, "there are." She wasn't laughing now. "Don't you know the story of the curse of Samson? That's why there are no people there any more." Then she told us all about the curse. And this was the story she told me – how much is true, how much legend, I do not know. All I do know is that I have never forgotten it.

"About a hundred and fifty years ago, they say there were just twenty or thirty people living on Samson – Woodcocks and Webbers mostly. A poor living they had, couldn't grow much except a few potatoes. Lived off limpets mostly. That's what turned their skin yellow. Did a bit of fishing. But it was a struggle to survive over there.

Well, one morning after a stormy night they woke up and saw this ship stuck fast on the sandbank. They rowed out to her and climbed on board. There were a couple of French soldiers on board. The men of Samson took them prisoner – we were at war with France at the time. Then they waited until the tide floated the ship off the sandbank, and set sail for the mainland. They were going to sail her to Plymouth and sell her. What luck! She'd make the island's fortune! Off they sailed into the sunset, leaving the women and children behind.

Well, that ship never reached the mainland. She went down on the Wolf Rock off Land's End. All the men of Samson were drowned, all the French soldiers. So this lucky ship that was to make everything right on Samson, bring them money to repair the houses, build a proper fishing boat, turned out to be nothing but a curse. With all the men drowned, just the women and old folk and children were left on Samson. They tried to survive but they couldn't. Just three years later, the last of the women left with her little boy, who was deaf, made deaf by the curse, she always said. As she pushed the little rowing boat off Samson, her little boy at the oars, she spat on the sand and cursed the place. She brought the boy to Bryher, and because he was deaf, he didn't like mixing with the other children. They'd tease him. He preferred the birds. He'd feed them. Wherever there were birds flying, the islanders on Bryher always knew he wouldn't be far away. When he grew up they called him, 'the

Birdman'." There was a long silence when she'd finished. "Oh, yes, there's ghosts on Samson all right, the ghosts of all those poor drowned men."

But it wasn't just that story, that happening, that enabled me to write the story so quickly; it was the islands themselves. I got to know both Samson and Bryher after that as well as I knew the countryside around my home in Devon. I came to know all the beaches and cliffs, Timmy's Hill, Watch Hill, Hell Bay, Green Bay, Rushy Bay, and the strange pool where the swans come in and land every day. I began my story in that pool, with these swans. There, the children wanted to sail their toy sailing boats, but the swans threaten them, and they are forced to sail them off Rushy Bay, opposite Samson Island, where no one is ever supposed to go. *Set foot on that place, you're cursed for ever!* they are told. *Never go there*. Well, one day they do. And that's where the Birdman comes in, and the cottages and the ghosts.

But what about the whales? you're thinking. Well, whales are washed up on the shores of Scilly – pilot whales mostly – and so are leatherback turtles.

It was the leatherback turtles that were a key ingredient in writing *The Wreck of the Zanzibar*, also set on Bryher and Samson. The waters round Scilly are notoriously difficult to navigate. There are dozens of wrecks, and a story to go with each one. And there are gigs (small boats for rowing or sailing), a gig for each island – used these days for racing, but in times gone by used to row out to rescue people from the wrecks, to claim salvage too. But only men were allowed to row in these gigs. There had been, I discovered, a wreck off Samson over a hundred years ago, in which the Bryher gig had rescued several cows. So I had a washed-up leatherback turtle, a girl determined to row out in a gig when it wasn't allowed and a great cow rescue off Samson: the ingredients of *The Wreck of the Zanzibar*. In that sense, a book is much like a cake. You can't make a good cake without the right ingredients. I had the right ones, just had to mix them and bake. If you see what I am saying!

I digress, but digressing is fun. Quite a lot of writing is digressing, I find!

Back to *Why the Whales Came*. The whales in the story are not pilot whales but narwhals. This is because I once came across a narwhal's tusk in a museum in Paris, a tusk of ivory that was part of the treasure of some long-ago king. These tusks were once thought to have come from unicorns. They were very valuable; they still are. Unicorns and narwhals have fascinated me ever since. (I have written a story called *I Believe in Unicorns*, more on that later). I discovered that the last narwhals found in British waters had been washed up in the Thames estuary in the mid-twentieth century. Someone had cut off their horns. This was a crime, I thought, a crime against nature itself, the kind of crime that brings a curse down on those who commit it. So, I thought, have narwhals come to Samson, have the islanders, who are struggling for survival, kill them and take their horns. Then they wake up the next morning to find a ship stuck on the sandbank, all of this watched and witnessed by a small boy, a deaf boy, that last boy to leave Samson, who grows up later on Bryher, who becomes the Birdman, his life blighted by the curse of Samson. I had my story. Now all I had to do was write it.

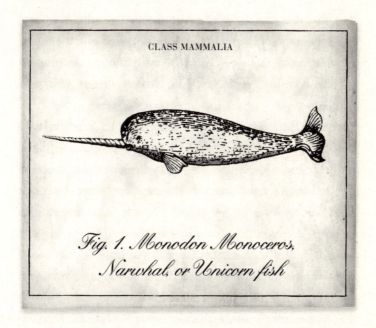

CLASS MAMMALIA

Fig. 1. Monodon Monoceros, Narwhal, or Unicorn fish

Research on narwhals

WHY THE WHALES CAME

The fire was our only comfort throughout the long and dreadful hours of the night. Each new settling of the burning embers sent an explosion of sparks high into the sky until all that was left was a perfect circle of glowing embers. Only fear kept us awake, fear of the unknown out there in the dark around us, and fear that one of us might fall asleep and leave the other to face the night alone. Every rustle behind us in the heather, the sudden squawking of a disturbed gull, even the soft groaning of a seal in the bay somewhere below us kept us both taut with terror. We talked all night long, as much as anything to keep out the noises of the night around us. I sought endless reassurances from Daniel and he did indeed seem to have an answer for everything. It was just that some-times I found it difficult to believe him.

"You think the Birdman's here then?" I asked. "How do you know it was him that lit the fire?"

"Well, he's the only one who ever comes to Samson, isn't he?" Daniel replied. "And someone built this fire, didn't he? It has to be him, stands to reason. And remember you were the one that said you heard Prince barking just after we landed. They're here somewhere, got to be. Soon as it's light, we'll find the house he stays in – the only house on the island with its roof on still – that's what he told us, remember? All we've got to do is find it and he'll be there. He can't leave the island in this fog any more than we can, can he? Don't worry, Gracie."

"But I still don't see why he lit this fire," I went on. "Not unless he's signalling to someone out at sea. P'raps that's it, Daniel. P'raps that's what he's up to. He could be, couldn't he, Daniel? I mean that's what those smugglers and wreckers used to do in the old days, isn't it? That's what I heard."

"A smuggler?" Daniel laughed. "The Birdman a smuggler? Don't be silly."

"Could be," I said. "Why not?"

"Gracie," Daniel said. "If you were a smuggler and you were signalling to a ship out there, would you do it in thick fog?"

"All right then," I went on. "If you know so much then, you tell me why he's gone and built a fire in the middle of nowhere?"

"Who knows?" Daniel shrugged his shoulders. "P'raps he's frightened of the dark. I know that's what I'd do if I found myself alone here in the middle of the night. Anyway, it's his island, isn't it? I mean he lived here, didn't he? He can do what he likes. He can build fires anywhere he likes. You still don't trust him, do you, Gracie? Not after all he's done for us, you still don't trust him."

"And what if he isn't here at all?" I said. "What if we

don't find him in the morning? I mean you'd think Prince would have heard us by now and come and found us, wouldn't you?"

"He's here, Gracie, honest he is. You'll see."

"But what if those stories are true?" I said, lowering my voice to a whisper. "What if all Father told me is really true and Samson does have a curse on it, like Charlie Webber told him. What's going to happen to us then? You've only got to set foot on the island and you'll be cursed for ever. That's what he said. That's what happened to Charlie Webber."

"Tommyrot," said Daniel. "It's all tommyrot. Everyone knows it's just stories."

"Then why doesn't anyone else ever land on Samson if it's all stories?"

"They're just scared, that's all," Daniel said. "Just scared."

"Well so am I," I said. "It's this place, Daniel, it doesn't feel right. And it's not just the dark either. I'm not the one who's scared of the dark, am I? There's ghosts here, Daniel. I can feel them all around us. The Birdman told us, didn't he? And one of them's his own father. That's what he said, didn't he?"

"Just imagining things I expect," said Daniel. "I mean if you were alone on this island for long you'd begin to imagine things wouldn't you? And after all he is old, isn't he? Anyway he never said he'd *seen* a ghost, did he?"

"No, but…"

"Well then," Daniel said. "Listen, Gracie, you ever seen a ghost? Have you?"

"No."

"So if you've never seen one, how do you know they exist? You don't do you?"

"P'raps not, but..."

"Well then, if you've never seen them and you don't believe they exist, you know he was just imagining things. Must have been, mustn't he? And all those stories your father told you about curses and houses burning down and the scarlet fever, they're just stories, Gracie. I mean everyone thinks the Birdman's mad, don't they?"

"Yes."

"Well, is he?"

"No."

"And Big Tim said you'd catch his madness if you touched him. Well you've touched him, haven't you, and have you gone mad?"

"No."

"Well then. Stands to reason, it's all just stories like I said. I mean, you can't believe in anything you can't see, can you? Well can you?"

"Anyway p'raps we've got nothing to worry about," I said. "P'raps we're not on Samson at all." But I knew full well we were. I could feel it. I could feel the ghosts watching us. They were out there in the darkness. I knew they were. I huddled closer to the fire hugging my knees, and prayed and prayed.

THE WRECK
OF THE ZANZIBAR

She told me to dig out a bowl in the sand, right under the turtle's chin, and then she shook out her net. He looked mildly interested for a moment and then looked away. It was no good. Granny May was looking out to sea, shielding her eyes against the glare of the sun.

"I wonder," she murmured. "I wonder. I shan't be long." And she was gone, down to the sea. She was wading out up to her ankles, then up to her knees, her shrimping net scooping through the water around her. I stayed behind with the turtle and threw more stones at the gulls. When she came back, her net was bulging with jellyfish, blue jellyfish. She emptied them into the turtle's sandy bowl. At once he was at them like a vulture, snapping, crunching, swallowing, until there wasn't a tentacle left.

"He's smiling," she said. "I think he likes them. I think perhaps he'd like some more."

"I'll do it," I said. I picked up the net and rushed off

down into the sea. They were not difficult to find. I've never liked jellyfish, not since I was stung on my neck when I was little and came out in a burning weal that lasted for months. So I kept a wary eye around me. I scooped up twelve big ones in as many minutes. He ate those and then lifted his head, asking for more. We took it in turns after that, Granny May and me, until at last he seemed to have had enough and left a half-chewed jellyfish lying there, the shrimps still hopping all around it. I crouched down and looked my turtle in the eye.

"Feel better now?" I asked, and I wondered if turtles burp when they've eaten too fast. He didn't burp, but he did move. The flippers dug deeper. He shifted – just a little at

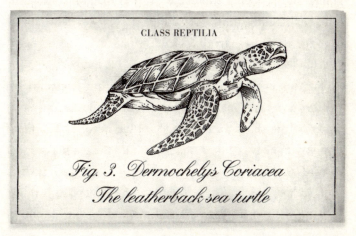

CLASS REPTILIA

Fig. 3. Dermochelys Coriacea
The leatherback sea turtle

Just like the Leatherback Turtles we found washed up on Samson Island first. And then he was scooping himself slowly forward, inching his way through the sand. I went loony. I was cavorting up and down like a wild thing, and Granny May was just the same. The two of us whistled and whooped to keep him moving, but we knew soon enough that we didn't need to. Every step he took was stronger, his neck reaching forward purposefully. Nothing would stop him now. As he neared the sea, the sand was tide-ribbed and wet, and he moved even faster, faster, past the rock pools and across the muddy sand where the lugworms leave their curly casts. His flippers were under the water now. He was half walking, half swimming. Then he dipped his snout into the sea and let the water run over his head and down his neck. He was going, and suddenly I didn't want him to. I was alongside him, bending over him.

"You don't have to go," I said.

"He wants to," said Granny May. "He has to."

He was in deeper water now, and with a few powerful strokes he was gone, cruising out through the turquoise water of the shallows to the deep blue beyond. The last I saw of him he was a dark shadow under the sea making out towards Samson.

I suddenly felt alone. Granny May knew it I think, because she put her arm around me and kissed the top of my head.

Samson

Life on Samson

Tiny Samson is now the largest uninhabited island on the Scillies. People lived on this mile-long island from about 2500 BC until 1855. Its last inhabitants, about forty people, lived in sturdy but basic cottages on a narrow strip of land between the island's two hills.

It is not known if the last families left voluntarily. Their landlord, Augustus Smith, had bought all the Scilly islands in 1834. Giving himself the grandiose title of "Lord Proprietor", he set about changing the islanders' way of life. He built a new quay on St Mary's Island, arranged for tree planting to protect agricultural land and built schools on the larger islands. However, he was not universally popular. He expelled people who could not find a local job and "cleared" other smaller islands. It could be that the Webber and Woodcock families, who were fishermen, were forced to leave Samson to enable Augustus Smith's plan to turn the island into a deer park. There is also a theory that a number of the island's men drowned in an attempt to rescue the crew of a ship wrecked on nearby rocks. Perhaps those who were left could no longer sustain their lives on the island.

In the event, the deer found Samson even more inhospitable than the earlier human inhabitants. At low spring tides, you can walk from Samson to the neighbouring island of Bryher. The deer did just that – at the first opportunity they escaped at low tide to other islands!

Today, Samson is managed by the Isles of Scilly Wildlife Trust and is a nesting site for over a thousand black-backed gulls, and masses of kittiwakes, terns, oystercatchers and ringed plovers. The only signs of its human past are some prehistoric graves and a few crumbling walls of old granite cottages, with their limpet shell middens on the doorstep, along with barns and boat sheds. Some claim that the ruins hold spirits and ghosts of past occupants.

In *Why the Whales Came*, the children are told that Samson was cursed because the islanders had slaughtered a group of beached whales. In those days, the quantity of food represented by a beached whale would have been seen by the hard-working and impoverished islanders as a godsend. Oil from the whale was used for heating and soap, bones were used for furniture and fencing and nothing was wasted.

Nowadays, twenty-three different species of cetacean (marine mammal) can be seen in British waters, but each year there are about 700 cases of whales and dolphins being stranded on our beaches. The numbers have increased by about 25 per cent in the last twenty years. Autopsies have shown that many of these animals have been injured by fishing nets. Most die before they reach shore, or before anyone can get to them to help, but there have been remarkable rescues.

We don't know why cetaceans lose their way and become stranded, but we do know that whales and dolphins use the Earth's magnetic field to navigate and find food. Sometimes they appear to misread the magnetic lines, and get lost. Another theory blames noise pollution such as underwater drilling and offshore wind farms.

The whale's own sonar system is thought to be badly affected by the sonar used by navy vessels. So our submarines, while detecting ships and other subs, may be interfering with the whale's sonar.

Many whale species are very social animals. They frequently travel in large family groups with a dominant leader. If the leader falls ill, or is confused and swims into shallow water, all the others often follow and the whole group may be beached together.

In the Thames, in 2006, there was the first sighting of a northern bottlenose whale, an endangered species since records began a century ago. This four-tonne, five-metre individual was probably separated from her pod in the Thames estuary. Thousands of Londoners thronged the Embankment to watch as a massive rescue attempt got underway. The whale was towed to a barge, which planned to carry the confused animal back out into the North Sea and to freedom. Sadly, the whale rapidly became disorientated and distressed. Eventually, it was decided that a vet should put her down to prevent her suffering any more. Michael's story *This Morning I Met a Whale* was inspired by this event.

My Friend Walter

THE DREAM

For about ten years before I came to live in Devon, I was a classroom teacher in junior schools. I was, if nothing else, a rather enthusiastic teacher, over-enthusiastic, some might say – and did. I loved to make my lessons lively, engaging. I had so many memories of my life as a small schoolboy, when I was mostly either bored or frightened by my teachers. So, as a teacher, I was determined to banish all fear and boredom from my classroom, for I knew that children could so easily come to dread their lessons, even be put off education for life. I had come perilously close to this myself. I know that above all a teacher has to always encourage the best in the child, has never to reinforce a sense of failure, has to pass on a passion for the subject, has to create an atmosphere in which creativity itself and the joy of discovery are all-important. In everything, I believed the child should feel supported and their efforts appreciated. So, when I taught, the children in my class knew I meant it, that I cared about the subject and about them. No one was treated as a success or failure, but rather as individuals who were trying the best they could – it was my job to help inspire them to do so.

One of the ways I tried to achieve all this was, as far as possible, to break away from the routine, the ordinary, the expected, to surprise the children. At every opportunity, I took them out of the classroom. So, for instance, before getting them writing about mud, we would troop down to the stream and paddle barefoot, then learn and sing a song together about "mud glorious mud", then come back, clear the desks to the walls of the classroom and stagger about pretending we were walking in deep mud, sinking into it. We would explore mud together. And when it came to history, I tried much the same tactic.

History for me at school had been a dull business, learning endless dates of battles and wars, of kings and emperors. So I knew all the battles the Duke of Marlborough had won – Blenheim, Ramillies, Oudenarde, Malplaquet, 1704, 1706, 1708, 1709. But I did not have a clue what the battles were for, nor who he was fighting. Just that he won, we won. I didn't discover till much later that history was full of great stories, remarkable people, and that other countries won battles too! Sometimes they even beat us. Outrageous!

I knew that what interested the children I was teaching was now, the world they knew and lived in, and they were fascinated by the future too. Science-fiction was for them infinitely more interesting than the past. The past was done, over with, full of characters who wore funny hats, people who did not belong in their world. They were all old and dead! I knew that if I was ever to excite them or even hold their interest, I had somehow to make these historical characters come alive.

So, when I was told to take my class on their annual school outing, that the coach had been booked, that I was going to the Tower of London, I thought this might be a wonderful opportunity to introduce the children to the stories of some of the famous people who had been kept there as prisoners – among them Elizabeth I, Lady Jane Grey, the Princes in the Tower, Thomas More, Guy Fawkes and Walter Raleigh. How could I best begin to prepare them for this trip? I wondered. Tell their stories, I thought. Dramatize them, cover the classroom walls with pictures of them, of the houses they were born in, of the Tower of London. And then I thought, Why not make life-sized figures of them? We made them out of straw, dressed them in cloaks and crowns and jewellery. So there they were, a dozen or more of these historical characters – historical scarecrows someone called them – names and dates on cards hung round their necks, so we all knew who they were.

Of all these characters, it was the story of Walter Raleigh that my class liked to hear about best of all. He was the kind of guy they could relate to, colourful, clever, wicked, brave. A multi-faceted hero, but a rogue too. He

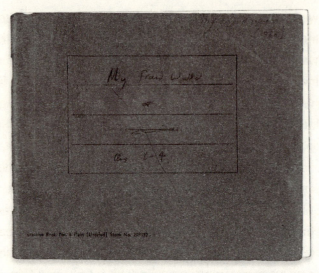

My notes for My Friend Walter

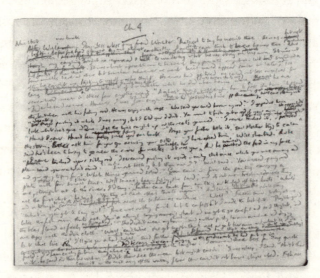

Don't worry, I can't read it either!

was the adventurer who sailed to South America, discovered potatoes growing and brought them back. Without Walter Raleigh we wouldn't be eating crisps today, I told them. And he brought back tobacco, and began the fashion of smoking it – hardly his greatest achievement, I know. He was a favourite of Queen Elizabeth I – explorer, soldier, sailor, writer who was a fine poet – and great historian. Raleigh was the one who sailed across the Atlantic and founded Virginia – named after the Virgin Queen, Queen Elizabeth I – in what is now the United States of America. Without Raleigh, Americans would probably not be speaking English today, of a kind. They'd be speaking Dutch or French instead. He grew up in deepest Devon on a farm, I told them, and he left it, went to court and did all this. So his life-sized straw-stuffed figure in our classroom was a particular favourite. But sadly, they all knew, he ended his days in the Tower – spending years as a prisoner in the Bloody Tower, before he had his head chopped off. I told them when, I told them why too. They were horrified at the cruelty, the injustice of it. We made an executioner's mask, cut out of black sugar paper, made an axe out of cardboard, painted a mural of the scene of the execution. I read them the poem he wrote the night before he died and had them recite it out loud.

"Even such is time, that takes in trust
Our youth, our joys, our all we have,
And pays us but with earth and dust…"

I told them how old and frail he was, how brave he must have been. All we read, all we painted and made and dramatized brought him alive for all of us.

So off we went one February morning by coach from our school in Wickhambreaux in Kent to the Tower of London. Every stone in the place breathes history. The children loved the armour and weapons in the White Tower, counted the ravens on Tower Green, visited the Crown Jewels, gasped and wondered at them; and then at my suggestion, and because it was cold and raining outside, we climbed the steps to the Bloody Tower to have our lunchtime picnic. We walked Raleigh's Walk, saw the rooms where he lived and slept for those long years of imprisonment. Some of them talked in whispers, I remember. I read again his last great poem, in the room where he wrote it. Then we had our picnic of sausage rolls and orange juice and apples and crisps, in his honour. And I went on talking, reminding them of all that Walter Raleigh had done, and of his sad and dreadful end. I was just telling them how it must have been: "... and, children, there is the very staircase he went down to be taken away to the scaffold." As I said this there was a great clap of thunder and the lights flickered. One or two children screamed, others giggled nervously. I don't know why I did what I did next. Maybe I thought it would make them laugh, maybe I just wanted to be wicked. "And do you know, children?" I went on, looking at my watch. "It's two o'clock. At exactly two o'clock every Thursday, they say –

and it is Thursday today, children – the ghost of Walter Raleigh comes back up these steps and into this very room, with his head under his arm." More thunder, more flickering of lights. I could hear a whimper or two. I saw the look on their faces. No one was laughing, no one was smiling. I knew at once I had gone too far. I got them out of there as quick as I could, reassuring them that it was just a silly story. Most were quiet in the coach all the way back to school, too quiet and not at all happy. We arrived, and got off the coach. As I watched the children walking away with their parents, I knew some of them would be telling that stupid story I had told in the Bloody Tower.

Sure enough, the next morning the head teacher called me in and gave me a right royal ticking-off. "You really are going to have to learn to think before you speak, Michael," she said. She was right, but I'm afraid it's not something I have learnt to do – even now all these years later.

But that visit, that story, had set my mind going. I had witnessed at first hand how powerful a ghost story could be – how deep down we worry about how ghosts might come to haunt us, to terrify us, that they are in some way evil, malign, maybe envious that we are alive and they are not. I wondered, why not try to tell a ghost story in which the ghost is friendly for a change, simply longing to visit his past, even trying to help? I thought about it for a while, but when it came to it, I either dismissed the idea or another more urgent story took its place. Yet Walter

Raleigh, and the Tower of London, and the children in my class at Wickhambreaux School, and that silly story I had told them stayed with me.

Five or six years later, when we had moved down to Devon, we decided to go for a day at the seaside. We had heard that the beach at Budleigh Salterton on the south coast of Devon was lovely. So we went. And sure enough, it was lovely, but the weather wasn't. So, unable to sit on the beach and swim, we stomped along the beach, threw stones into the waves, and watched the gulls being

Hayes Barton, birthplace of Walter Raleigh

buffeted about in the sky. I do remember there was an upturned boat high up on the beach, an old one, clearly not seaworthy any more. We sat down beside it for a while – to get out of the wind while our children played. And that was when it came into my head: a picture, a famous picture, called *The Boyhood of Raleigh* by John Everett Millais. It is of Walter Raleigh as a little boy, sitting, if I remembered rightly, with a friend on the beach, both listening intently to an old sailor telling tales of his adventures across the seas. He was pointing out to sea,

living his story as he told it, telling them of his great explorations and his extraordinary adventures. And all the while the young Walter was thinking, When I grow up…

I recalled then that visit to the Tower, those times spent teaching my class, how they and I had come to know Raleigh so well. And then it occurred to me. This might even be the very beach Walter Raleigh sat on when he was listening to that old sailor. After all, Raleigh had lived in Devon, on a farm, and hadn't it been somewhere near Budleigh Salterton? Had I remembered right? I had! I had! The beach was cold. We needed somewhere else to go by now anyway. We needed tea. I asked around. There was a very good place for tea in a farmhouse not far away, we were told, in a village called East Budleigh. East Budleigh wasn't far. As we neared the village, there was a sign: HAYES BARTON, BIRTHPLACE OF WALTER RALEIGH. CREAM TEAS. Too good to be true. But true all the same.

So we had our tea in the farmhouse where Walter Raleigh had grown up. After tea I asked if we could possibly see round the house. I said I was a writer and explained how Raleigh had interested me for a long time. The woman there was very kind, took us upstairs and walked us along a corridor into a bedroom. "Here is where Walter was born," she told us. "And that is his cradle." There was a wooden cradle by the bed, Raleigh's cradle. As I stood there, I felt the hairs standing up on the back of my neck, on my arms. I had been in the room at the Tower where Walter Raleigh had spent the last night of his life, and here I was in the room where he had slept the first night of his life! I reached down and touched the cradle, rocked it gently and told myself that now I could do it, must do it. I must somehow help the ghost of Walter Raleigh escape from the Bloody Tower and come home, home to Devon, to East Budleigh, to Hayes Barton, to his childhood home. I could make him live, and breathe, again. I could bring history to life.

I had never done this before, never written a ghost story. I had read a few, of course. Among my favourites were *A Christmas Carol* by Charles Dickens and "The Canterville Ghost" by Oscar Wilde. I had particularly loved these because they had benign ghosts, well-meaning ghosts, who somehow managed to be scary, to frighten the living daylights out of those they needed to frighten in the story – the reader too – but in the end they were doing it to help rather than simply to haunt.

A few books later and I was to write another ghost story: *The Ghost of Grania O'Malley*. Like Walter in *My Friend Walter*, this eccentric Irish pirate chief, also from the time of Queen Elizabeth I, returns to her birthplace – Clare Island, off the coast of Galway – to set things right, to help. I remember thinking as I was writing it, I wonder if Walter Raleigh ever met Grania O'Malley when she went to meet Queen Elizabeth at Greenwich, which she did. Maybe there's another ghost story in there somewhere to be told one day. Those two would have got on so well together, Walter and Grania. Both rogues, both pirates, both brave. Or maybe they would have hated each other. Who knows? Still dreaming that one up. We'll see.

MY FRIEND WALTER

"I have been searching for you." He looked at me more closely and smiled and shook his head. "Long ago I knew someone of the same name," he said. "She was older, I grant you, yet the likeness is unquestionable. You have her eyes, you have her face." His voice was strangely reedy and high-pitched, and he spoke with a burr much as we do in Devon. He seemed to be waiting for me to say something, but it was hard to know what to say, and so I said nothing. The old man began to chuckle as he looked around the room. "If Sir Walter himself could be here," he said, "I wonder indeed what he would think of his family."

"Sir Walter?"

"Sir Walter Raleigh!" he said rather sternly. "You have heard of him I trust?"

"Yes, I think so," I said. "Wasn't he the one that laid his cloak in a puddle so Queen Elizabeth could walk across without getting her feet wet?"

The old man looked at me long and hard and then sat back on the sofa and shook his head sadly. "Is that all you know about Sir Walter Raleigh? Well, you should know more. Do you not know that he is an ancestor of yours?"

"Of mine?"

"A distant relative I grant you, but everyone in this room has the blood of Walter Raleigh running in their veins, albeit thinly." He drew on his pipe and sighed as he looked around him. "It is hard to believe it, but it is so." He turned to me again. "He lived close by for some time, you know."

"Close by?" I said.

"In the Tower of London. If ever a man served his country well it was Walter Raleigh – and how did they repay him? They locked him up and cut off his head."

"Cut off his head? But why?"

"That is indeed a long story and a hard one for me to tell." He leaned forward again and spoke gently. "But since you have some connection with him by blood, perhaps you should go and see where he lived all those years ago. Thirteen years he was there. Thirteen long, cold years in the Bloody Tower. You should go there child. You should see it." He gripped my arm so tightly that it frightened me, and looked at me earnestly. "He is part of your history. He is part of you. Will you go?"

"I'll try," I said, and he seemed happy with that.

He looked past me. "I long for something to drink, child; but there is a crush of people about the table."

"I'll fetch it," I said. "Tea?"

He smiled at me. "Wine," he replied. "Red wine. I drink nothing else. I shall be here or hereabouts when you return." When he stood up he was a lot taller than I expected. I looked up into his face. His beard was white and pointed, and he seemed for a moment unsteady on his feet. "Back in a minute," I said.

I suppose I was gone a little longer than that because there was a queue for the wine, but when I came back he was nowhere to be seen. I asked after him everywhere but no one seemed to have noticed a tall old man in a black cloak carrying a silver-topped cane. I thought I had found him once and tugged at a black-cloaked figure talking to Aunty Ellie, but he turned out to be a vicar in his cape and so I offered him the wine anyway to cover my embarrassment. Aunty Ellie was delighted at my politeness. She introduced me as her little niece, her "little china doll"; and I was once more yoked to her skirts and paraded around amongst my inquisitive relatives. But I remember little enough of the party after that for all I could think of was the tall old man who appeared and then disappeared, who had insisted that I visit the Tower where Walter Raleigh had been locked up all those years. The more I thought about it, the more I wanted to go; but I wondered how on earth I was going to persuade Aunty Ellie to take me.

In the end, though, it was Aunty Ellie herself who suggested it. She had met with a long-lost cousin of hers whom she had not seen since she was a child and I suppose they wanted something to keep me happy, or quiet, whilst they reminisced about the childhood summer holidays they had spent together by the sea at somewhere called Whitstable. We could either go on a trip up the river or to the Tower,

Aunty Ellie said. Which did I want? "The Tower," I said. And so I found myself that afternoon inside the Tower of London walking past red-coated, bearskinned guards whose eyes wouldn't even move when I looked up into them, past Beefeaters who smiled down at me and curled their abundant moustaches as if they were Father Christmases.

As we stood in the queue waiting to see the Crown Jewels, I tried to ask Aunty Ellie about Walter Raleigh. After all, if he was related to me he was related to her too. She told me not to interrupt and finished telling her blue-haired cousin, Miss Soper I was to call her, all about her life as a midwife, about how she had looked after almost all the newborn babies born in Devon for over thirty years and how so many of them were named after her. "Now dear," she said, turning to me at last, "what was it?"

"Someone at the party told me we were related to Walter Raleigh." Aunty Ellie opened her mouth to speak, but Miss Soper got there first.

"Indeed, we are, dear," said Miss Soper. "But thankfully only distantly, and on his wife's side. He was a terrible rogue, that one. He was imprisoned here, you know."

"I know," I said.

"And he was a traitor," said Miss Soper. "That's why he had his head chopped off. We are more proud of our Sir Francis Drake connection, aren't we Ellie? The Sopers are related much more directly to the Drakes than the Raleighs. Now there was a man if there ever was one. Francis Drake." She took a deep breath. "Drake is in his hammock and a

64

thousand miles away..." and Miss Soper began to recite a poem in such a loud and impassioned way that the whole queue gathered around her to listen, and then clapped when she had finished. "I think I drank a teeny weeny bit too much wine at the party."

"I think so too," said Aunty Ellie, "But what does it matter? Oh, it's so good to see you again, Winnie, after all this time. You haven't changed a bit." And they hugged each other for the umpteenth time and I began to wish I was with someone else.

We saw the Crown Jewels and ooohed and aaahed with the others as we filed past all too quickly. There wasn't time to stop and stare. There were always more people behind, pressing us on, and Beefeaters telling us to move along smartly. The Crown Jewels were splendid and regal enough but they looked just like the pictures I had seen of them, no better. I was impatient to get to the Bloody Tower to see where Walter Raleigh had been imprisoned, and it was already getting late. When we came out of the Crown Jewels Aunty Ellie said there'd only be time for a short visit to the Bloody Tower.

So I found myself at last inside the room where Walter Raleigh had spent thirteen years of his life. There wasn't much to see really, just a four-poster bed, a chest and a tiny window beyond.

I walked up and down Raleigh's Walk, a sort of rampart that overlooks the River Thames, and I wondered again about the old man no one else had seen at the party.

Storm clouds had gathered grey over the river and brought the evening on early. The river flowed black beyond the trees and people hurried past to be under cover before the rain came. I was alone and I was suddenly cold. Aunty Ellie and Miss Soper had gone on without me. They would wait for me outside by Tower Green, they said. They had found the Bloody Tower grim and damp, not good for her rheumatism, Aunty Ellie said. "Don't you be too long," she'd told me. "We've got to get back."

I was wondering why Walter Raleigh hadn't just made a rope out of sheets and let himself down over the wall. It's what I would have done. I leaned over the parapet. "Too far to jump," said a voice from behind me. A tall figure was walking towards me, his black cloak whipping about him in the wind. He was limping, I noticed, and carried a silver-topped cane. "So," he said. "So you came. Allow me to present myself." He bowed low, sweeping his cloak across his legs. "I am, or I was, Sir Walter Raleigh. I am your humble servant, cousin Bess."

The ghost in the tower

The Bloody Tower (one of twenty-one towers that make up the Tower of London) is thought to be home to Sir Walter's ghost. If Sir Walter's ghost does parade around the Tower, he must be a very busy travelling ghost, as he goes regularly to Exeter as well, namely to the Royal Clarence Hotel (now called the ABode), the city's oldest hotel, an elegant building overlooking the cathedral. The hotel was built in 1769 on the site of Walter Raleigh's father's house, and the coughing noises that have been heard at the hotel, in empty rooms and with no possible source, have been attributed to Sir Walter Raleigh, perhaps because he popularized tobacco smoking in his lifetime!

His ghost has also been seen at another of Sir Walter's homes, Sherborne Castle. There he is said to wander the grounds, enjoying the surroundings, until he gets to his former smoking spot, known as "Raleigh's Seat". In the eleventh century, a Norman nobleman gave the castle to the Bishop of Salisbury. Legend has it that "whosoever shall take those lands from the bishopric should be accursed". The bad luck Raleigh had after taking over the castle makes the curse almost believable...

Sir Walter fell out of favour and was imprisoned in the Tower of London for thirteen years during the reign of James I. In fact, he lived there in relative comfort, with his wife, Elizabeth Throckmorton, and their two sons, Walter and Carew, the younger born there in 1605. Sir Walter was finally beheaded in 1618.

In life he had the freedom to wander the Tower of London at will, and his ghost continues to do so, looking exactly as he does in his portrait hanging in the Tower. Sir Walter's ghost has been seen on the ramparts known as Raleigh's Walk, where he exercised during his imprisonment. He also walks the Byward Tower and the Seven Tower Green, now used as a lodging for the Yeoman Warders. There are claims that some Tower of London ghosts are seen headless, and heard rattling chains! The wife of one Warder was scared to take a bath because she claimed to have been physically touched by an entity she thought was a man from Sir Walter's time. How the apparition could be identified as Sir Walter, as it was headless, is anyone's guess!

The Tower of London, the site of aristocratic executions for centuries, claims to be the most haunted place in Britain. Other ghosts include St Thomas à Becket and Queen Anne Boleyn, who is buried under the chapel's altar. Her ghost has been spotted there on many occasions. No doubt she is aggrieved by her execution in the Tower in 1536.

The "Princes in the Tower" also haunt the buildings. The sad mystery of these two little princes has intrigued historians for hundreds of years. The two were Edward V, aged thirteen, and his younger brother Richard. Edward only reigned for around two months in 1483, before disappearing with his brother from the Tower some time later. The two little princes were never seen again and it is generally assumed that they were murdered. No one really knows who by, although popular suspicion fell on their uncle and Lord Protector, Richard, Duke of Gloucester, later Richard III.

In 1674, the skeletons of two young children were discovered in the White Tower under the stairs leading to the chapel. They were reburied in Westminster Abbey, but it is claimed that their spirits live on. The two young princes have been seen holding hands, wearing white nightgowns and cowering in various rooms of the Tower. From the fifteenth century to the present day there have been reports of two small figures gliding down the stairs. If people reach out for them, they back up slowly to the wall and disappear. In 1990, two Coldstream Guards said they heard two young children giggling just outside the Tower.

Sir Walter's ghost at the Tower is in distinguished company!

Waiting for Anya
&
The Dancing Bear

THE DREAM

I have set my stories all over the world, and down through the ages too, from ancient times to yesterday. I have never invented worlds of fantasy, nor travelled into the future. Maybe I lack the imagination to do that. I need the canvas of places I know, or can find out about. I need the past or the present as firm foundations upon which I can build my stories. And the more connected places and events are to my own life, to my memory, half imagined or otherwise, or to the memory of others, the more confident I feel that I can dream up my plot through the people and places that will animate it. I have returned often in my stories to those places and people I know best, my home in Iddesleigh, in Devon, and to the Isles of Scilly, to memories of post-war London, and the Essex coast near Bradwell, where I grew up, to my years in boarding schools – all of these old familiar places, from which so many of my stories grow.

However, from time to time, and always by happy accident, it is spreading my wings and journeying over the seas that has provided me with fresh ideas and pastures new. My second country is France. It was the first foreign country I ever visited, when I went to the seaside in Normandy, to Sables-d'Or-les-Pins, as a small boy. Here I first discovered chocolate eclairs, and tasted my first sip of cider. Later, after I learnt to speak the language a bit, it became the only foreign country where I could communicate properly – Clare could already speak it fluently, as fast as the French do, so that helped. The more we went there, the more I felt at home. We made friends there, and often through them, became ever more aware of its people and culture, of how deeply connected we are to France historically, by language, by war, by kings and queens. As a writer, I am often translated into French. I have been into schools and colleges in France, attended book fairs and conferences all over the country, in the great cities, in tiny villages. In *Sparrow*, I even retold the story of Joan of Arc – an unlikely, and some said, illadvised enterprise for an English writer.

I have a French side to the family too, four grandchildren, who have a family house in the Béarn region of France, in the South-West, not far from the Pyrenees and the Spanish border. It was after a family wedding down there many years ago that I happened upon a small remote village in the foothills of the Pyrenees, called Lescun. This tiny place was to provide me with the background to two of my favourite stories, but more than that, it provided me with the stories themselves. It was as if the village and the stories were simply waiting there for me to turn up and discover them.

Clare in the Pyrenees

We nearly didn't get to Lescun at all. I had found the place on the map, chosen it because there was a small inn there where we could stay. I could see it was so close to the mountains that we could walk up into them from the village, up to the Pic d'Anie, and over the border into Spain. I had always had the rather ridiculous notion that it would be fun to stand with one foot in one country and one in another. Silly, I know. But here was my chance.

We lost our way – it was before satnav made that well-nigh impossible. I confess I was becoming just a little shirty with Clare, my map-reader, who as usual was insisting that we had to be very close to Lescun by now and that one way or another we would soon get there. When I'm negative she becomes positive, which is inclined to make me even more negative. I was becoming, I fear, ever more silent, impatient and thin-lipped.

Then she spotted a strange sign by the side of the road – a huge cut-out figure of a bear, holding a pot of honey in his paw, and an arrow, beside him, pointing off the road to the right. Across his stomach was painted one word in large letters, which read: MIEL.

"Honey," Clare said. "We like honey, don't we, dear? Let's turn right here." I was sulking too much even to argue by now. We turned off the road and drove into a village called Borce – just a few houses, a shop, a café and a village green. And on the village green there was a large cage. We got out of the car to have a closer look. There was a bear in the cage, and a notice on the bars: JOJO. EUROPEAN BEAR, FOUND AND REARED AS AN ORPHAN CUB BY A GIRL FROM THE VILLAGE. DO NOT FEED THE BEAR. The bear looked old, his fur tatty and ragged and matted. He seemed rather sad, heartbroken even, from the look in his eyes. He sat there swaying, longing to be let out, to be free. Clare bought her honey in the café, while I stood there looking into that bear's eyes, already determined there and then to tell the story of the little girl and the bear cub.

A question or two over a coffee in the village café gave me a helping hand with my embryonic story. The bear cub had been found, it seemed, many years ago by a little girl who was playing Poohsticks by a stream on the edge of the village. She had picked the cub up in her arms, easily enough in its weakened state, and brought it back into the village. It caused quite a stir. Everyone came running. One of the old farmers said, "Knock it on the head – we don't like bears here, they kill our sheep." But someone else said, "No, let's keep him. We'll make a cage for him, call him JoJo, put his picture on our pots of honey, call it 'JoJo's Honey' and sell all the honey our bees can make. Then we'll put a notice down by the road, telling all those gullible tourists driving by to come and buy our honey." So that's what they had done, and of course that's why we were there. As we were leaving the café, Clare happened to ask: "Are we anywhere near a village called Lescun, by any chance?"

"Oh, yes," they said. "Just a kilometre up the road, before you come to the mountains. You can't miss it."

Clare didn't say, "I told you so", but I could tell she wanted to.

We found Lescun up the road, just as we had been told, and there, right in the centre, was the little village inn. As we walked in we saw two bearskins stretched out on the walls, and a huge black and white photo of village hunters, standing in the square in front of the inn, rifles at their sides, a dead bear stretched out on the ground at their feet. Maybe the mother of JoJo, I thought, and then looked away. It wasn't a photograph you wanted to look at twice.

Next morning after breakfast, taking a picnic with us, we walked up out of the village towards the Pic d'Anie and the mountains. We were followed all the way by a huge white sheepdog, I remember. He was most definitely keeping an eye on us, we felt. We saw shepherdesses sitting in fields, knitting, their sheep all around them on the hills, bells tinkling softly, as we followed the trail up onto the high pastures, where we found cows being milked and cheese being made. We stopped and watched for a while, and then climbed on and up, until we were on top of the Pic d'Anie, the frontier of France and Spain. Now I could stand there, arms raised, one foot in Spain, the other in France, and breathe in the air of both!

We stayed a couple of nights in Lescun, and in that time got talking to people. We learnt that the village had been occupied by Germans during the Second World War. They had taken over the priest's house by the church. They were patrolling the hills all around, trying to prevent people escaping over the border into neutral Spain –

shot-down Allied airmen, Jews, Frenchmen escaping transportation to Germany. There was a cross by the side of the road outside the village where an escaping Jew had been shot and killed. We were also told that, although few knew about it at the time, there had been a safe house outside the village, a farmhouse where an old lady had courageously hidden away many of those who were trying to escape, before arranging for a guide to take them over the mountains to freedom – this at the risk of her life.

The bear story was one thing. I decided this was another. I put JoJo out of my mind, for the moment. I knew that in Lescun I had stumbled upon a remarkable story. I needed to learn more. It was difficult, though, to ask about how it was occupied. The subject is a sensitive one in France, was then, is now. But then, by great good fortune, I was given a window of opportunity. At supper one evening, the hotel manager's daughter, a girl of about ten or eleven, approached our table. "Excuse me," she said, "but my father says that when you came to the hotel, and signed in, he recognized your name from a book I am reading. This one." She held out a copy of *Cheval de guerre* (*War Horse*). "I wonder if you would please sign it for me." So I did, with pleasure. "And," she went on, "my father says you are invited to our house tomorrow for wine and pâté." She said she would come and fetch us, which was how we found ourselves sitting in a farmhouse kitchen at midday the next day, eating wonderful home-made pâté and sipping delicious wine. Her father was there too – it was he who was the most talkative and friendly, friendly enough for me to dare to ask him a question. "Did you live here in the war when the village was occupied?"

"Yes," he said. "I was a boy. "The German soldiers used to give us sweets. We did not want to like them, but we did – the soldiers, I mean, not the sweets. They were mostly old soldiers, not fighting soldiers. They just wanted to go home. People got on quite well with them – some of the Germans had fought in the First World War, and so had many of the older men in the village. They were in a strange way all old comrades. Then one day after long years of occupation, we woke up, and they were gone. War over. We rang the church bell, put out the flag, had a big party."

I left the village, my head full of the story that was already taking shape. One of our French family, the grandmother, later told me how as a child she had stood at the roadside and watched the Germans come marching in. "I don't like to admit it," she had said, "but in a horrible way, when I think about it, we children admired them in their smart black uniforms, handsome, victorious." I was having quite unexpected and honest insights into how it was for children then to see their country occupied.

On the way up through France back to England, we stopped by a village called Oradour-sur-Glane, a village left in ruins as a memorial to the eight hundred or so villagers massacred by SS troops in 1944. The village was burnt out entirely, the charred remains of a few cars still there, the church and the barns where so many had been killed, still charred and gaping, open to the skies. This was the other face of the occupation. We stopped too by a wood and walked into its silence. Here were graves in among the trees. Here was all that was left of a concentration camp, a holding camp for those prisoners, mostly Jews, destined for Auschwitz or Treblinka or Bergen-Belsen – death camps.

In *Waiting for Anya*, I would tell my story of a shepherd boy in Lescun, of a bear who is shot, of the Nazi occupation of the boy's village of Lescun, of the safe house he stumbles upon where Jewish children are kept hidden, of the secret he must keep. In *The Dancing Bear*, I would tell another kind of story altogether, but they both took root in and around Lescun, that little village in the mountains, which we so nearly didn't find.

WAITING FOR ANYA

Then one blustery Autumn day, after the sheep had come down from the pastures and he was spreading out the bracken for the bedding in the barn, he saw Widow Horcada scurrying past, black scarf over her head, flowers in her hand. He knew she'd be making for the churchyard to put flowers on her husband's grave. She'd stop to do her shopping on the way back, she always did. Jo knew he had a clear half hour to get up there and back: he could do it if he hurried. She'd never see him, not if he was careful. Rouf tried to come with him as he always did. He shut him in the barn and shouted to Maman that he wouldn't be long.

He kept under the cover of the trees as long as he could. From there he could see without being seen. Her pigs were foraging in the field below the house and the cow was lying curled asleep in the middle of them. There was no one about. He threw caution to the wind because he had to – there was no time for anything else. He hared across the field until he reached the safety of the barn wall where he knew he could not be seen from the house. He ran around the back of the barn and into the courtyard behind. There was no sound except for the contented grunted of rooting pigs. He was creeping past the barn door when he heard something shuffling around inside. The bear cub, it must be the bear cub.

He looked about him and then opened the door slowly. Like all the barns it was long and low and dark, with bracken on the floor and hay in the wooden rack that ran the length of the wall. But there was no bear cub, and no other animals either. Yet he was sure he'd heard something, quite sure. He pushed the door wide open so as to throw as much light as possible down the barn. There was one small dirty window at the far end, and the shutters were banging open and shut, first one and then the other. Jo peered into the darkness. He would go no further. He could see well enough from the doorway. He was turning to go when he trod on something. He bent down and picked up a shoe, a child's shoe. The strap was broken. He thought little of it at first. He would have dropped it and left had he not heard the breathing – a regular wheezing breathing.

It came quite definitely from the hayrack about halfway down the barn. Jo took a few steps towards it and the breathing stopped. He thought of the bear cub and of the hibernation Monsieur Audup had told them about, but he thought that it couldn't be the bear cub because it wasn't winter yet and anyway a bear cub would hardly be sleeping in a hayrack – but then perhaps it would. He took a few more tentative steps forward and peered into the hay. The breathing began again a little further on and quite suddenly he found himself not looking at hay at all but at two eyes that stared back at him unblinking and terrified. Jo could do nothing for a moment but stare back into them. They were not the eyes of a bear for the face that went with them was pale and thin under a fringe of dark hair.

Jo backed away slowly, swallowing his fear. He had the presence of mind to close the door quietly and it was just as well he did for across the yard Widow Horcada was bent over, holding a bucket under an outdoor tap. She had her back to him and was humming quietly to herself. For a few moments he stood looking at her disbelieving. How could she be back so soon? It wasn't possible. Yet there she was in front of him. She had only to turn round. It was just a few steps to the corner of the barn and safety. He'd make it if he could move silently. Without taking his eyes off her he began to inch his way along the wall.

He knew he should have looked where he was going. He told himself so as the fork he blundered into clattered to the ground. Jo looked at the Widow Horcada, the bucket fell out of her hand as the black shawl swung round. Jo dropped the shoe, stumbled over the fork and ran and ran. He rounded the corner of the barn, but there he was stopped in his tracks, for up the hill, a large basket in one hand, a stick in the other, came Widow Horcada. She looked up, saw him and shouted at him. He could not hear what she was saying. Jo turned again and ran back into the yard – it was the only way he could go. She was there too and coming towards him. He looked now from one to the other. Fear crept up his spine like a warm cat and he felt the hair rise on the back of his neck. Never in all his life had he felt like screaming until this moment. He wanted to but he could not. And then one of them spoke, the one striding across the yard towards him.

"It's me." It was a man's voice. "It's me." And he pulled the shawl off his head. The red beard was longer than Jo remembered but it was the same man. "Don't you remember me?" he said.

THE DANCING BEAR

It was a Sunday morning in April. We were in the café before lunch. The old man was going on about Roxanne again, and how she ate him out of house and home. He'd had a bit too much to drink, I think, but then he was often that way.

"Gone off again, she has," he grumbled. "God knows what she gets up to. Nothing but trouble, that girl."

Just then we heard shouting in the village square and, glad of any diversion, we all went out to look. Roxanne was staggering towards us, clutching a bear cub in her arms, with its arms wrapped around her neck. She'd been scratched on her face and on her arms, but it didn't seem to bother her. She was laughing and breathless with joy.

"Bruno!" she said. "He's called Bruno. I was down by the stream. I was just throwing sticks and I felt something stroking my neck. I turned round and there he was. He patted my shoulder. He's my very own bear, Grandpa. He's all alone. He's hungry. I can keep him, can't I? Please?"

If we hadn't been there – and half the village was there by now – I think the old man might have grabbed the bear cub by the scruff of the neck and taken him right back where he came from.

"Look at him," he said. "He's half starved. He's going to die anyway. And besides, bears are for killing, not keeping. You know how many sheep we lose every year to bears? Dozens, I'm telling you, dozens."

Some people were beginning to agree with him. I looked at Roxanne and saw she was looking up at me. Her eyes were filled with tears.

"Maybe" – I was still thinking hard as I spoke – "if you kept him, you know, just for a while. It wouldn't cost much: some waste milk and an old shed somewhere. And just suppose" – I was talking directly to the old man now – "just suppose you made 'bear' labels for your honey jars – you could call it 'Bruno's Honey'. Everyone would hear about it. They'd come from miles around, have a little look at the bear and then buy your honey. You'd make a fortune, I'm sure of it."

I'd said the right thing. Roxanne's grandfather had his beehives all over the mountainside, and everyone knew that he couldn't sell even half the honey he collected. He nodded slowly as the sense of it dawned on him. "All right," he said. "We'll try it. Just for a while, mind."

France during
World War Two

Germany invaded France on 10 May 1940. A little over a month later, Maréchal Pétain, the new prime minister of France, asked for surrender terms. The armistice, signed on 22 June 1940, split France in two. The north and west of France, including the Channel and Atlantic ports, were to be under German occupation. The rest of France – "Vichy France" – was "free" to be governed by the French.

Charles de Gaulle, an officer in the tank corps in the French Army, refused to surrender. He fled to England, from where, on the eve of the French surrender, he broadcast a radio message to the French people. This historic speech gave hope to many who disagreed with Maréchal Pétain, and helped to start the Resistance movement, with people fighting secretly to do anything possible to obstruct the Germans and support the British.

At first, resistance was patchy and disorganized. People escaped into the country and the mountains, joining the "Maquis", groups of Resistance fighters in remote areas. (The word *maquis* is from the Corsican for "bush", evoking an image of woods and mountains.) French Resistance fighters blew up bridges, derailed trains, collected information for the British, kidnapped and killed German officers. As the war progressed Resistance groups grew more organized and effective, but many fighters were captured, tortured and shot, or sent to concentration camps.

The Nazis followed a policy of "collective punishment" or civilian "reprisals" for any resistance actions across occupied Europe. On 10 June 1944, following the kidnapping of a German officer by the French Resistance, a Nazi Panzer (armoured tank) division rolled into the village of Oradour-sur-Glane. There was no evidence that Oradour locals had been involved in the kidnapping or the Resistance movement, but that day, 642 men, women and children were murdered. Nazi troops herded the men of the village into a barn and shot them before the building was set ablaze. Women and children were locked inside the church while the village was looted. Soldiers then set off an incendiary device in the church, trapping them in the flames. Finally the rest of the village was destroyed. The ruins can still be seen today.

Many French people chose a non-violent, but equally dangerous, form of resistance to Nazi occupation: they helped people escape from

German-occupied Europe. At first these were British soldiers cut off from their units during the evacuation of Dunkirk, escaped prisoners of war, shot-down airmen. As the Allies intensified their bombing campaign from 1941, more and more Allied airmen were shot down. Helped by Resistance networks, many of them were escorted out of France and guided over the Pyrenees to neutral Spain. The "Comet" network, involving some 2,000 Resistance members, helped 700 Allied servicemen into Spain, hiding them, feeding them and providing them with forged identity cards and money. But it came at a price: 800 Comet members were arrested, and 140 were executed.

Meanwhile, other escapees included French civilians trying to avoid forced labour in Germany, and victims of discrimination of all kinds – foreigners, anyone who had been denounced to the authorities, and Jews. Vichy France was the only place in Europe without a German military presence that nevertheless voluntarily cooperated in the rounding-up and deportation of Jews, a cause for guilt in France to this day.

Many of these escapees braved the hazardous trip across the mountains of the Pyrenees. The Pyrenees, with their steep and treacherous paths, were hostile and well guarded, a formidable challenge, especially in winter and in the dark. Hundreds of the escapees were already malnourished and exhausted after weeks on the run hiding in barns and attics.

However, even after reaching Spain, escapees were not necessarily safe. Spain was technically neutral in the war, although ideologically leaning towards Germany. Those who were captured by Spanish frontier guards were returned and handed over to the German authorities. Nevertheless, particularly in the early part of the war, Spain allowed a large number of Jewish refugees to cross Spain on their way to Portugal. Later, German pressure reduced the number of Jews admitted entry into Spain.

Many French Jews decided not to escape through the mountains, but joined the Resistance movement themselves. Jews in France constituted only 1 per cent of the French population, but they comprised over 15 per cent of the Resistance.

It is thought that the efforts of Resistance networks helped around 33,000 men, women and children to escape successfully along the entire length of the Pyrenees. As one escapee, Jean Souque, said, "You never really know what freedom is until you've lost it."

The White Horse of Westbury

The Butterfly Lion

THE DREAM

I was in Hay-on-Wye at the literary festival, strolling through the streets past all the second-hand bookshops, when I happened to glance in at the window of one of them and caught sight of a book called *The White Lions of Timbavati*. On the front cover was a striking photograph of a white lion in the African bush. He was looking directly at me, staring at me. I was interested, intrigued. I'd never heard of white lions before. I had thought until then that all lions were tan in colour, or dusty gold. I went in and asked if I could have a closer look. The book turned out to contain a study made over several years of a pride of white lions in South Africa, and there were numerous photographs throughout, of white lions with their cubs, sleeping through the heat of the day, hunting, then sleeping again. It was £4.45. I bought it and took it back to my hotel room.

After that, I took the book with me wherever I went.

These rare and beautiful creatures became ever more magical to me as I turned the pages, and I kept dipping into it, kept wondering at them, at their magnificence. So it was that I had the book with me and was reading it again, a couple of weeks later, when I found myself on the train travelling home from London to Exeter. Just before we came into Westbury Station in Wiltshire, the train stopped. I looked up from my book, to see where we were, I suppose, and there, right across the hillside, carved out of the chalk, was this huge white horse. White horse. I looked down at the cover of my book. White lion. I looked up again. White horse, white lion, white horse. From that moment, I knew I was going to tell a story about some great white lion carved out of a chalky hillside. But no story came. My white lion remained simply an image in my head, not a story. Try as I did, I could make nothing more of it.

Then I heard a story, a true story that enabled me to bring that white lion on the hillside to life. I was at a dinner party, and everyone was exchanging stories, I remember, of grandparents. Who knows why! A particularly boring fellow opposite me was sounding off, at length, and in a voice like a trombone, about a grandfather of his who had been in the trenches in the First World War. The tone of his storytelling was so ponderous and pompous that I nearly stopped listening altogether. But I am very glad I didn't. I know I only went on listening because he said this story was about a lion. It was, it turned out, about a lot more than that.

His grandfather, it seemed, had been sent to the Front in France as a young eighteen-year-old officer. After just a couple of days in the trenches, a shell exploded near by, and he was wounded in the leg. He was stretchered to a field hospital, treated there, and then taken to a large convalescent hospital in a chateau, some thirty miles behind the lines. As part of his treatment, the doctors made him walk into the nearest village every day, with his walking stick, to build up the strength in his leg.

One day, having walked the mile or so from the chateau to the village, he was sitting, having a glass of wine in a café, when he heard the sound of shooting. Wondering what was going on, he got up and limped off round the corner into the square. Drawn up around the village square were a dozen or so wagons and cages from a travelling circus. And then he saw an old Frenchman going from cage to cage shooting the animals one by one, and crying his heart out as he did so.

Enraged, the young soldier wrenched the rifle out of his hand, "Why?" he cried. "Why are you doing this?"

"Listen," said the old circus keeper, "these are my animals, my family. But I can't feed them any more. No one comes to the circus. I have no money. And even if I had money, there is no meat to buy, no straw or hay to buy. Everything goes to the soldiers and the horses at the Front. My animals are starving. I have no choice but to shoot them."

There was just one circus animal still alive, the old circus lion.

"Well, you're not shooting that lion," said the young man.

"Then you look after him," the Frenchman replied. "I cannot."

Not long afterwards, villagers and soldiers witnessed an extraordinary sight. Coming down the street towards the grand house that served as military headquarters was a young soldier and an old man, the circus owner, who was leading the circus lion. People disappeared into their houses, and shut the doors and windows. Children were hauled off the street. As they approached the headquarters, the commanding officer came running down the steps, demanding to know what was going on.

"Sir," said the young soldier, saluting. "This is a circus lion. It belongs to me now, because this Frenchman, who is the circus owner, cannot feed him any more. So I arranged that we would look after the lion – he was going to have to shoot him otherwise. And the lion is the emblem of England, isn't it, sir? So we could not let that happen, could we, sir?"

"I should jolly well think not," said the commanding officer. So they looked after the old lion, and in time sent him back to England, where he lived out his life in a zoo.

"Well, what do you think of that?" said the teller of the tale when he had finished. All of us had listened to every word. Not surprisingly, after a story like that, no one else seemed to have a grandfather story to tell. I later found out there was truth in his story, that something like that had actually happened.

So now I had a story to tell, but not the confidence to tell it. The truth was, I knew little or nothing about lions, or about Africa. Help came, by great good fortune – I have had a lot of this! – from a chance meeting in a lift in Dublin. I was there to give a talk at a conference. That was now over, and I was making my way up to my room after breakfast, when into the lift stepped someone I knew, a face I instantly recognized. But I hadn't a clue who this person was. She was maybe about my age, exceedingly beautiful and elegant. All I knew was that this was a face I had loved. As the lift went up, I struggled to recall her name. I did, just in time, but I was so overwhelmed at being so close to someone I had so much admired that I couldn't think what to say. So I said the first thing that came into my head: "I think your Born Free Foundation is wonderful," I told her.

"Thanks so much," said Virginia McKenna, great and beautiful star of the film *Born Free*, and many other films and plays, and founder of the Born Free Foundation. The lift stopped, the door opened, and off she went. Off I went too, distraught at my clumsiness.

I was packing my suitcase a few minutes later and saw there on my bed a copy of the book I had just published, *The Dancing Bear*. Leave a copy for Virginia McKenna, I thought. Her whole life has been about caring for wild animals, fighting to ensure they are not locked up in cages or treated cruelly. I knew that was why she and her late husband, Bill Travers, had set up the Born Free Foundation. So I wrote a little dedication to her in my book and left it for her at the reception desk.

A week later I received a wonderful letter from her, saying how much she had liked *The Dancing Bear* and how heartened she was by my kind words. If ever I needed it, she wrote, if ever I was to think of writing a book about a lion, she would be only too pleased to help, because she knew lions quite well, had lived with them and worked with them, and loved them. I needed no further encouragement. I asked for her help by return of post. And help came. Armed now with all this new inside knowledge about lions from Virginia McKenna, with my story of the white horse carved out on that hillside in Westbury, with that story I'd heard round the dinner table about the young soldier in the First World War, surely I could do it. Surely I could begin. But I couldn't.

I needed to find the voice for my story. 1914 is a long time ago. I couldn't start: "Once upon a time..." It wasn't a fairy story. Someone in the story had to tell it, someone who was there, alive at the time. But who? Someone old now, with a tale to tell, I thought. Memory helped me there, memories of me as a schoolboy, a small frightened boy running away from boarding school – as I had – meeting an old lady a mile or so away from the school who took pity on me and looked after me. She brought me to her home in the village, gave me tea and sticky buns, calmed me down and told me about the photo on her mantelpiece of her husband in uniform and how he had gone off to the First World War and came home deaf from the guns. Then she drove me back to my school, so that no one ever knew I had run away.

The voice of the storyteller in *The Butterfly Lion* is hers, and the little boy in the story is me. I even call myself Michael. I often do that in my stories. It helps me feel I am inside the story as I am writing, that I am living it. There are more Michaels in my stories than I care to remember. I am not very inventive with names. Often I write in the first person. So then it makes sense to be Michael, even Michael Morpurgo sometimes. I am Michael Morpurgo, for instance, in another story set in my boarding school, the story I call *My One and Only Great Escape* – also about my running away. I was never very good at running away. But, though I did not realize it at the time, it helped me write my stories, and more than once too. If I had not run away, I think I should never have found a way to write *The Butterfly Lion*.

The rugby team at The Abbey School,
before my 'great escape'
(I'm in the front row, on the left, the one with ears!)

THE BUTTERFLY LION

I was still deciding which direction to take when I heard a voice from behind me.

"Who are you? What do you want?"

I turned.

"Who are you?" she asked again. The old lady who stood before me was no bigger than I was. She scrutinized me from under the shadow of her dripping straw hat. She had piercing dark eyes that I did not want to look into.

"I didn't think it would rain," she said, her voice gentler. "Lost, are you?"

I said nothing. She had a dog on a leash at her side, a big dog. There was an ominous growl in his throat, and his hackles were up all along his back.

She smiled. "The dog says you're on private property," she went on, pointing her stick at me accusingly. She edged aside my raincoat with the end of her stick. "Run away from that school, did you? Well, if it's anything like it used to be, I can't say I blame you. But we can't just stand here in the rain, can we? You'd better come inside. We'll give him some tea, shall we, Jack? Don't you worry about Jack. He's

99

all bark and no bite." Looking at Jack, I found that hard to believe.

I don't know why, but I never for one moment thought of running off. I often wondered later why I went with her so readily. I think it was because she expected me to, willed me to somehow. I followed the old lady and her dog up to the house, which was huge, as huge as my school. It looked as if it had grown out of the ground. There was hardly a brick or a stone or a tile to be seen. The entire building was smothered in red creeper, and there were a dozen ivy-clad chimneys sprouting skywards from the roof.

We sat down close to the stove in a vast vaulted kitchen. "The kitchen's always the warmest place," she said, opening the oven door. "We'll have you dry in no time. Scones?" she went on, bending down with some difficulty and reaching inside. "I always have scones on a Sunday. And tea to wash it down. All right for you?" She went on chatting away as she busied herself with the kettle and the teapot. The dog eyed me all the while from his basket, unblinking. "I was just thinking," she said. "You'll be the first young man I've had inside this house since Bertie." She was silent for a while.

The smell of the scones wafted through the kitchen. I ate three before I even touched my tea. They were sweet and crumbly, and succulent with melting butter. She talked on merrily again, to me, to the dog – I wasn't sure which. I wasn't really listening. I was looking out of the window behind her. The sun was bursting through the clouds and lighting the hillside. A perfect rainbow arched through the sky. But miraculous though it was, it wasn't the rainbow that fascinated me. Somehow, the clouds were casting a strange shadow over the hillside, a shadow the shape of a lion, roaring like the one over the archway.

"Sun's come out," said the old lady, offering me another scone. I took it eagerly. "Always does, you know. It may be difficult to remember sometimes, but there's always sun behind the clouds, and the clouds do go in the end. Honestly."

She watched me eat, a smile on her face that warmed me to the bone.

"Don't think I want you to go, because I don't. Nice to see a boy eat so well, nice to have the company; but all the same, I'd better get you back to school after you've had your tea, hadn't I? You'll only be in trouble otherwise. Mustn't run off, you know. You've got to stick it out, see things through, do what's got to be done, no matter what." She was looking out of the window as she spoke. "My Bertie taught me that, bless him, or maybe I taught him. I can't remember now." And she went on talking and talking, but my mind was elsewhere again.

The lion on the hillside was still there, but now he was blue and shimmering in the sunlight. It was as if he were breathing, as if he were alive. It wasn't a shadow any more. No shadow is blue. "No, you're not seeing things," the old lady whispered. "It's not magic. He's real enough. He's our lion, Bertie's and mine. He's our butterfly lion."

"What d'you mean?" I asked.

She looked at me long and hard. "I'll tell you if you like," she said. "Would you like to know? Would you really like to know?"

I nodded.

"Have another scone first and another cup of tea. Then I'll take you to Africa where our lion came from, where my Bertie came from too. Bit of a story, I can tell you. You ever been to Africa?"

"No," I replied.

"Well, you're going," she said. "We're both going."

Suddenly I wasn't hungry any more. All I wanted now

was to hear her story. She sat back in her chair, gazing out of the window. She told it slowly, thinking before each sentence; and all the while she never took her eyes off the butterfly lion. And neither did I.

White lions

Thirty years ago, there were 200,000 lions living in the wild; today there are only 15,000. In thirty-five African countries, where once they roamed free, the lion is now extinct or has virtually disappeared. And although it may be unthinkable that lions ever become completely extinct, they are now listed as "vulnerable" in the International Union for Conservation of Nature's Red List of Threatened Species.

A wild lion has a "home range" of about 240 kilometres, the area regularly travelled by a single lion in its food gathering, mating and caring for young. This brings lions into conflict with farmers and with the increasing need, driven by population growth, for land building and agriculture. "Anyone who is trying to farm livestock in Africa finds it very difficult to co-exist with lions," comments Luke Hunter of Panthera, one of the groups trying to save the lion from extinction. He also notes a "very widespread killing of lions, mostly in a conflict situation". Poachers and big-game hunters also add to the risks for these big cats.

The lion most likely to die out unless we take more positive action is the white lion. White lions are not albinos. Albino animals – and people – have an inherited disorder characterized by the complete or partial absence of pigment in the skin, whereas white lions owe their remarkable colouring to a genetic twist. A pigment gene gives them blue or green-grey eyes instead of brown, and a pelt that remains white all their lives. It is their very prettiness and apparent cuddliness that have been their downfall since their first contact with Europeans in 1938.

White lions probably evolved many millennia ago. Despite this, there was an unsupported belief among some conservationists that white lions could not survive in the wild, on the grounds that their colouring would make it difficult to remain camouflaged when they were hunting. Most white lions were rounded up and sold to zoos – if they were not killed by big-game hunters first.

A few wild white lions can be found on the edge of a South African National Park. To the local tribe, the Shangaan, the area is special. They name it Timbavati, meaning "the place where something sacred came down to earth".

For centuries, white lions have been part of the African oral tradition. The medicine men traditionally believed the lions to be animal angels. One legend says they were the first creatures to be created by the gods - and when life becomes extinct the roar of the white lions will be the last sound on Earth. Tribal elders believe that the white lions are here to deliver a message for humanity. In spiritual terms their white colouring represents purity and enlightenment. White represents sunlight and contains all the colours of the spectrum in one; white is beyond colour, creed, race, or gender.

Sadly, rich hunters pay huge sums of money to slaughter lions - even though it is illegal to hunt them in the wild almost everywhere in Africa - and white lions are especially prized by hunters. A stuffed lion can sell for £40,000.

Many lions are captured in the wild as cubs, or bred in captivity, brought up as tourist attractions in lion ranches. They are bottle-fed, taught not to fear humans, and spend their days being petted and photographed by unwitting visitors. The animals involved are very vulnerable. No longer fearful of humans, they will approach them expecting to get fed, but instead receive a bullet, or an arrow from a hunting bow. One rancher revealed: "We keep them up until six months for attractions for the people so they can play with them and then we sell them to other lion parks. What they do with the lions is up to them."

The Global White Lion Protection Trust has spent the last twelve years buying two thousand acres of land in Timbavati and preparing to release white lions, hoping that they might re-establish themselves. Reintroduction into the wild of animals born or reared in captivity is always difficult. Their dependence on human contact can mean the loss of both their hunting instincts and their fear of people – both essential qualities for survival.

Nevertheless, the initial success of the programme was capped in 2014, when the first ever photographs of white lion cubs born in their natural habitat were published. Conservationist Linda Tucker, who founded the Trust, said: "The birth of these second-generation white cubs to a wild white lioness is fantastic news. It brings huge hope for the future of white lions. They recognize me, but I keep my distance and allow them their independence. I look at them like any mother with a brood of growing youngsters. And, in the end, the most loving gift you can give is freedom."

Kensuke's Kingdom

To begin ....

disappeared on the night of my tw[...]
th day. June 28th 1988. Only now
n years later can I at last tell th[...]
traordinary story, the true story. Kens-
[...]de me promise I would keep silent,
[...]thing about him or his kingdom un[...]
least ten years had passed. By then,
[...]d would be all over for him anyway
[...]would't matter any more. But I was
~~came looking for him~~ even after
~~to bring apart back~~ [...] to reveal
was. ~~this~~ hide him his friends needed
And peace and people, he said, rarely
~~So I promised; But I have kept my prom~~
~~But is a risk [If Ten years have pa~~
say anything now? Why not let sl[...]
? I s-ppose it's
want the world
[...] to that, for [...]

Kensuke's Kingdom

THE DREAM

Some books that you read when you are young make such an impression that they never leave you. Some are life-changing, both literally and imaginatively. The first book I ever really loved was Robert Louis Stevenson's *Treasure Island* – I must have discovered it when I was nine or ten.

Until then I had been addicted to comics. I liked being read to, but I had a horror of words packed tight on a page. I preferred pictures to tell the story rather than words. For a while, I managed to read nothing but Enid Blyton adventures – great page-turners. But *Treasure Island*, I could tell, even then, made all the pictures I wanted and needed in my head, and was much more engaging and compelling than Blyton books, because the characters were so well drawn that I cared about them, identified with them. I *was* Jim Hawkins in the Hispaniola hiding in that barrel of apples on deck, overhearing Long John Silver and his mutinous, villainous cronies hatching their murderous plans. And the island itself – I knew Treasure Island like the back of my hand. I lived on that island, knew its beaches and caves and the stockade. That island was a world of its own, and I loved that.

Then there was *Lord of the Flies* by William Golding. I read this as a teenager, as many of us do, and was struck at once not only by the dark power of the story, but also the landscape. Golding's island is not simply scenery against which the story is played out. It is the wilderness and wildness of the island, the isolation from the world and the imprisoning sea itself that determine the behaviour of the boys.

Islands fast became a fascination. I read all the books I could about them. Then later, when I was grown-up, about thirty, I was lucky enough to visit some islands that were isolated and wild, where the sea rules. Every summer we would go to the Isles of Scilly for our holidays, to stay on Bryher, the smallest of the five inhabited islands, rearing cliffs at Hell Bay at one end, and beaches of the finest sand at the other at Rushy Bay. I got to know that island and its people in all weathers, when the fog rolled in and the lighthouse hooted its warning, when storms raged and threatened to flood and overwhelm, when the sun shone over a sparkling green sea. And we caught crabs and shrimps in the rock pools, went fishing for mackerel. Bliss it can be on such days. But the sea always rules. Tides, the wind, the weather dictate the lives of islanders and visitors. There are times when you cannot leave the island for days on end.

The more I got to know the Scillies, the more I became aware of the effect of isolation on how islanders feel, how they see the world, their sense of independence, their toughness. I listened to their stories, stories of wrecks and treasure, of great tragedy and supreme courage. There were ancient burial chambers, field systems now swallowed up by the sea, but visible. The Romans had been here, King Arthur too, maybe, and pirates and monks. Scilly for me was a treasure house of stories, both true and legendary. I immersed myself in the place. So it was hardly surprising that in the end, I sat down and wrote my own stories about Scilly, on Bryher mostly. I wrote *Why the Whales Came*, then *The Wreck of the Zanzibar*; *The Sleeping Sword*; *Arthur, High King of Britain*; *Half a Man*; and recently, *Listen to the Moon*. But there was one island story I could not set on Scilly.

Like many writers, I receive letters from readers from time to time. I like them, because mostly, people write because they have loved the stories. So, I confess it, I love getting fan mail – makes a fellow feel good, especially if he is having difficulty with his new story. About a year after *The Wreck of the Zanzibar* came out, I got a letter from a boy which went something like this.

Dear Mr Morpurgo,

I read your book *The Wreck of the Zanzibar*. It is the best book I ever read, better than all the Harry Potter books put together. BUT, it is about a girl. I am a boy. Will you please write me a story about a boy who gets stuck on a desert island?

Yours sincerely…

What a great idea! I thought. Until I discussed it with Clare, my wife. She said it wasn't an original idea. Didn't I realize there was *Treasure Island*, *Lord of the Flies* – both about boys on desert islands, classics, known and loved all over the world, both by literary giants. That, of course, was precisely why I liked the idea. All right, so Stevenson and Golding were great writers, but I could have a go, couldn't I?

But try as I did to dream up my story of my boy on the desert island, I couldn't find a way to make it work. Everything I thought up seemed to have been done before. It was beginning to look as if Clare had been right – she usually is. I couldn't even find a way of getting my boy onto the island. Then I struck lucky. At a very dull party I got talking to a stranger, a young man, and asked him, as you do, what he did. He told me that he had just returned from five years' sailing around the world on a yacht, stopping off on uninhabited islands in the Pacific. I remember, as he was telling me, that I felt the hair on the back of my neck standing up.

"Just you, on your own?" I asked him.

"No, with my wife too!"

"The two of you, then?"

"No, three. Our son came along."

"A boy?" I said.

"Sons usually are," he replied. "Oh, yes, and the dog – the dog came too. The dog fell overboard once or twice."

"Really?" I said.

Suddenly the dull party was dull no more. I quizzed the poor stranger for an hour or more and came away knowing I could do this now. Unseen, in the dark of night, the boy would somehow fall off the yacht, dog too, and there he was in the sea, watching the boat sail away into the darkness, his mum and dad on board, his screams unheard. Swim, swim, swim … sharks, sharks, sharks. Island, island, island! I had my boy on the island, and with a dog too. I added a football, because I felt like it. That was a bonus!

Once I got home and thought about it, I realized this wasn't enough in itself to make a story. You can't make bread with just flour, you need yeast, salt, water, oil. All I had was a boy and a dog on an island. Then what? Again, I simply could not go any further. I very nearly abandoned the idea altogether. But it obsessed me, would not leave me alone.

From time to time, I cut out stories that interest me from newspapers, true stories. I kept asking myself who else could be on this island? Maybe it wasn't deserted but already inhabited? That was when I remembered the story I had cut out of a newspaper, about a Japanese soldier who, after the end of the Second World War, refused to believe the war was lost, and remained at his post on an island in the Pacific. Over twenty years later he had been discovered and brought back to Japan. I had my yeast, my salt, my water, my oil! My boy thinks himself alone with his dog on this island, but it turns out that there is also a Japanese sailor there, who has stayed on the island after the war, hidden himself away from the world and made the place his own, his kingdom. He does not want this intruder on his island. He feeds him, but ostracizes him. So, a young boy of today from one culture, one time, has to get along with an ancient Japanese warrior from another time, another culture, who does not want the boy there, nor his dog. Conflict! I had conflict. In my story, in almost any story, conflict is important, essential.

Before I can begin a story, I have to have names. I have already said that I am not good at choosing names for my characters. With *Kensuke's Kingdom* I struggled for weeks, searching for names that might work. Without them, I couldn't write even my first sentence. In the end, in desperation, I called the boy Michael, as I do! It was a start. Then I happened to be listening one day to a song on our Buddy Holly CD, *Peggy Sue*. Great name for a boat, I thought. It was difficult, though, to find a name for my marooned Japanese sailor. Then I got lucky again – luck, happenstance, always plays its part in the making of my stories, a large part. I went one day to a school to do a talk, and afterwards was signing books for the children. I looked up and there was this tall Japanese boy.

"What name shall I write in your book?" I asked him.

"Kensuke," he said. He spelt it for me. I liked the sound of it, the look of it.

"Can I borrow your name?" I asked him.

"What for?"

"To use in my next book," I told him.

"Can I have a copy of the book when it comes out?" he asked me. I agreed.

Only the dog's name left to find. All I could think of was Rover or Sally or Scoobydoo, until one dark evening in winter when I was walking down the lane to the milking parlour on the farm, with some of the city children who had just come down for their week on the farm. Our dog, Bercelet, came along with us, as she often did. The children huddled together close to me as we walked – the darkness clearly made them nervous – there are no streetlamps in the countryside. One boy, the biggest of the group, was particularly nervous and talked a lot.

"That dog, what's his name?" he asked me.

"Bercelet," I replied.

"Bercelet! Funny name!" he laughed. "What sort of dog is that, then?"

115

"A lurcher," I told him.

"Lurcher!" He laughed again, then said, "I got a bigger one than that back home, an Alsatian."

"What's he called?" I asked.

"Stella Artois," he said. Now I was doing the laughing. I had my dog's name, Stella Artois. The next day I sat down to write my story onto the paper, in my scrawly tiny writing. I called it *Kensuke's Kingdom*.

KENSUKE'S KINGDOM

The terrors came fast, one upon another. The lights of the *Peggy Sue* went away into the dark of the night, leaving me alone in the ocean, alone with the certainty that they were already too far away, that my cries for help could not possibly be heard. I thought then of the sharks cruising the black water beneath me – scenting me, already searching me out, homing in on me – and I knew there could be no hope. I would be eaten alive. Either that or I would drown slowly. Nothing could save me.

I trod water, frantically searching the impenetrable darkness about me for something, anything to swim towards. There was nothing.

Then a sudden glimpse of white in the sea. The breaking of a wave perhaps. But there were no waves. Stella! It had to be. I was so thankful, so relieved not to be all alone. I called out and swam towards her. She would keep bobbing away from me, vanishing, reappearing, then vanishing again. She had seemed so near, but it took several minutes of hard swimming before I came close enough to reach out and touch her. Only then did I realize my mistake. Stella's head was mostly black. This was white. It was my football. I grabbed it and clung on, feeling the unexpected and wonderful buoyancy of it. I held on, treading water and calling Stella. There was no answer. I called and I called. But every time I opened my mouth now, the seawater washed in. I had to give her up. I had to save myself if I could.

There was little point in wasting energy by trying to swim. After all, I had nowhere to swim to. Instead, I would simply float. I would cling to my football, tread water gently and wait for the *Peggy Sue* to come back. Sooner or later they would come looking for me. I mustn't kick too much, just enough to keep my chin above the water, no more. Too much movement would attract the sharks. Morning must come soon. I had to hang on till then. I had to. The water wasn't that cold. I had my football. I had a chance.

I kept telling myself that over and over again. But the world stayed stubbornly black about me, and I could feel the water slowly chilling me to death. I tried singing to stop myself from shivering, to take my mind off the sharks. I sang every song I could remember, but after a while I'd forget the words. Always I came back to the only song I was sure I could finish: "Ten Green Bottles". I sang it out loud again and again. It reassured me to hear the sound of my own voice. It made me feel less alone in the sea. And always I looked for the grey glint of dawn, but it would not come and it would not come.

Eventually I fell silent and my legs just would not kick any more. I clung to my football, my head drifting into sleep. I knew I mustn't, but I couldn't help myself. My hands kept slipping off the ball. I was fast losing the last of my strength. I would go down, down to the bottom of the sea and lie in my grave amongst the seaweed and the sailors' bones and the shipwrecks.

The strange thing was that I didn't really mind. I didn't care, not any more. I floated away into sleep, into my dreams. And in my dream I saw a boat gliding towards me, silent over the sea. The *Peggy Sue*! Dear, dear *Peggy Sue*. They had come back for me. I knew they would. Strong arms grabbed me. I was hauled upwards and out of the water. I lay there on the deck, gasping for air like a landed fish.

Someone was bending over me, shaking me, talking to me. I could not understand a word that was being said. But it didn't matter. I felt Stella's hot breath on my face, her tongue licking my ear. She was safe. I was safe. All was well.

I was woken by a howling, like the howling of a gale through the masts. I looked about me. There were no masts above me, there were no sails. No movement under me either, no breath of wind. Stella Artois was barking, but some way off. I was not on a boat at all, but lying stretched out on sand. The howling became a screaming, a fearful crescendo of screeching that died away in its own echoes.

I sat up. I was on a beach, a broad white sweep of sand, with trees growing thick and lush behind me right down to the beach. Then I saw Stella prancing about in the shallows. I called her and she came bounding up out of the sea to greet me, her tail circling wildly. When all the leaping and licking and hugging were done, I struggled to my feet.

I was weak all over. I looked all about me. The wide blue sea was empty as the cloudless sky above. No *Peggy Sue*. No boat. Nothing. No one. I called again and again for my mother and my father. I called until the tears came and I could call no more, until I knew there was no point. I stood there for some time trying to work out how I had got here, how it was that I'd survived. I had such confused memories, of being picked up, of being on board the *Peggy Sue*. But I knew now I couldn't have been. I must have dreamed it, dreamed the whole thing. I must have clung to my football and kept myself afloat until I was washed up. I thought of my football then, but it was nowhere to be seen.

Stella, of course, was unconcerned about all the whys and wherefores. She kept bringing me sticks to throw, and would go galloping after them into the sea without a care in the world.

Then came the howling again from the trees, and the hackles went up on Stella's neck. She charged up the beach barking and barking, until she was sure she had silenced the last of the echoes. It was a musical, plaintive howling this time, not at all menacing. I thought I recognized it. I had heard howling like it once before on a visit to London Zoo. Gibbons, "funky gibbons", my father had called them. I still don't know why to this day. But I loved the sound of the word "funky". Perhaps that was why I remembered what they were. "It's only gibbons," I told Stella, "just funky gibbons. They won't hurt us." But I couldn't be at all sure I was right.

From where I now stood I could see that the forest grew more sparsely up the side of a great hill some way inland, and it occurred to me then that if I could reach the bare rocky outcrop at the summit, I would be able to see further out to sea. Or perhaps there'd be some house or farm further inland, or maybe a road, and I could find someone to help. But if I left the beach and they came back looking for me, what then? I decided I would have to take that chance.

The real Kensuke

Second World War Japanese soldiers, especially officers, fiercely adhered to a rigid code of "No surrender". Japan had the oldest continuous hereditary monarchy in the world, and had never been invaded or lost a war. Japanese soldiers were fervently loyal to their Emperor, and believed in a variant of the Bushido code (literally, "the way of the warrior"). The most honourable fate for a warrior was to die taking enemies with him. Ordinary death in battle was the next most honourable fate; surrender unthinkable. Japanese troops who found themselves in a hopeless situation often adopted a suicide (or *banzai*) charge. They would die rather than surrender. Very few Japanese officers were captured alive until the final months of the war, and even then not many.

Towards the end of 1944, American forces were sweeping through the Pacific Islands to drive back the Japanese. The island of Guam was of strategic importance. Its airfields could handle large bombers, it had a deep harbour and its capture would assist the push towards the Philippines and Taiwan. When the attack began, the Japanese

Guam garrison numbered 22,000. Over 18,000 were killed in the subsequent fierce fighting. As only 485 were taken prisoner, some just melted into the jungle.

On 24 January 1972, two fishermen from Talofofo village on Guam were checking their shrimp traps when they heard a sound in the tall reeds. Out came an old and wild-looking Japanese man, who tried to grab one of the hunter's rifles.

Eventually, the story of Shoichi Yokoi's twenty-eight years of survival became known. Yokoi, an apprentice tailor, was born in 1915, and conscripted in 1941. When US forces invaded, soldiers such as Yokoi became cut off from their commanders during the fierce fighting, and had to fend for themselves.

Yokoi's long separation from the world began. He and a handful of other soldiers hid in the jungle. They took enormous care not to be detected, erasing their footprints as they moved through the undergrowth. They killed local cattle to eat. Later, fearing American patrols and local hunters, they withdrew deeper into the jungle, supplementing their diet of nuts and berries with venomous toads, river eels and rats.

Yokoi knew, from leaflets dropped by plane in 1952, that the war was over. But neither he nor the others would give up, because they thought the news might be false Allied propaganda. "We Japanese soldiers were told to prefer death to the disgrace of getting captured alive." Over time their numbers dwindled to three, who shared a cave. Eight years before Yokoi was captured, the two other men died, but he continued to survive completely alone.

One of Michael's inspiration triggers for Kensuke was a press article about another Japanese soldier found years after the war was over. After Yokoi's return, there were searches for soldiers hiding out on islands and in the jungle. Another straggler turned up two years later in the Philippines. Unlike Yokoi, whose rifle had rusted and become useless, Lieutenant Hiroo Onoda had kept a working firearm and was accused of killing several villagers before he was discovered in the jungle. Onoda survived on coconut milk, bananas and stolen cattle.

Neither Yokoi nor Onoda found adjusting to life in modern Japan easy. Yokoi became a popular television personality, and advocate of simple living, but he disliked the country's rapid postwar economic and industrial development. Japan had become a powerhouse of capitalism and technology. Yokoi became increasingly nostalgic about the past, and returned to Guam on several occasions before his death in 1997. There is a small museum on the island displaying Yokoi's prize possessions from those years in the jungle.

Onoda, like Yokoi, returned triumphantly to his homeland as a symbol of the irrepressible soldier, and, like Yokoi, did not like what he found there. "Japan's philosophy and ideas had changed dramatically. That philosophy clashed with mine, so I went to live in Brazil." In South America he set up a cattle ranch. Eventually, he returned to Japan, teaching survival skills to youngsters.

Onoda had only surrendered when his ageing former commander visited him and read the thirty-year-old orders stating that combat activity had ceased. Onoda remembers the time with a mixture of emotions: "*I became an officer and I received an order. If I could not carry it out, I would feel shame. Every Japanese soldier was prepared for death, but as an intelligence officer I was ordered to conduct guerrilla warfare and not to die... We really lost the war! How could they have been so sloppy? Suddenly everything went black. A storm raged inside me. What had I been doing for all these years? Gradually the storm subsided, and for the first time I really understood. My thirty years as a guerrilla fighter for the Japanese army were finished. This was the end. I pulled back the bolt on my rifle and unloaded the bullets.*"

Billy the Kid

THE DREAM

I'm not sure I ever wrote a story more inspired by the lives of others. For me now, when I read *Billy the Kid*, every page is a reminder of family and friends, who they are and were and the stories they have told me.

As with many of my books, I would never have come up with the idea in the first place without Michael Foreman. He rang me one day, nearly twenty years ago now, I suppose. "Hello, Michael, it's the other one," he began. "I want you to come with me to Stamford Bridge to see Chelsea play." Now, I had never been to a proper football match, and Michael knew I wasn't that interested in football. He knew my game was rugby. He, however, is a Chelsea fan through and through, a season ticket holder. He's mad about it. I thought that was why he was asking me really, to convert me from rugby to football. But then he explained, "I've got something I want to show you – an idea for a story." He wouldn't tell me on the phone.

I had to come to the match if I wanted to find out more. So I did. With him, I joined the blue tide flooding the streets around Chelsea, heard the thunder of clapping and chanting in the stadium, and there I was in my seat waiting for the game to begin.

Michael and the other one

If I'm honest, and don't tell Michael, the game was quite dull – very few goals were scored, and when there was one, everyone all around me was on their feet instantly, so that I could not even see what was going on. The half-time whistle went. "All right," I said, "What am I here for? What's the story?" Michael was pointing up to the director's box. "See those half-dozen old men in scarlet uniforms?" he said. "They're Chelsea pensioners – old soldiers, all of them. They live in a sort of old people's home for veterans, just down the road. Very famous." "I know who they are," I told him. "I've seen them about in their uniforms." "Well," he went on, "the club gives the old fellows free seats in the director's box at all the home games…" "But what's your story idea?" I asked. "Look down that end of the grounds." He was pointing. "The Shed End there, they call it. What do you see?" There was a solitary Chelsea pensioner sitting there in his scarlet uniform.

"All right," I said, knowing he wanted me to ask the obvious question. "What's he doing there, all on his own?" "That's why I've dragged you all the way from Devon," he replied. "To see him. That old bloke is always sitting there on his own. And here's why. When he first came to be a Chelsea pensioner, ten or so years ago now, they knew he was a bit of a Chelsea fan, so they told him that he could have a free seat with the others in the director's box at Chelsea. And he said something like, "Well, you can stuff that. Full of posh people. I wouldn't sit up there, not if you paid me. I want to go where my dad took me when I was a little kid, to the Shed End behind the goal." So they told the club, and the club agreed, and now he sits there every home game. And he's happy."

Michael turned to me. "I want you to tell that man's story – I mean his whole life story, from the old days when he was a little boy coming here with his dad, right up to now. I think he's about eighty now, maybe older. Fill in the years for me, Michael, and we'll make a book of his life."

Well, I knew at once I wanted to do it, that was for sure. I was very moved by the idea, and honoured that Michael had entrusted me with it. But I had no clue where to start. On the train back to Devon the next day, I remember jotting down the names of four people: my Uncle Francis, my Uncle Pieter, Les Farley – an old man from my village in Devon – and Uncle Mac, who was not my uncle, but had been like a father to me when I was young. All of them had fought in the Second World War, and might, had they all survived, now have been the Chelsea pensioner I had seen sitting there on his own, at the Shed End. Their lives, their stories, might play a part, in some way or other, in my Chelsea pensioner story, I thought. Somehow, I wanted to weave their lives together, a way of remembering them maybe. Their life stories had been part of my life for so long. I'll tell you something about each of them.

The first two life stories belong together because they were brothers, my two uncles, Francis and Pieter. At the outbreak of the Second World War, my Uncle Francis was a teacher, and my Uncle Pieter was an actor. Francis was a committed socialist and pacifist, and decided that he could not join up. Pieter, on the other hand, was quick to join the RAF. I can only imagine the difficulties and arguments there must have been within the family as these two brothers went their separate ways. Pieter was killed in 1940 when his plane crashed in St Ives in Cornwall. He was twenty-one. He lived on only in my mind – because, of course, I never met him – and in his photo which was always kept on the mantelpiece as I was growing up, a poppy beside it. My mother, his sister, grieved for her dead brother for the rest of her life.

On learning of the death of his younger brother, Francis decided he could no longer stay out of the conflict, that he had to play his part. He spent most of the rest of the war as a secret agent in France, living and fighting with the French Resistance. He was captured by the Germans and condemned to death. But, at the last moment, he was rescued, saved by a friend, a Polish secret agent called Christine. After the war he went back to teaching again.

I grew up with the stories of these two lives, and wrestled with the dilemma they faced. To fight or not to fight? For how long do we give peace a chance? In my own life, in an attempt to answer these questions, I have tried both the soldier's way and the teacher's way. Billy, my Chelsea pensioner, I decided, might have to face the same dilemma, so I gave him a younger brother who joins up at the beginning of the Second World War, but is then killed at Dunkirk. So Billy joins up, and his life changes for ever.

In my mind he now becomes Les Farley, the old farm labourer from my village, who I came to know, who was working on a farm at the start of the war. He joined up and after training was shipped off to North Africa, to Tobruk. He and his pals landed with rifles, but no ammunition, and the next morning found themselves facing the Panzers of Rommel's army. They were all taken prisoner. Within a week or so, they were prisoners of war of the Italians, all taken to a prison camp in the north of Italy. After two years of a poor diet and living in wretched conditions, they woke up one morning to discover the Italian guards had gone. Italy, they were told, was now out of the war. The gates of the prison camp were open. So thousands of British prisoners of war simply walked out, Les among them. They walked in twos and threes all across northern Italy, avoiding the German soldiers who were now invading. An Italian farming family hid Les and his pals for the winter months, at great risk to themselves of course.

Then, with the coming of spring, they left Italy and made for the South of France, where, rumour had it, the Americans were landing. For weeks, they were looked after by the French Resistance – the "Maquis" they were called – then handed over to the Americans. From Marseilles, Les and his friends were shipped back to England, to Liverpool. There, Les was able to go home for a week's leave. When Les walked back into the village, no one could believe their eyes. He had been reported as dead, missing in action, two years before. After the war, Les worked for the rest of his life on farms all around, on ours too for a while. He suffered health issues all his life on account of his time as a prisoner of war. Read *Billy the Kid*, and you will get to know him a bit, just as you will get to know my uncles.

And you will also meet Uncle Mac, for Billy is Mac too. In fact, he is more Uncle Mac than anyone else. Mac was a family friend, always kind and gentle, never judgemental. A real friend and support to a young boy trying to grow up and find his feet in the world, and he was funny too. But he was sad as well – I could see that in his face sometimes. I didn't know why till I was much older, old enough, I suppose, to be told such things. There were times, I knew, when I went to see Mac and Edna, his wife, and their family, when Mac would not be there. He was a physiotherapist, and a good one too. But for reasons I did not understand, he was sometimes away for weeks at a time. And no one spoke of him then, which I knew was strange.

I must have been maybe twelve or thirteen when at last I learned why Mac was often not there. He was sick, I was told. He had a drink problem. He was an alcoholic. Then I was told how and why the illness had begun. It seems that in the war, Mac had been a young soldier in the Royal Army Medical Corps. He had been in one of the very first ambulances to drive into Bergen-Belsen, a Nazi concentration camp (the camp where Anne Frank had died only weeks before the camp was liberated), where it was discovered that thousands upon thousands of people, Jews and others, had been kept in the most appalling conditions. The British soldiers who first entered that camp were faced with unimaginable horrors, thousands dead, thousands dying, and Mac had to try with the others to look after them, bury them. It was a horror that was to haunt him for the rest of his life. The drink helped him forget, but in time he could not live without it.

Writing all these life stories into the making of Billy, I wrote my story, wrote it fast, his character coming more alive in my head with every word I wrote. But then, try as I did, I could not find a way to end his story. Somehow, the life of the old soldier had to end up back in Chelsea – after all, that was where I had seen that old Chelsea pensioner. I could not figure out how to do it, not without contriving something that was forced, and therefore impossible for me to believe. To write a story, I have to first believe absolutely in it, in the characters, in how the story plays out. I must never make things happen, never play God. It is always a difficult line to draw. I like my stories to grow organically out of the characters and the situations they find themselves in, that they have created. I want the characters to find their own way towards the denouement. I try not to impose one, try not to create a neat ending, but to let the ending happen, to surprise myself with it. With *Billy the Kid*, this didn't seem to be happening. I was stuck.

I don't know why but time and again when I get stuck, something happens, always something totally unexpected that shines a new light on the story. In the case of *Billy the*

Kid, that occurred in France at a literary festival in Aix-en-Provence.

I hadn't wanted to go. I wanted to finish my *Billy the Kid* story, the one I couldn't finish. But I had to go. I had promised. So, when I had done my talk at the festival, there I was, having supper in a country inn just outside the town with all the other writers from the festival. They all spoke French loudly and very fast, and I was quite tired. My hostess took pity on me and introduced me in English to her husband across the table. "Here's one of the men I live with," she said, laughing. "He is my husband." "And who is the other one?" I asked. Her husband spoke up. "He is not here," he replied. "He likes to stay at home." And then he told me this story by way of explanation – so that there should be no misunderstanding, he said.

It seems that five years before, this couple had bought a plot of land just outside the town of Aix, and they had built a house there at weekends, just the two of them, which is why it had taken nearly five years to build. Anyway, two years into the project they had dug the foundations and built a cellar there for their wine. They arrived one Saturday morning to get on with the next stage, when they discovered an old tramp sleeping in the cellar they had made. He was very friendly, offered to share with them his wine and his salami. "Hope you don't mind if I stay here," he said. "It's out of the wind, and soon you will put a roof on and I shall be dry. I will help you, if you like. I have been a bit of a builder, bricklayer, carpenter."

It was difficult to say no. So they said yes. And the old tramp stayed on and helped them with the building work just as he had said.

Soon, the sitting room was built and the tramp moved in, living there with his sleeping bag and his bottles. But of course the time came, a couple of years further on, when the house was finally finished and they had to ask him to leave, explaining that they needed the house for themselves. They liked him a lot by this stage, so it was not easy to ask him to go. "I could go," said the old tramp, "but I should be very sad to leave. Could you not build me a little shed down the bottom of the garden? I could live in there. I won't be any trouble. And you're sort of like family now." Well, they couldn't say no. They showed me a photo of this old tramp, lying out in the sun beside his shed at the bottom of the garden, looking as happy as you like. "Does he still drink?" I asked. "Oh, yes," they said. "But we told him, only one bottle of beer a day. And he keeps to it – mostly." Now I could go home and finish my story of Billy the Kid. I had an ending. Lucky man, again!

And again too, because that same evening in the country inn outside Aix provided me with the idea for a short story I was to write later, called *Meeting Cézanne*. It involves Picasso, who used to eat at this inn and draw pictures sometimes on the paper tablecloths, and Cézanne, who didn't. Shan't say another word about it. Read it. Digressing again.

BILLY THE KID

I could have sent a telegram home, but I didn't. I thought I'd just walk in and surprise them. It was tea time. I never even knocked on the door. Emmy was there, they were all there. God, did I get a hugging – three of them all at once, and Mum going on and on about how I was just skin and bone. Emmy wept buckets, and even Ossie had to dry his eyes. I'd never seen him do that before. And he called me a young scallywag for not warning them. I gave Emmy back her gold cross and said it had worked, which it had. But she wouldn't have it back, said I had to keep it. Back at Chelsea they treated me like a conquering hero. The war would be over soon enough now, six months, a year at the most, everyone knew it. They told me there'd always be a place for me back at the club when I'd finished with the army. I played a couple of practice games with some of the lads. I wasn't as sharp as I had been – I wasn't strong enough to be sharp – but I could still tease them with my dribbling.

I was soon out of puff though. I knew I'd have a lot of training, a lot of catching up to do if I was ever going to get back into the first team. But I'd do it. Nothing in the world was going to stop me from pulling on a Chelsea shirt again, not lousy Mr Hitler, nor his lousy war.

Home was difficult. They all knew I was going soon. So every day, every moment was precious, too precious for all of us. We couldn't be normal. And Joe's bed was still there across the room, and so was his box of cigarette cards on his shelf. I found myself talking to him even more now, sometimes aloud. I dreamt of him too, and I dreamt of Lucia and the shots echoing around the mountains.

I hate goodbyes, so I left a letter for each of them and crept out of the house before dawn. Once I was on the train to Dover, I was back in the army, back to left right, left right, saluting officers and polishing boots. So they sent me off to war for the second time. How I wish they never had.

I thought the fighting would be mostly done with by now, and so it was. But there were still so many wounded to look after – our lads, and Germans, and refugees. We were treating as many refugees as soldiers. I drove ambulances, swabbed down floors, made beds, buried people. That was when I first started to drink with the lads. I never had before. When the work was over we'd get together and drown our sorrows. The drink was cheap, and I discovered I had a bit of a taste for it. No more than that. Not then. Not yet.

We'd heard about the camps, concentration camps where they'd been exterminating Jews and anyone they didn't like; but I don't think any of us really believd it. You had to see it to believe it. But when I saw it, I still couldn't believe it. I didn't want to believe it.

As we drove in though the gates of Belsen in our convoy of ambulances, they came wandering towards us like ghosts, walking skeletons, some of them in striped pyjamas, some completely naked. They were staring at us as if we had come down from some other planet. The children would come up to us and touch us, just to make sure we were real, I think. You couldn't call them children – more like little old people, skin and bone, nothing more, hardly living. They all moved slowly, shuffling. A strange silence hung over the place, and a horrible stench.

It was our job to do what we could for the sick, to get them eating again. As for the dying, we were usually too late.

We buried the dead in their thousands, in mass graves. You didn't want to look, but you had to. Once you've seen such things you can never forget them. They give out no medals for burying the dead, but if they did I'd have a chestful. There was one little boy I found in his bunk. I thought he was asleep. He was curled up with his thumb in his mouth. He was dead. I wrote home, but I couldn't tell them what I'd seen. I just couldn't.

When I left Belsen a few days later in a convoy of ambulances I was full of hate and anger, full of horror, and full of grief too for the little boy with his thumb in his mouth. I drank every evening now, drank to forget.

Chelsea pensioners

Until the seventeenth century, the state made no specific provision for old and injured soldiers, who had to survive on handouts from the parish or from charities. Pensions for all ex-forces personnel were not introduced until after the First World War. Until then it would have been a common sight to see maimed and disfigured veterans begging on the streets.

Tradition credits Nell Gwyn, "pretty, witty Nell", with using her influence over her lover, King Charles II, to establish the Royal Hospital Chelsea. Nell started life selling oranges at the Drury Lane Theatre, became an actress at fifteen and eventually rose to be the best known of the king's many mistresses. In 1681, King Charles authorized the building of the Royal Hospital Chelsea, for the "succour and relief of veterans broken by age and war". The buildings were designed by Sir Christopher Wren, one of the most famous English architects. Once the buildings were furnished, 476 retired non-commissioned officers and men went to live there in 1689. Each pensioner had a six-foot-square "berth" in wards known as "Long Wards".

By the time the hospital was completed, there were more pensioners than places available in the hospital. Eligible ex-soldiers who could not be housed in the hospital were called out-pensioners, receiving their pension from the Royal Hospital but living outside it. In-pensioners surrendered their army pension and lived within the Royal Hospital. In return, veterans received board, lodging, clothing and medical care.

Until recently, if any of the pensioners from the last 300 years had been able to revisit the hospital, they would have found that little had changed. However, parts of it were heavily damaged during both World Wars and in 2009, considerable rebuilding and extension took place.

The hospital still maintains a "military-based culture which puts a premium on comradeship". The in-pensioners are formed into four companies, each headed by a Captain of Invalids, responsible for the day-to-day organization and welfare of his charges.

In 2009, the first women in the hospital's 317-year history were admitted as in-pensioners. Dorothy Hughes, who had been on an Anti-Aircraft Battery in the Second World War, was the first. She was followed by Winifred Phillips, of the Women's Royal Army Corps. But curiously the records show that another woman, Mrs Christian Davies, was admitted in 1717, and was awarded a pension for her service and wounds received in the army. She died in 1739 and was buried with full military honours.

Pensioners regularly attend events leading up to Armistice Day, including the National Service of Remembrance at the Cenotaph. For the last hundred years the annual Chelsea Flower Show has been held in the grounds of the hospital. It is at these events that many of us see the pensioners' unique public uniform for the first time, the distinctive scarlet coat and black tricorn hat designed by the first Duke of Marlborough in the eighteenth century. They have blue coats for everyday use.

Chelsea football team's first club crest, used until 1952, featured a Chelsea pensioner, inspiring the club's original nickname – "The Pensioners". The picture of a pensioner appeared in match-day programmes. The nickname was dropped under the instructions of Ted Drake, who became Chelsea's manager in the 1950s. Drake felt that the "Pensioners" tag was a bit embarrassing for a young, fit and successful football team!

Residents of the hospital can still be seen attending Chelsea's home games at Stamford Bridge. When Chelsea won the Premier League title in 2005, Chelsea pensioners formed a guard of honour as the players came out for the trophy presentation. A few years later, in tribute to the trademark coats worn by the pensioners, Chelsea's kit for the 2010–2011 season featured a red trim on the collars.

The link between club and hospital continues to this day, with the club allocating eight free seats for pensioners at each home game. The hospital holds a fortnightly lottery, and the lucky winners get to see the game live!

Two Chelsea Pensioners chatting
at the Royal Hospital Chelsea

Chapter One.

Ten o'clock. Five past ten ~~~ gone now, and I'm alone. I have a ~~

ahead of me, and I ~~will not~~ waste a single moment of it

it away. I shan't dream it away. ~~For now~~

sleep. ~~Even if I wanted to I couldn't~~ Nve, and

it, because I haven't much ~~moment~~

~~than each I that that~~ every ~~of thing~~ is

~~it before~~

I joined up I had drifted through my days

through my nights, sure that my tomorrows

be better, and all my yesterdays too — sure

my tomorrows would become my yesterdays. I

eighteen years of yesterdays and tomorrows,

I want to remember as many of them

Private Peaceful

THE DREAM

Having published *War Horse* in 1982, I thought I was done with the First World War. I did not want to spend any more time in the trenches, among the suffering and the dying. I really did not want to revisit the world of that war in my stories again. But a few years later, whether I liked it or not, *The Butterfly Lion* simply led me back to those times, into that dreadful war.

After those two books, all my instincts were never to go there again. And indeed, for a while, my writing did take me elsewhere. But circumstance, in a way a direct legacy of having written both *War Horse* and *The Butterfly Lion* – as well as other stories I had written about the Second World War – brought me back to Belgium, back to Ypres, which I had often visited for research purposes. With Michael Foreman, I had been invited to a conference at the In Flanders Fields Museum in the old Cloth Hall in Ypres. Writers and illustrators came from all over the world to talk about writing about war for young people. I was invited, I am sure, because of *War Horse* and *The Butterfly Lion*; Michael Foreman because of his great classics, *War Boy* and *War Game*.

It was at this conference that I first met the *a cappella* singers Coope, Boyes and Simpson, whose songs from and about the First World War I knew and loved already. I did not know it then, but they were to become good and dear friends, later playing a huge part in the *Private Peaceful story*, and that we would end up performing together, interweaving my stories and their glorious music.

After the conference was over, Michael Foreman and I decided to spend some time visiting the In Flanders Field Museum. We were in for a shock. This museum pulled no punches. As we walked in, there was an in-depth introduction to the causes and preparations for the First World War in all the countries concerned. This told us at once that this was to be very different from other war museums. This was the story of the war as seen from all sides, not simply from a British or British Empire perspective. In that sense, it was unsettling, because both Michael and I were used to only the British take on the war. And disturbing, of course, is how a museum about war should be, unsettling and enlightening.

As we moved deeper into the museum, the thunder of war came ever closer and the world about us grew darker. Then we were plunged into the fury and chaos of battle, into the horrors of trench warfare, into the pity, into the slaughter and the suffering, on all sides. Separated now in the darkness, Michael and I each heard the poetry of Wilfred Owen and John McCrae, heard the songs of the men marching off to war, the bands playing, and then read the letters home, from soldiers, nurses, understood how it had been for local families to be caught up in the fighting, to have their land and homes laid waste about them. All around us were the uniforms, the weapons, the photographs and paintings, the sound of shelling and machine gun fire, the songs, the poems. It was a vision of hell. We emerged, speechless, an hour or so later, near the exit. Tears would not let us speak. I stayed to look at the last few exhibits as Michael left, saying we'd meet in the square.

There was a rather insignificant-looking letter in a frame on the wall, I noticed. I have no idea why I stopped to read it – perhaps I was still composing myself before meeting up with Michael again, I don't know. It was a small, typed letter, just a few lines. It read something like this:

Dear Mrs ——,

I regret to have to inform you that your son, Private ——, was shot at dawn for cowardice on the morning June —— 1916.

It was signed by a lieutenant.

Above the letter in the same frame, was the envelope. The envelope, I could see, had been ripped open, the tear jagged. It was that tear, as well as the cruel brevity of the letter, that I found so hard to take. I could visualize so clearly this mother standing on the front step of her terraced house, in Salford, I think it was, dreading a letter like this, knowing the news such letters might bring, then plucking up the courage to rip the envelope open. In those few words her life and the life of her family were shattered, the loss, the grieving, the shame overwhelming her.

I had met at this conference Piet Chielens, the director of the museum, who was, I knew, one of the world's great experts on the First World War. I asked him more about this letter and it was he who told me there had been about 300 British soldiers executed in the First World War for cowardice or desertion, two for falling asleep on sentry duty. He showed me transcripts of some of their trials, some lasting less than half an hour. Half an hour for a man's life. I read accounts of the executions, some in open country up against a hedge, some in the courtyard of prisons, some in farmyards. The firing squad was sometimes made up of soldiers from their own company, pals, comrades in arms forced to shoot one of their own.

I visited the graves of one or two of these unfortunate men – "worthless", one of them had been called at his court martial. Further research convinced me that these proceedings had often been no more than mock trials. Many soldiers on trial had clearly been suffering from shell shock, some had already been treated in hospital for it. Many were not even legally represented. There was a clear purpose in these trials. Examples had to be made, discipline had to be kept. There was little justice in these court martials, but rather a determination to convict and punish, as a warning to others. I soon discovered that many of the families of these unfortunate men had been seeking justice for them ever since, petitioning the government again and again over the decades since the war, to pardon these executed men, to acknowledge the injustice, the cruelty. No such pardons had been given.

I think it was this injustice that made up my mind. I would write the story of one of these men, tell his tale from cradle to grave, so that he was not simply a name on a gravestone, but a child, a boy, a young man. I would set my story in a place I know well, in my home village of Iddesleigh, from where many men had left their farms and marched off to that war, yes, the same village where Joey and Albert had grown up together in *War Horse*. My soldier would live with his family, in the cottage where I live, with his brothers, his mother and his forester father. Like the millions who went to war, his life at home would be centred round family, school, friends, community, the farms and the countryside, an ordinary enough life, before the war took him away and destroyed him.

The name of Private Peaceful I found by accident in

the Bedford Cemetery near Ypres. It seemed at once the
right family name for him. He became, as I was creating
him, as I was writing him, my Unknown Soldier. He has
now become that, I am pleased to say, for many others
too.

So often, though, ideas, not just for names but for people, come from readers I meet, readers who write to me. I
was in my dreamtime – that period of research I live
through with each book, of thinking myself, feeling
myself, into the story, dreaming it up, becoming familiar
with my characters and the places they live in and have
their being. I was trying to create the Peaceful family, to
get to know them, their circumstances at home, their
place in the community, their relationships to one
another. I was still struggling with this, when one day I
received a letter from a mother. She had been reading
The Butterfly Lion to her children, and said it was the only
book she and her children could all enjoy listening to
together. This was largely because she had a teenage boy
called Joe – who had Down's syndrome – who found listening to stories very challenging. But with this story, she
wrote, he simply loved listening along with his siblings,
rocking back and forwards, humming contentedly
throughout, and asking to hear the story over and over
again. She would love it, this mother wrote, and so would
all her children, if one day I could somehow write a boy
like her Joe into one of my stories. For family reasons, I
already had a great interest in such children and it didn't

take me long to decide to create a character like her Joe. "Big Joe", I called him, and he became the heart of the Peaceful family. He became the catalyst for me. The Peaceful family were no longer fiction to me. Everything revolved round their love for Big Joe. I could begin my story of Private Peaceful. Big Joe was all the spur I needed.

Now I could become one of the Peaceful brothers, living through a night when there could be no sleep, when the last thing I want is for dawn to come. By reflecting on my childhood at home in Devon, by living my life again, I might postpone dawn as long as possible. To do this, I would become young Private Peaceful, speak it down onto the page in his voice, see and feel it as he did.

I was visiting Ypres a while after the publication of the book, and was being interviewed for radio by the BBC in one of the dozens of cemeteries around Ypres, when a coach pulled up on the road by the gateway into the cemetery. Out of it poured a school party of fifty or more teenage children – English, and from Epsom I saw from the coach. They invaded the quiet of the cemetery, behaving, I thought, rather boisterously and noisily. We had to stop recording. I was about to go over and ask them to quieten down, not because of the interview, but because loud laughter and banter seemed disrespectful in such a place. Then an extraordinary thing happened. They hushed, quite of their own accord. Loud voices became whispers as they moved among the gravestones. Some held hands. Most did not speak at all. The place, the graves, the dead had touched them.

Seeing the microphones, I suppose, the accompanying teachers approached and recognized me. "This is extraordinary!" they said. "You are not going to believe this. We have all come to Ypres because we read *Private Peaceful* back at school." He had become the Unknown Soldier for everyone. They had just come from Bedford Cemetery, where they had laid a wreath they had made on Private Peaceful's grave, along with messages and letters the children had written to him. "You have to go and see them, read them," the teachers said. So I did. I knew as I crouched there, reading their letters to him, that *Private Peaceful* had been worth writing.

And some time after publication, and after Simon Reade's 2004 play of *Private Peaceful* had been touring the country for several seasons, the government at last relented and granted pardons to those unfortunate men so cruelly executed in the First World War. They were not worthless. It was official. Of course, it was the sustained campaign by their families that had brought about this change of heart. But I hope and believe the book, the play and the concerts of *Private Peaceful* played their part in it too.

PRIVATE PEACEFUL

"I want no tears, Tommo," he whispers in my ear. "This is going to be difficult enough without tears." He holds me at arm's length. "Understand?"

I can do no more than nod.

He has had a letter from home, from Molly, which he must read out to me, he says, because it makes him laugh and he needs to laugh. It's mostly about little Tommo. Molly writes that he's already learning to blow raspberries and they're every bit as loud and rude as ours when we were young. And she says Big Joe sings him to sleep at night, *Oranges and Lemons* of course. She ends by sending her love and hoping we're both well.

"Doesn't she know?" I ask.

"No," Charlie says. "And they won't know, not until afterwards. They'll send them a telegram. They didn't let me write home until today." As we sit down at the table he lowers his voice and we talk in half-whispers now. "You'll tell them how it really was, won't you, Tommo? It's all I care about now. I don't want them thinking I was a coward. I don't want that. I want them to know the truth."

"Didn't you tell the court martial?" I ask him.

"Course I did. I tried, I tried my very best, but there's none so deaf as them that don't want to hear. They had their one witness, Sergeant Hanley, and he was all they needed. It wasn't a trial, Tommo. They'd made up their minds I was guilty before they even sat down. I had three of them, a brigadier and two captains looking down their noses at me as if I was some sort of dirt. I told them everything, Tommo, just like it happened. I had nothing to be ashamed of, did I? I wasn't going to hide anything. So I told them that, yes, I did disobey the sergeant's order because the order was stupid, suicidal – we all knew it was – and that anyway I had to stay behind to look after you. They knew a dozen or more got wiped out in the attack, that no one even got as far as the German wire. They knew I was right, but it made no difference."

"What about witnesses?" I ask him. "You should have had witnesses. I could have said. I could have told them."

"I asked for you, Tommo, but they wouldn't accept you because you were my brother. I asked for Pete, but then they told me that Pete was missing. And as for the rest of the company, I was told they'd been moved into another sector, and were up in the line and not available. So they heard it all from Sergeant Hanley, and they swallowed everything he told them, like it was gospel truth. I think there's a big push coming, and they wanted to make an example of someone, Tommo. And I was the Charlie." He laughed at that. "A right Charlie. Then of course there was my record as a troublemaker, 'a mutinous troublemaker' Hanley called me. Remember Etaples? Had up on a charge of gross insubordination? Field Punishment Number One? It was all there on my record. So was my foot."

"Your foot?"

"That time I was shot in the foot. All foot wounds are suspicious, they said. It could have been self-inflicted – it goes on all the time, they said. I could have done it myself just to get myself out of the trenches and back to Blighty."

"But it wasn't like that," I say.

"Course it wasn't. They believed what they wanted to believe."

"Didn't you have anyone to speak up for you?" I ask him. "Like an officer or someone?"

"I didn't think I need one," Charlie tells me. "Just tell them the truth, Charlie, and you'll be all right. That's what I thought. How wrong could I be? I thought maybe a letter of good character from Wilkie would help. I was sure they'd listen to him, him being an officer and one of them. I told them where I thought he was. The last I'd heard he was up in a hospital in Scotland somewhere. They told me they'd written to the hospital, but that he'd died of his wounds six months before. The whole court martial took less than an hour, Tommo. That's all they gave me. An hour for a man's life. Not a lot, is it? And do you know what the brigadier said, Tommo? He said I was a worthless man. Worthless. I've been called a lot of things in my life, Tommo, but none of them ever upset me, except that one. I didn't show it, mind. I wouldn't have given them the satisfaction. And then he passed sentence. I was expecting it by then. Didn't upset me nearly as much as I thought it would."

I hang my head, because I cannot stop my eyes filling.

"Tommo," he says, lifting my chin. "Look on the bright side. It's no more than we were facing every day in the trenches. It'll be over very quick. And the boys are looking after me all right here. They don't like it any more than I do. Three hot meals a day. A man can't grumble. It's all over and done with, or it will be soon anyway. You want some tea, Tommo? They brought me some just before you came."

So we sit either side of the table and share a mug of sweet

strong tea, and speak of everything Charlie wants to talk about: home, bread and butter pudding with the raisins in and the crunchy crust on top, moonlit nights fishing for sea trout on the Colonel's river, Bertha, beer at The Duke, the yellow aeroplane and the humbugs.

"We won't talk of Big Joe or Mother or Moll," Charlie says, "because I'll cry if I do, and I promised myself I wouldn't." He leant forward suddenly in great earnest, clutching my hand. "Talking of promises, that promise you made me back in the dugout, Tommo. You won't forget it, will you? You will look after them?"

"I promise," I tell him, and I've never meant anything so much in all my life.

"You've still got the watch then," he says, pulling back my sleeve. "Keep it ticking for me, and then when the time comes, give it to Little Tommo, so he'll have something from me. I'd like that. You'll make him a good father, like Father was to us."

It is the moment. I have to do it now. It is my last chance. I tell him about how Father had died, about how it had happened, what I had done, how I should have told him years ago, but had never dared to. He smiles. "I always knew that, Tommo. So did Mother. You'd talk in your sleep. Always having nightmares, always keeping me awake about it, you were. All nonsense. Not your fault. It was the tree that killed Father, Tommo, not you."

"You sure?" I ask him.

"I'm sure," he says. "Quite sure."

We look at one another and know that time is getting short now. I see a flicker of panic in his eyes. He pulls some letters out of his pocket and pushes them across the table. "You'll see they get these, Tommo?"

We grip hands across the table, put our foreheads together and close our eyes. I manage to say what I've been wanting to say.

"You're not worthless, Charlie. They're the worthless bastards. You're the best friend I've ever had, the best person I've ever known."

I hear Charlie starting to hum softly. It is *Oranges and Lemons*, slightly out of tune. I hum with him, our hands clasping tighter, our humming stronger now. Then we are singing, singing it out loud so that the whole world can hear us, and we are laughing as we sing. And there are tears, but it does not matter because these are not tears of sadness, they are tears of celebration. When we've finished, Charlie says: "It's what I'll be singing in the morning. It won't be God Save the ruddy King or All Things bleeding Bright and Beautiful. It'll be *Oranges and Lemons* for Big Joe, for all of us."

The guard comes in and tells us our time is up. We shake hands then as strangers do. There are no words left to say. I hold our last look and want to hold it forever. Then I turn away and leave him.

When I got back to camp yesterday afternoon I expected the sympathy and the long faces and all those averted eyes I'd been used to for days before. Instead I was greeted by smiles and with the news that Sergeant Hanley was dead. He had been killed, they told me, in a freak accident, blown up by a grenade out on the ranges. So there was some justice, of a sort, but it had come too late for Charlie. I hoped someone at Walker Camp had heard about it and would tell Charlie. It would be small consolation for him, but it would be something. Any jubilation I felt, or any of us felt, turned very soon to grim satisfaction, and then evaporated completely. It seemed as if the entire regiment was subdued, like me quite unable to think of anything else but Charlie, of the injustice he was suffering, and the inevitability of what must happen to him in the morning.

We have been billeted this last week or so around an empty farmhouse, less than a mile down the road from where they're keeping Charlie at Walker Camp. We've been waiting to go up into the trenches further down the line on the Somme. We live in the bell tents, and the officers are billeted in the house. The others have been doing their very best to make it as easy as they can for me. I know from their every look how much they feel for me, NCOs and officers too. But kind though they are I do not want or need their sympathy or their help. I do not even want the distraction of their company. I want simply to be alone. Late in the evening I take a lamp with me and move out of the tent into this barn, or what is left of it. They bring me blankets and food, and then leave me to myself. They understand. The padre comes to do what he can. He can do nothing. I send him away. So here I am now with the night gone so fast and the clock ticking towards six o'clock. When the time comes, I will go outside, and I will look up at the sky because I know Charlie will be doing the same as they take him out. We'll be seeing the same clouds, feeling the same breeze on our faces. At least that way we'll be together.

Treatment of soldiers in the trenches

In the First World War, 306 British soldiers were shot for desertion, mutiny or cowardice. By contrast, not one American or Australian soldier was executed.

Initially, these executions were kept secret from the public: "I had my first direct experience of official lying when I read some twenty reports of men shot for cowardice or desertion. A few days later the responsible minister denied that any sentence of death for a military offence had been carried out in France." (Robert Graves, *Goodbye To All That*, 1929)

Rifleman Henry Williamson recollected the process of an execution: "He was tied to a post against a wall in his civilian clothes, and we were told to fire at a piece of white cloth pinned over his heart. We didn't know what the rifles were loaded with. Some were loaded with ball, others with blank." Afterwards, if the victim was still alive, the officer in charge would shoot him with his revolver.

Private William Holmes witnessed another execution: "These two youngsters had only been with us two weeks. When they knew we were going to do this attack, they were literally crying their eyes out." They ran away, but were captured, then "Their caps were taken off, every insignia of their regiment was torn off, to disgrace them. The verdict ... described how they had let their mates down." The platoon drew lots for the firing squad. They "were sick with the whole thought of it. They were going to go and shoot their own mates. But there you are... For the mere disobedience of an officer you could be shot."

Journals, and details of the trials, suggest the disturbing conclusion that class and race prejudice played a major part in the decision to execute a man. A disproportionate number of those executed were working class privates from Scotland, Ireland and Wales. Of the 306 men executed, only three were officers. Fifteen officers sentenced to death received a royal pardon. Privates noticed that officers received lighter sentences. In 1916, General Haig ordered that more officers should be executed to "strengthen the fighting spirit of the troops".

Many of the victims were shockingly young. Private Thomas Highgate was executed, aged a mere seventeen, thrity-five days into the war, the first soldier to face a firing squad. He fled the carnage of the Battle of Mons and hid in a barn. He was undefended at his trial, because all his comrades from the Royal West Kents had been killed, injured or captured. Another Private, Herbert Burden, had lied about his age to join up. When he was shot ten months later, he died officially too young to be at the Front.

Many trials breached army regulations. An order in January 1915 had effectively reversed the principle that the accused is innocent until found guilty. But regulations stipulated formal legal representation. Most of the accused were not legally represented, although some did have a "prisoner's friend" (an officer who represented a defendant at a court martial). The condemned had the right to petition the king for mercy, but in practice no one did, suggesting that they were not informed that appeal was available.

In general, the trials were perfunctory and often unjust. In November 1916, Private Peter Goggins and Corporal John McDonald were on guard duty. Sergeant Joseph Stones ran past their position shouting, "Run for your lives, the Huns are on top of you!" They retreated to a reserve trench twenty yards away. Stones gave evidence that he had ordered the retreat, but both men were charged with desertion, and Stones was sentenced to death for throwing away his rifle. All were executed to "set an example". Private Rochester witnessed the executions, and reported that "the chaplain who prayed with them before their deaths remarked that he had never met three braver men".

Many argue that we should not apply our modern codes of behaviour to the actions of previous generations, and that we should not even try to right the wrongs of the past. Correlli Barnett, co-author of the BBC television series *The Great War*, said that to obtain a mass pardon for men accused of cowardice or desertion was "pointless" after all these years. Others, particularly relatives, disagreed. When the suppressed documents of the court martials were released in 1990, the campaign for official pardons was invigorated.

The Shot at Dawn Memorial was established in 2000 at the National Memorial Arboretum in Staffordshire, in memory of those executed during the First World War. Five soldiers from New Zealand had already won a pardon earlier in 2000, as did twenty-three Canadians a year later. But successive British governments took until 2006 "to acknowledge that injustices were clearly done in some cases, and to acknowledge that all these men were victims of war" (Defence Secretary, Des Browne). All 306 British soldiers executed by their own side in the First World War were finally granted posthumous pardons.

The Shot at Dawn Memorial

The Amazing Story of Adolphus Tips

THE DREAM

Let me tell you about some wonderful neighbours we once had living down our little lane in Devon. They were Commander and Mrs Simpson. He had been in the Royal Navy, his wife had been in the world of politics and his sister who had lived with them had been a head teacher. They were all getting on in years, the sister well into her nineties. He, it turned out, had been an explorer as well as a naval officer, and had as a young man discovered and mapped an unknown inland lake in Greenland. They were all supremely interesting people, and kind with it. But in the end, our little lane in the middle of nowhere was just too remote for them, too far from shops and the doctor. After only a few years, they moved to a village in South Devon closer to their family,

169

and more convenient for them. We would go to see them from time to time in their new home in Slapton Sands; but then, sadly, soon afterwards, and in quite quick succession, they died.

I was asked by the family to speak at Commander Simpson's funeral service in the church at Slapton. I was honoured to be asked, but knew I would find it difficult to say what I wanted to say about him, about all of them, without finding myself overcome by the moment. So, just before the service began, we went into the village pub, down the road from the church, and had a sandwich and a beer. "Dutch courage" they call it – not sure why. Anyway, we were sitting there in the pub when I happened to notice some small black and white photographs on the wall. They intrigued me. They were old photos, clearly taken during the Second World War, because they were of American soldiers in the uniforms of the time. On closer inspection, I saw these soldiers were in the village of Slapton itself. They weren't marching about, none were carrying weapons. They were with local villagers, carrying furniture, piling it up on carts.

I asked about the photos at the bar. "What were they doing here, these American soldiers?" I asked. By way of answer, the barman produced a book from under the counter, and put it down in front of me. It was called *The Land That Changed Its Face*, by Grace Bradbeer. "Here's a little book that'll tell you all about it," he replied. "Local history. All in there. Five pounds."

Well, after that, I couldn't very well not buy the book, could I? As it turned out, I am so glad I did!

I didn't get a chance to read it at once, of course. The funeral was very moving, the Commander's naval sword on the coffin. At the burial, Bercelet, our lurcher dog, who he loved and who loved him, lay at the graveside, head resting on her paws, watching. As soon as I got home, I read the little book from cover to cover. Here, in brief, is the remarkable story I found in it.

In 1943, the villagers of Slapton, and six other villages near by, were called together and informed that they had six weeks to move out as the American army needed the villages, the farms, the beaches as an exercise area. They had to practise landings from the sea, in preparation for the projected liberation of France and Europe the next year. The beach at Slapton was perfect for this, because it resembled the kind of beaches they were going to land on in Normandy.

The families moved out to wherever they could go, friends, relations. All the farm animals were evacuated, houses and churches sandbagged and protected as much as they could be. It was a difficult and traumatic time for everyone. One farmer killed himself, I later heard. He could not and would not leave the house he had grown up in.

But there was another personal story in the book that I found almost incredible. A small girl, a farmer's daughter, was preparing to leave the farm with her whole family on the very last morning before the perimeter wire was to be closed, before they were to be separated entirely from their farm for months, years, maybe – they did not know. The last cart, piled high with their belongings, was about to pull away when the little girl said, "Where's my cat?" The family searched everywhere, in the farmhouse, in the barns, all over the farm. They could not find her. They called for her again and again. She would not come back. In the end, time ran out and they had to leave. The little girl was distraught of course. This was her precious beloved pet, a ginger cat called Adolphus Tips, and she was having to abandon him.

The months of training began, the American soldiers landing on the beaches from landing craft, with live shells being fired over their heads onto the countryside beyond, onto the farms and houses and churches and schools. They had to make these exercises, these war games, as real as possible. For ten months, the villagers and farmers had to stay away, and the exercises and the shelling went on. The little girl feared the worst. How could any cat survive that? Then, in June 1944, the Americans, as well as other Allied soldiers – British, Canadian, French, Indian, African – thousands of men – set off in their ships on D-Day to Normandy to liberate the continent, the biggest invasion armada the world had ever seen. A few months later, the perimeter wire was lifted and the local people, villagers and farmers, were all allowed back home. Many homes were in ruins. Most were damaged.

The little girl returned, still hoping but not believing for one moment that her beloved cat could have survived. The windows and doors of the farmhouse were all blown out, the barns destroyed. But as they walked up the path to the front door, the cat came bounding out of a broken window to greet them. Adolphus Tips had survived. How wonderful was that! What a story! What a name! Adolphus Tips! I knew at once that I had to tell his story, the story of the little girl and of the local people and the American soldiers too, so far from home.

I remembered then, as I thought about it, the first American soldiers and sailors and airmen I had ever seen. Just after the Second World War, there were hundreds and thousands of American servicemen and women still in England. I remembered how smart they were, how smiling and confident they seemed, how they liked kids and always had chocolate to give you, Hershey's bars. And I remember in particular the black soldiers. I think the first black person I ever talked to was a tall black soldier in the Warwick Road in London. He asked me the way to Piccadilly Circus, and I was so flummoxed by how tall he was and how different he looked from anyone else I had ever seen, and by how strangely he spoke, that I just pointed up the road and said, "That way." I had no idea whatsoever which way I pointed. Maybe he's still looking for Piccadilly!

I read all I could about the millions of US troops who came across to England and I went to the Normandy

American Cemetery and Memorial overlooking Omaha Beach, where so many Americans had died, maybe some of those very soldiers who had practised their landings at Slapton, maybe some of the soldiers in those photographs in the pub. I stood there by the gravestones and thought about how young they were and about how old they would now be fifty years later, grandfathers, perhaps, like me, and about how lucky I was to have lived my life in comparative peace and how they had missed so much.

I returned often to Slapton, to walk the beach, to see where the old hotel had been, to see the tank they discovered after the war and dragged up onto the seafront, which stands now as a memorial to the American soldiers who died. And one day, there happened to be an American veteran there at the tank, visiting. I went closer.

He wore a cap from his old uniform and was wearing his medals. He was telling his family how he had been there on this beach as a young man, how he had lost so many good friends, the best friends he ever had.

I went up to the village shop of Slapton and what did they have for sale? A picture of Adolphus Tips, the cat who would be at the centre of my story. With that picture, that cat, looking up at me, I sat down and wrote his story, a story of then and now, of sadness and hope, and of a great and hidden tragedy too.

I dedicated the book to our old friends, the Simpson family, without whom I would never have written the story. I hope they would have liked it. I think they would. I think they would like the play too. Kneehigh Theatre have made a wonderful stage adaption, which they call 946. It is on now, as I write this, in a huge circus tent that seats five hundred people, in a field in Cornwall. A field where, very probably, some of those Americans camped all those years ago.

THE AMAZING STORY OF ADOLPHUS TIPS

Wednesday, May 10th 1944

Adie still hasn't come back to see us again. I've been hoping and hoping every day. I wonder if he ever will. I can't stop thinking of him walking away down the lane, and that maybe it's the last time I'll ever see him. Mrs Blumfeld keeps saying the invasion must happen soon, any day now, she says – when the weather's right. They've got to wait till the weather's right. It's rough out at sea today. I hope it stays rough for ever, and then Adie won't have to go on the invasion, and he'll be safe.

I helped Barry and Mum pull off a calf this afternoon. The calf was walking inside ten minutes. I've seen lots of lambs born, lots of calves, and each time it surprises me how quickly they can get up and walk on their wobbly legs. What takes us a year or more, they can do inside an hour.

Mum's a bit down. It's because she hasn't had a letter

from Dad since he left. We don't even know where he is. We think he's in England still, but we don't really know. We were kneeling there in the field, watching the calf trying out his first skip and falling over himself, and Barry was laughing. But Mum and me weren't laughing because our minds were elsewhere. If Barry hadn't been there I think I'd have told her there and then: "I know what it feels like, Mum, to miss someone you really really love."

I can't tell Barry that I love Adie, that's for sure, because he's too young and he wouldn't understand, and even if he did understand he'd be upset. He's never said it, but I know he wants me to be his girlfriend. I never will be, not now. Barry's more like a brother to me, more like a friend, a really good friend. With Adie, it's different, so completely different.

Saturday, May 20th 1944

Mrs Turner has come to stay, Barry's mum (she likes us to call her Ivy). Last Tuesday she just turned up out of the blue, to give Barry a nice birthday surprise, she said – that's in two days' time. She gave him a surprise all right. She gave us all a surprise. We got back from school and there she was sitting with Mum at the kitchen table, her suitcase beside her. She hugged Barry so tight and for so long that I thought his eyes might pop out, and she pinched his cheek, which I could see he didn't like at all. She's got lots of powder on her face and bright scarlet lipstick, which Barry's always wiping off his face after she kisses him, and that's very often. And her eyebrows are pencilled on, not real, just like Marlene Dietrich in the films, Mum says.

Barry hasn't said much since she's been here, nor has anyone else. No one can get a word in edgeways. His mum never stops talking. She could "talk the hind legs off a ruddy donkey" – that's what Grandfather says. And she smokes all the time too, "like a ruddy chimbley" – Grandfather says that too. Ivy's nice though. I like her. She came with presents for everyone, and told us again and again how kind we'd been to look after Barry for her. All through supper tonight she told us story after story about the Blitz in London, about the air-raid sirens, running to shelters and sleeping at nights down in the underground stations. She talks in a "townie" accent just like Barry does, only a lot louder and for a lot longer. She's very proud of her big red London bus. "I'm tellin' you. Ain't nothin' goin' to stop my number seventy-four from gettin' where she's goin'," she said this evening. "'Oles in the road, busted bridges, tumbled-down houses. They can send over all the hexplodin' doodahs they like. Will they stop my bus from gettin' where it's goin'? Not bloomin' likely, that's what I say."

Barry tries to stop her talking from time to time, but it's no use. In the end he just goes out and lets her get on with it. He spends even more time now out on the farm with Grandfather and Uncle George. Barry's mum makes no bones about it: she doesn't like the country one little bit, and farms in particular. "Smelly places. All that mud. All them cows. And the bloomin' birds wakin' you up in the mornin'." Yesterday she was washing up at the sink with Mum after supper when all at once she burst into tears. "What is it?" Mum asked, putting an arm around her.

"It's all that green," she said, pointing out of the window. "It's just green everywhere. And there's no buildin's. And it's so empty. I 'ate green. I don't know why, I just 'ate it."

She hardly ever goes out, just stays in the kitchen, smoking and drinking tea. Mum likes her a lot because she's good company for her and because Barry's mum loves to help out. She likes to be busy, fetching and carrying, scrubbing floors, ironing and polishing. She's black-leaded Uncle George's stove for him so he's happy too. Barry never actually says he wants her to go home, but I can feel he does. I don't think he's ashamed of her exactly, but you can tell he's uncomfortable with her around. He either wants to be at home with her in London, or down here with us, but not both. That's what I think anyway.

Preparation for
D-Day landings

In 1943, the Allies were preparing to invade German-occupied countries and liberate Europe. They were about to launch a huge seaborne attack, "Operation Overlord", on German-occupied France. Nothing on this scale had ever been attempted and it needed careful planning and preparation. One dress rehearsal for the landings the Allies would need to make in France took place on a stretch of the Devon coast at Slapton Sands. This resulted in the death of 946 American servicemen - one of the worst military training disasters of the twentieth century.

In 1943, Slapton Sands was a quiet backwater. It seemed an ideal place to practise beach landings because its unspoilt gravel beach was similar in layout to Utah Beach on the coast of Normandy. This was where the Americans planned to land.

Before "Exercise Tiger" could begin, the villages and farms had to be cleared of the civilian population. A compulsory mass evacuation was carried out, involving 180 farms and 3,000 local residents. Many had never even left their villages before. Pam Will-Strete was the last child to leave: "For the children it was like going on holiday, but parents were upset and it was very traumatic for the elderly." Residents were only given six weeks' notice to move their belongings, pets, farm equipment and animals. It was particularly hard on farming families. Gordon Luscombe remembers that they couldn't get anyone to help with their animals because "everyone was in the same boat. The animals had to be sold, but we had to almost give them away because there were so many for sale." No one knew if and when they would return to their homes.

Exercise Tiger started as it ended, disastrously. Live ammunition is commonly used in military training to acclimatize troops to the sights, sounds and smells of a bombardment. After the use of live rounds, there should have been time to declare the beach safe and then to land the American troops. However, the officer in charge had delayed the bombardment, because some British vessels were late arriving. Crucially, the radio message notifying the delay did not get through to all the landing craft because the radio frequencies to be used were mistyped in the orders. As a result, the landing craft were using a different radio frequency from the ships further away, and many were still dropping off men when the bombardment started. The terrible mix-up of timings meant that as the American soldiers came onto the shore, the British were still bombing the beach.

A nine-boat patrol of German motor torpedo boats, attracted by high levels of radio traffic, slipped undetected through the Royal Navy's protective screen. Unwarned, the landing craft carried on towards the shore, and became sitting ducks for the nine German E-boats.

In the ensuing attack, there was little time to launch lifeboats. With many trapped below deck, hundreds of sailors and soldiers went down with their ships. Some jumped into the sea, but most drowned, weighed down by their uniforms, or hampered by badly fitted lifebelts. Hundreds died in the attack, among them many irreplaceable specialist engineers. The loss of the three LSTs (landing ships for tanks) meant that there were fewer reserve boats for the actual D-Day landings in Normandy, less than two months later.

An overwhelming worry was that ten of the senior officers on the torpedoed ships knew the details of the invasion plans. If any of them had been taken prisoner by the Germans, all the invasion plans might be at risk. After huge efforts to recover corpses from Lyme Bay, the bodies of all of these officers were identified, but many of the hundreds who died were laid in unmarked graves in Devon.

All survivors were sworn to secrecy at the

risk of court martial, and the invasion of Normandy went ahead successfully. Ironically, more lives were lost during the dress rehearsal at Slapton Sands than on Utah beach during the real invasion.

In the 1970s, a guesthouse owner, Ken Small, was told by a local fisherman about a metal object sunk three-quarters of a mile offshore. This turned out to be an American Sherman tank. Small managed to arrange for the tank to be salvaged and a special service was held at Slapton Village Church, where a memorial plaque to those who lost their lives during the D-Day practice landings was unveiled. It was not until 2012 that an official American memorial plaque to the 946 dead was erected, not on Slapton Sands, but at Utah Beach, in Normandy. Many residents of Slapton Sands never returned to their homes and farms and those who did often found them bombed or damaged. But one special resident did return - Aldolphus Tips, a local cat!

I Believe in Unicorns

THE DREAM

I am not sure when I first saw the cartoon. Probably in a book of cartoons or a magazine in a dentist's waiting room or maybe it was a doctor's, but anyway, it was when I was young. I think it was in a magazine called *Punch*. I was flipping through it, looking at the pictures, when I came across a small sad drawing, a cartoon that I have never forgotten. It was of a couple of unicorns, standing abandoned, on a small rock in the sea, all that remained above water of a mountaintop, the world flooded all around them, and Noah's ark floating away into the distance. That image stayed in my head as I was growing up, as I was trying to work out how true these ancient biblical stories I was hearing and reading were, or how metaphorical.

In time, of course, Charles Darwin's *On the Origin of Species* made it all clear to me, that creatures – ourselves too – have evolved and adapted, that those who were strong or clever had far better chances of survival. Others, I knew, had been hunted to extinction, or died out as a result of some cataclysmic event, dinosaurs and mammoths and sabre-toothed tigers among them. But unicorns were unique. Unicorns for me were always fabulous, in both senses of the word, but lived on in my hopes and dreams on the cusp of reality and fantasy. And while I might have realized quite early on that unicorns were imaginary, legendary, I had always harboured a childish hope that they might have once existed, which was why, I suppose, that little cartoon had resonated so much with me, why I could not get it out of my mind. Here, at least, was a credible biblical explanation of their extinction – they had existed, but the last of them had died in the Great Flood. They had simply missed the boat.

So unicorns have always fascinated me, whether it was the sight of a unicorn opposite a lion in a royal crest – symbols of purity and strength respectively – or a unicorn woven into an ancient tapestry, sitting at the feet of a princess, symbol again of purity, of all that is virtuous and true. And then I came across, quite by accident, a unicorn's horn. A real unicorn's horn. It was in Paris. I was visiting a museum there, the Musée de Cluny, to see again these glorious "La Dame à la licorne" tapestries that I love. There she was, the princess, her faithful unicorn at her side, in a meadow landscape of grass and wildflowers and trees, with all manner of wild creatures about her, rabbits, deer, birds. I stood marvelling at the beauty of it again for a while, then wandered away, through one great chamber in the museum to another. That was when I saw the unicorn's horn, leaning up against a wall in a corner of a room, about three metres long, made of ivory, tapering in a perfect spiral to a perfect point.

I later learnt that these horns were rare and therefore very valuable and much prized, an essential artefact in any respectable king's treasure, evidence of great wealth and status. They were found washed up on beaches, and thought in ancient times to be evidence that unicorns really existed. Much later, it was discovered that these horns were, in fact, the tusks of a narwhal – actually not tusks at all, but rather strangely extended teeth used for ice-breaking in the Arctic North where they live.

All this simply served to fuel my passion for these mythical creatures, and none of this dampened my lingering hope that maybe, just maybe, unicorns might once have roamed the Earth, and might somehow have been transformed into, evolved into, narwhals. Well, why not? I thought. Did we not once crawl up out of the sea? So the opposite could happen, surely. Fantastical, I know, but that is the "stuff dreams are made on"! However absurd, I wanted to believe in unicorns, and believe in them absolutely.

There are, of course, many different ways a child can

grow up to love stories and poems. Sometimes – most often, perhaps, as with me – it is a mother or father who reads to a child at bedtime. With some poems that I read even now – "The Listeners" by Walter de la Mare, "Jabberwocky" by Lewis Carroll, "The Way Through the Woods" by Rudyard Kipling – I can hear my mother's voice in my head as I read. She read them over and over to us. They were passed on with love. Then, if we are lucky, there is a great and inspiring teacher who gifts us a passion for literature, not simply because literature is in the curriculum, but, as the great poet W. B. Yeats says, for that teacher, "Because a fire was in my head". Such teachers, and there are very many of them, are never pretending. They mean it, and we know they mean it. They know how enriching to our lives is the power of great stories and poems, how literature is one of the great pathways to knowledge and understanding.

We know the best parents and the best teachers do this, change lives. So often forgotten are the best librarians, those dedicated people who go quietly about their business of trying to encourage reading. For many children who are not read to at home, or who have been frightened off books, or bored by them, at school, a good library and good librarian can change the life of a child, by judicious and sensitive recommendations, by arranging book groups, by readings, by inviting authors in to talk to children. Like so many of my fellow writers, this is how I have come across so many librarians, as an invited author, reading to children who sit there in their anoraks, expectant, cross-legged on the floor, covering the carpet from bookshelf to bookshelf. The librarian knows and I know that maybe for one of those children sitting there, to whom books have always been boring, life might suddenly be transformed. Maybe that child will love a story for the first time, and become a reader for life, or a writer. Librarians, for me, are the unsung heroes in all this. Which is partly why I found myself one day writing about a librarian who was to become, most definitely, the hero of my story.

I have so often found that if I leave the door open, and do not force myself to contrive a story just because I think it's a good idea, then sooner or later, something, someone, some happening nudges me, gives me the opportunity to sit down at last and tell the story that has been evolving in my head for so long. And the more unexpected and remarkable these happenings are, the better it is for my story. I have such a happening to tell you. A few years ago, I was invited along with my friend, the poet Kevin Crossley-Holland, to go to Moscow to talk to librarians and teachers and students. I had never been to Russia before and was honoured to be asked. Hundreds of librarians were coming, I was told, from all over Russia, to hear talks given by writers from many different countries. It was a gathering inspired by the First Ladies of the United States and Russia, and many other countries including Britain. There was a great banquet in the

Kremlin on the first night, and speeches, and much vodka and caviar – really! – and all the guests, First Ladies apart, were librarians and writers. It was magnificent, not at all like any librarians' conference I had ever been to before, a pure celebration of the importance of their work. But it was at a final celebratory dinner a few nights later, after we had all given our lectures, that the great happening happened.

It was a prize-giving dinner. Twenty or so of these four hundred selected librarians were apparently prize-win-ners. One by one, and to great applause, each went up to receive a public accolade and was then presented with a scroll to take away. Of course, the prize-giving was in Russian, which I didn't understand, and it all took a rather long time, as these things often do. So if I'm honest I found it all rather boring. I was pleased, as we all were, I think, when we came at last to the final prize-winner of the evening – so my Russian host explained. As his name was announced, 400 librarians rose to their feet as one, clapping and huzzah-ing and banging their tables, as a diminutive man in an ill-fitting suit made his way slowly to the podium. He was cheered all the way. I turned to my host and asked who he was, why everyone was so especially enthusiastic about this prize-winner.

"Ah," she said, "this man is the most famous librarian in all of Russia." "Why?" I asked. She explained. "He is a librarian in a small town two thousand miles away. One day, a few years ago, his library caught fire. And do you know what he did, this man? Against the advice of the fire brigade, he went in and out of that library, rescuing books from the flames. The townspeople were so inspired by his courage that they too joined in. Some went in and out with him, coming out with armfuls of books. Others made a line across the square and they passed the books from hand to hand. Tens of thousands of books were saved, until the firemen finally stopped them, telling them it was just too dangerous to go into the building any more. Later, in the square, with the library now almost completely destroyed, the librarian told the people that they had to take the books home and look after them, until a new library was built – and it has been now – and then they should all bring their books back. And that is what happened. And that is why he is being given the first prize this evening. He is everyone's hero."

I was not bored any more. Here was a man who loved books and who had risked his life to save them. There is a story, sadly a true story, of a time in Nazi Germany when books that were not approved by the Nazi authorities were gathered together in a huge pile and burnt in public. Here I had heard the opposite story, of books being saved from the flames, great books, beloved books, fiction, non-fiction, poetry, religious books, history books, art books, scientific books, all saved, because that man knew how important books are to us all, as individuals, as a society.

Now began the weaving process I love so much, that dreamtime during which I don't write a word, but rather walk the lanes near my home talking my story out loud, weaving it as I go. Sheep are great listeners, cows less so, I find. So I had a unicorn, a librarian, and a little boy quite like I had been, who didn't much like books or school, who preferred always to be outside. It wasn't difficult to become him. Tomas, I called myself. I like to be out in the mountains with my bee-keeping father. But my mother thinks that maybe I should go to the library to listen to a story. Be good for me, she says. Something different. Set it, I thought, in the Balkans, in Croatia, maybe, or Bosnia, where a brutal civil war had been raging at the time. And somehow weave in the story of the unicorn left behind by the ark, and the story of the burning books in Nazi Germany. Weave it all in, I thought, and mean every word of it in the telling, as a parent might do when reading aloud to a child, or a teacher, or a librarian. And above all, as you write it, believe in that unicorn.

I BELIEVE IN UNICORNS

One afternoon the unicorn lady took out from her bag a rather old and damaged-looking book, all charred at the edges. It was, she told us, her very own copy of *The Little Match Girl* by Hans Christian Andersen. I was sitting that day very close to the unicorn lady's feet, looking up at the book. "Why's it been burnt?" I asked her.

"This is the most precious book I have, Tomas," she said. "I'll tell you why. When I was very little I lived in another country. There were wicked people in my town who were frightened of the magic of stories and of the power of books, because stories make you think and dream; books make you want to ask questions. And they didn't want that. I was there with my father watching them burn a great pile of books, when suddenly my father ran forward and plucked a book out of the fire. The soldiers beat him with sticks, but he held on to the book and wouldn't let go of it. It was this book. It's my favourite book in all the world. Tomas, would you like to come and sit on the unicorn and read it to us?"

I had never been any good at reading out loud. I would always stutter over my consonants, worry over long words.

But now, sitting on the magic unicorn, I heard my voice strong and loud. It was like singing a song. The words danced on the air and everyone listened. That same day I took home my first book from the library, *Aesop's Fables*, because the unicorn lady had read them to us and I'd loved them. I read them aloud to my mother that night, the first time I'd ever read to her, and I could see she was amazed. I loved amazing my mother.

Then one summer morning, early, war came to our valley and shattered our lives. Before that morning I knew little of war. I knew some of the men had gone to fight, but I wasn't sure what for. I had seen on television tanks shooting at houses and soldiers with guns running through the trees, but my mother always told me it was far away and I wasn't to worry.

I remember that moment. I was outside. My mother had sent me out to open up the hens and feed them, when I looked up and saw a single plane come flying in low over the town. I watched as it circled once and came again. That was when the bombs began to fall, far away at first, then closer, closer. We were all running then, running up into the woods. I was too frightened to cry. My father cried. I'd never seen him cry before, but it was from anger as much as fear.

Hidden in the woods we could see the tanks and the soldiers all over the town, blasting and shooting as they went. A few hours later, after they had gone, we could hardly see the town any more for the smoke. We waited until we were quite sure they had all gone, and then we ran back home. We were luckier than many. Our house had not been damaged. It was soon obvious that the centre of town had been hardest hit. Everyone seemed to be making their way there. I ran on ahead hoping and praying that the library had not been bombed, that the unicorn lady and the unicorn were safe.

As I came into the square I saw smoke rising from the roof of the library and flames licking out of the upper windows. We all saw the unicorn lady at the same moment. She was coming out of the library carrying the unicorn, staggering under its weight. I ran up the steps to help her. She smiled me her thanks as I took my share of the weight. Her eyes were red from the smoke. Between us we set the unicorn down at the foot of the steps, and she sat down exhausted, racked with a fit of coughing. My mother fetched her a glass of water. It must have helped because the coughing stopped, and all at once she was up on her feet, leaning on my shoulder for support.

"The books," she breathed. "The books."

When she began to walk back up the steps I followed her without thinking.

"No, Tomas," she said. "You stay here and look after the unicorn." Then she was running up the steps into the library, only to reappear moments later, her arms piled high with books. That was the moment the rescue began. People seemed suddenly to surge past me up the steps, and into the library, my mother and father amongst them.

It wasn't long before a whole system was set up. We children made two chains across the square from the library to the café opposite, and the books everyone rescued went from hand to hand, ending up in stacks on the floor of the café. The fire was burning ever more fiercely, the flames crackling, smoke billowing now from the roof. No fire engines came – we found out later the fire station had been hit. Still the books came out. Still the fire burned and more and more people came to help, until the café was filled with books and we had to use the grocer's shop next door.

Book censorship

Governments, and those with power, have often used censorship and suppression of art and literature to try to control the general population. In Nazi Germany, a massive propaganda campaign was orchestrated to win the loyalty and cooperation of Germans. The Propaganda Ministry took control of all forms of communication. Viewpoints in any way threatening or contradicting the beliefs of the regime were eliminated from all media. This escalated into planned book burning.

On 10 May 1933, Nazis raided libraries and bookstores across Germany. They marched by torchlight in night-time parades, chanted slogans, and threw books into huge bonfires. More than 2,500 authors were on the banned list. Authors such as Jack London, H. G. Wells and Leo Tolstoy were amongst those whose works were destroyed. These actions shocked the world, with people recalling Heinrich Heine's prophetic words: "Where they burn books, they will in the end burn people."

A more recent example of book burning to destroy ideas, and a culture, comes from the Bosnian war. In the capital, Sarajevo, Muslims, Christians and people of other faiths had lived together in harmony for centuries. The siege of Sarajevo by the Serbian National Army began in 1992. The city would suffer for four years, the longest siege in modern warfare. By the time the peace accord was signed, 250,000 people in Bosnia, mainly civilians, had been killed. The war had created two million refugees. And, in Sarajevo alone, more than two million books were burnt, lost or destroyed.

The moving story of how a small group of men and women did their best to save a collection of unique manuscripts and books is one of the few life-affirming stories to come out of that terrible conflict.

Mustafa Jahic was overjoyed when he was appointed director of the Gazi Husrev-beg Library in Sarajevo. "My father dreamed of my life being surrounded by books. When I got the chance to care for the library I was the happiest man in the world." The library contained, in the words of Hosa Popara, the Keeper of Islamic Documents, the memories of "all the generations that have gone before for the last 1,000 years". The library also represented the best of many ethnic groups and cultures.

The books, many intricate and beautifully illustrated, were hundreds of years old, but many were unidentified and uncatalogued. Culturally, the most important document was the earliest handwritten history of Bosnia, by Salih Muvekit. In Turkish, it had never been translated into Bosnian. Dr Lamija Hadžiosmanović was asked to translate the history. She was allowed to take the original to her apartment, so she could work on it at home, but the siege of Sarajevo started soon afterwards. A neighbour warned her that she was in immediate danger. Lamija escaped with a few clothes and some food but forgot to take the manuscript with her. The neighbourhood then fell into Serbian hands.

Meanwhile, Mustafa Jahic realized that the library was at great risk from artillery bombardment. With a group of trusted friends and employees of the library, a plan was hatched to move more than 10,000 unique manuscripts to a safer location across town, specifically, to the building where the library had first been housed in the sixteenth century. The plan was dangerous. Shellfire was constant and snipers were on the lookout for targets on the streets. The team had no proper containers and no transport. The decision to use banana boxes to transport the books, and to make all the journeys on foot, street by street, box by box, increased the risks.

Destruction of books can rob people of their sense of historic identity. After the siege, Jahic stated his passionate belief: "A unique book that is destroyed can never be restored again... So for me to save a single book became tantamount to saving a human life. It steered me through the war. To compare manuscripts with people might not be appropriate, but we can say that books are our past, our roots. Without the past, we have no present and no future."

In August 1992, the National and University Library in the city hall of Sarajevo was set on fire. As one firefighter said: "I felt so helpless. The culture of our people, the identity, the history of Bosnia for centuries in one place ... was being swallowed by the fire and the flames." Although firefighters and library staff managed to salvage some items, more than 90 per cent of the National Archives were lost in the blaze.

Fearing that their library would be next, Jahic and his team started the whole removal process again. This time the invaluable books would be hidden in a fire station. They also decided to try to microfilm the manuscripts secretly so that, if the worst happened, something at least would survive. They smuggled equipment and chemicals into the city through tunnels and underground passages, a Herculean venture because of the constant power cuts.

The team saved 10,067 irreplaceable manuscripts but not Salih Muvekit's *History of Bosnia*, left behind in Dr Hadžiosmanović's apartment. In an extraordinary final twist, Dr Hadžiosmanović returned to her apartment four years later to find everything of value seemingly destroyed or stolen. Even her favourite dress was riddled with bullet holes. Serbian soldiers had lived in her apartment. The place was wrecked. But among the mud and dust on the floor, under a metal platter, was a pile of discarded books. Underneath the pile were the undamaged *History of Bosnia* manuscripts. When she gave them to the director the next day, he wept with joy and relief.

Alone on a Wide Wide Sea

THE DREAM

It was while I was out on a book tour in Australia some fifteen years ago that I first heard about child migration from Great Britain to Australia after the Second World War. The children who were sent away – banished, exiled, call it what you will – were all vulnerable. Some were orphans, some simply unwanted in this world. Homes were found for them across the seas in Canada, South Africa and Australia. It was thought that in these far-flung places they would find a fresh start, a new family, happiness. The way to hell is very often paved with good intentions.

For some of these migrant children, it turned out to be the best thing that could have happened to them. But many of them ended up with broken hearts and broken lives. They were often appallingly treated, exploited for their labour, and suffered great cruelty and abuse. One later wrote, "We were stripped of a nationality, culture and birthright. Many of us were stripped of our family name and even our birth date. We were stripped of our personhood, human rights and our dignity. We were referred to as migrant boy number 'so and so' or migrant girl number 'so and so'. And so we arrived, strangers in a lost land and with no way back."

Such words stirred in me the idea that maybe I could trace in a story the life of one of these migrant children from on board one of the ships at Liverpool in 1947 to a farm in the outback of Australia, where he struggles to survive and find himself, as he tries to build a new life and have at last his own family and some happiness.

The main problem I had in dreaming up the story in my mind was that I knew Australia – its people, its language, its history and its culture – only as a visitor, a researcher. I could find no way to get closer to my story. I was a stranger to it, too much of a stranger. I put the story on the back burner, as I so often do. I came quite close to abandoning the idea altogether. Then, quite out of the blue, I got lucky, twice – which enabled me to write two Australian stories. First, I met a man, an Australian of my generation – old, that is – both of us then the wrong side of sixty – a real live ancient mariner whose extraordinary ocean adventures gave me the key to my migrant story. His name was Alex Whitworth, his fellow ancient mariner, Peter Crozier, also well into his sixties. Their boat was called the *Berrimilla*. Remarkably, I was able to follow these two adventurers online, as it happened, reading their log as they sailed around the world.

So here is their story in a nutshell. And, in truth, their yacht was scarcely bigger than a nutshell! Just thirty-one feet. They set sail from Hobart, Tasmania, in 2004, their aim to sail around the world to England and back. On the way, Alex would run the marathon in the Falklands, reach England and compete in the Fastnet Race, then once they had sailed back home to Australia, take part in the Sydney to Hobart Race. And, he said, I could follow them if I liked, on the *Berrimilla* website, where their progress around the world would be updated daily. This I did, checking their site, catching up from time to time on everything that was happening to them. Much of it was technical, and since I'm not an ancient mariner myself, not of great interest to me. But other details most certainly were. Their bulletins gave us wonderful insights into storm and calm, into cold and wet, into moments of high drama (being knocked down by huge waves, and recovering). Their courage and extraordinary powers of endurance were utterly amazing to me, and their modesty too. And I learnt so much as well of the mundane but important and constant business of repairing the boat, keeping it shipshape.

It was in the Southern Ocean that there began a happening so unlikely that it only could belong in the pages of fiction, and fiction that strained credibility at that. But this happened, really happened. Sitting on deck one night Alex and Peter spotted a moving light in the sky, not a shooting star, something else. Their first thought was that this was the International Space Station flying overhead. One said to the other as they sipped their Guinness, "Be good to talk to those guys up there. What do you think?" So they emailed HQ in Hobart, asking if it would be possible to be put in touch somehow with the astronauts up there. The reply was: "Why not? No problem. We'll ask NASA." So they did. The astronauts came back: "Great idea." There then followed an email and satellite radio conversation lasting some weeks between those two old Australian blokes in their tin can of a boat sailing around the world, and these rather younger astronauts flying around the world in their tin can of a space station. All adventurers, kindred spirits, enduring great hardships and danger, and dealing with it as best they could. Comradeship, friendship grew between sea and space, between old and young, between yacht and space station.

Weeks later, after a stop in the Falklands for repairs and to replenish stores – and of course to run the marathon – the *Berrimilla* finally arrived at Falmouth in Cornwall, in the pale light of early morning. No one there, no press, no fuss, none of that. It wasn't a race. No big deal. This was just two old fellows doing their thing. They tied up and on shaky legs were making their way down the quay when they saw figures walking towards them, a family. It was the American astronaut, Leroy Chiao, with whom they had struck up such a close relationship during their epic journeys. He had since landed and had brought his whole family over from the US to Falmouth to welcome his new Australian friends in the *Berrimilla*. They are still friends, all these years later. And if you're wondering, yes, they did complete the Fastnet Race – did well in it too, and, shortly after, sailed all the way back to Australia, where they competed in the Sydney to Hobart Race as well. All true, all remarkable and all so unlikely, I thought, which was why it was so perfect for my story. Alex helped massively with my research, even drew the *Berrimilla* for the book.

It was this real-life adventure that gave me the idea to have a return journey of some kind in my child migrant story, so that the story would be circular, the journey of the migrant boy in 1947, and then a lifetime later, his daughter's return journey, sailing single-handed, fulfilling a wish and a longing.

My other Australian inspiration came from a lady who I went to stay with while I was on that book tour of Australia. She ran a project in the bush outside Melbourne, where city kids would go to live the life of pioneer Australian children a century or so before. They cooked for themselves, grew food, explored the bush, lived uncomfortably. I stayed there a couple of nights, read *War Horse* to the children round the campfire and bottle-fed a wombat on my lap. And this wombat was special, so special I wrote a book about him, *Wombat Goes Walkabout*. But that's another story! This extraordinary lady, at the same time as looking after all these city children during their week's stay, used to go out in the mornings and rescue surviving marsupials – possums, wombats, kangaroos – from the roadside. Often, the mothers were dead, run over, the babies still alive. She would bring them back, feed them, care for them and then, when they were strong and grown, take them back to the bush. The old wombat I fed was the only orphan she had not managed to return to the wild. I think he was too fond of her and the good life. That amazing and eccentric lady found her way into *Alone on a Wide Wide Sea*, became a vital part of it, of my migrant child's life.

With all this in mind, I could begin my story. The title comes from the poem *The Rime of the Ancient Mariner* by Samuel Taylor Coleridge. I had to learn the whole poem when I was a boy at school. Much of it I had forgotten, but not the albatross that is killed by the ancient mariner, and not the line, "Alone on a wide wide sea". The poem itself is in my story, vivid in Alice's memory, as it is in mine, connecting her so strongly to Arthur, her beloved father, the migrant boy. He had taught her about sailing boats, building boats; he had taught her his favourite poem too.

And so I could become my migrant boy, endure with him the journey to Australia, the hardships of life in the outback, live his life, his sorrows and joys, then become his daughter, and sail with her back to England, retracing her father's journey, an epic voyage of discovery, to find his roots and hers.

Michael in the Australian bush – with a friend

ALONE ON A WIDE
WIDE SEA

We had been travelling through hilly country for a day or two now, and Big Black Jack was finding it very hard going, and not just because of the hills either. We knew already that kangaroos made him nervous, but there hadn't been many of them until now. Now they were everywhere, and he was not happy. In the half-dark we could see their shifting shapes, and so could Big Black Jack. We could feel him tensing beneath us. We'd talk to him to try to calm him, smooth his neck, pat him gently, but nothing seemed to work. His ears would be twitching frantically. He'd toss his head and snort at them. Worst of all, he'd just stop without any warning. Falling off was all too easy. It amused the children hugely, but was painful for us. In the end Marty and I decided it would be better altogether, and safer too, to give Big Black Jack a rest, and walk. So during the last couple of nights of our journey we walked with the bushmen, one of us leading Big Black Jack. He seemed happier that way. He puffed less and snorted less. The last night we were with them I felt as if I really was one of them, sharing the silence and the stars.

The next morning at sun-up we were coming to the top of a high hill. It had been a long steep climb. Below us was a wide green valley with a stream running through, and trees, more trees than I'd ever seen in my life. In front of us on the crest of the hill the bushmen had stopped and were talking among themselves. I thought we'd be resting here for a while, and was only too happy about that because my legs were tired, and I was longing for food and for sleep. I sat down to investigate a thorn in my foot which had been troubling me. Beside me Big Black Jack was cropping the grass contentedly.

Suddenly Marty called out. "They're going! They're leaving us!" Sure enough, the bushmen were walking away from us back the way we'd come, the children looking over their shoulders at us from time to time as they went. We called after them again and again, but they didn't stop. Then they rounded the side of the hill and were gone.

"Why?" Marty said. "Why here? Why did they leave us here?"

We stood there in silence, each of us trying to make some sense of what was happening to us, of why they had treated us this way. We felt utterly bewildered. The parting had been so unexpected, so sudden and strange. No goodbyes, not even the wave of a hand.

That was when Big Black Jack began snorting again. I looked around for kangaroos. There were none, not that I could see anyway. But Big Black Jack had stopped eating in mid-chew. He had his head up now and his ears pricked. He whinnied loud and long, so that the valley rang with it. He was lifting his nose, sniffing the air, and listening. We could hear kookaburras and galahs, all the cackle of the bush at daybreak, but certainly nothing out of the ordinary. But then we heard the sound of whistling, of someone singing, a woman singing, and with it the tread of a horse in among the trees below us, of a saddle creaking. Big Black Jack whinnied again.

A great bay horse was coming out of the trees and up the hills towards us, on its back a rider in a wide-brimmed straw hat. But it wasn't the horse or the rider that we were looking at so much as the cavalcade that was following along behind, a cavalcade of creatures, all of them infants: wombats, wallabies, joeys. And as the rider came closer I could see there was a koala clinging on round her neck, looking at me over her shoulder. She rode right up to us, let the horses touch noses and check each other over. Meanwhile she took off her hat and looked us up and down. I haven't forgotten the first words she spoke to us:

"Strewth," she said. "Look what the cat brought in. But maybe it wasn't the cat, right? How'd you get here?"

"It was the bushmen," Marty told her.

"I thought as much. Are you waifs and strays then? They only bring me waifs and strays. They know I collect them, see. They don't eat the little ones, not unless they've got to. Good people they are. Just about the best, I'd say.

Where are you from?"

"England," I said. There was a wombat rooting around my feet now.

"S'all right. He won't bite," she told me. "You've come fair ways then."

"We were at Cooper's Station," Marty said. "We escaped."

"I know Cooper's Station. Mr Bacon's place, right? Where's he's got all those orphan kids." She looked us up and down.

"He used to be the preacher in town before they moved out there," she continued. "If there's one thing I can't abide it's fanatics of any kind, and religious ones are the worst of all. Running away from that place seems a pretty sensible thing to do. You'll be looking for somewhere to stay then."

Marty and I looked at one another. She was turning her horse now and walking away from us, her little animals following her. "Well, are you coming or aren't you?" she called out. "If you are, then bring the poor old black horse with you. He needs feeding up by the looks of him. Come to that, so do you. Couple of raggedy little scarecrows, that's what you are. I'll soon fatten you up. Come along if you're coming. Don't spend too long thinking about it. Haven't got all day."

Lost children

Australia was one of the most distant parts of the British Empire. For generations, successive British governments used their Empire as a dumping ground for the unwanted and dispossessed in Britain. Transportation to Australia was initially to build a population in a distant possession and to get rid of criminals, many of whom would have otherwise been hanged for their crimes. In early times these unfortunates could even include children as young as seven who had been convicted of minor crimes.

From 1618 until as late as 1970, about 150,000 children, who had committed no crimes, were transported to British colonies, mainly Canada and Australia, as part of official "child care" practice. Britain is the only country in the world to have done this over a sustained period, rather than as a policy of last resort during times of war or civil unrest.

These children were poor, unwanted, orphaned, or just "difficult". It was thought that children who were not part of conventional families posed a danger to society as well as to themselves. Many responsible for their deportation persuaded themselves that it was a better future for the children than staying in care homes in the UK. But, in fact, it was also cheaper to send children to Australia than to care for them in Britain. In 1950, children cost five pounds a day in the UK but only ten shillings in Australian institutions.

Voluntary societies engaged in child deportation were given UK government sanction and support. The Australian government also provided subsidies. Australia was desperate to expand its workforce, wanting – in its words – "good white stock". The Bishop of Perth stated in 1938: "... it is necessary to look for external sources of supply. And if we do not supply from our own stock we are exposed to the menace of the teeming millions of our neighbouring Asiatic races."

In the days before telephones, computers and world travel, children shipped overseas were permanently separated from everyone and everything they knew. When they reached Australia, they were housed in residential schools, or with host families, until they were of employment age. They experienced a harsh climate, long hours of hard physical work, loneliness, lost identities and the pain of living with a family but not being of the family.

In 1956, British officials went to Australia to investigate. Their conclusions were damning. One home was described as isolated with "deplorable conditions", and the boys "appeared unhappy". Accommodation at another was "primitive", with managers "rigid and narrow in outlook". Although ten of the worst places were blacklisted, more children were sent to them while the government debated what to do with the damning report.

The scale of deportation was later brought to light by a Nottinghamshire social worker, Margaret Humphreys. She set up the Child Migrants Trust in 1987 to assist separated families, and to pressurize governments to investigate. Many former child migrants began to draw public attention to their distressing experiences. Their pain, hurt and anger was clear.

Although a few migrants did exceptionally well, all experienced trauma and many were abused. Tony Jones was told by the Church of England that he was an orphan. He wasn't. The authorities assured him there were no records. That was another lie. His mother was too poor to look after him and placed him in a children's home. She did not consent to his deportation; indeed, she was never asked. Tony arranged a reunion, but his mother died two weeks before he arrived: "I saw my mother in the coffin. It's the most heartbreaking time of my life. They knew she was alive."

Tony Costa said, "I still wake during the night in a cold sweat, in a state of night terror featuring the monsters of my childhood – though it was never any kind of childhood. I was desperately trying to understand what crime I had committed to warrant such a heinous punishment."

Child-care charities and governments finally

started to condemn what they had once so enthusiastically endorsed. In 2009, the Australian prime minister apologized: "Sorry that as children you were taken from your families and placed in institutions where so often you were abused. Sorry for the physical suffering, the emotional starvation and the cold absence of love, of tenderness, of care. We look back with shame that so many of you were left cold, hungry and alone, and with nowhere to hide and nobody to turn to." Sometime later, the British prime minister also apologized. The work of reconciling lost children with their families overseas still continues but will soon end as those affected are now so old.

Kaspar: Prince of Cats

THE DREAM

Odd things happen in life, if you allow them to. I like odd. Like many writers and illustrators and storytellers, I often get invited to talk or read at festivals, or teach creative writing for a week somewhere, or go into schools on World Book Day. And sometimes I get asked to be "writer in residence" somewhere, in a museum, art gallery or college maybe – I have done it at Tate Britain, for instance. Over weeks and months, you give a series of master-classes or lectures, readings or tutorials, all designed to encourage those who come along to write themselves. I enjoy it because it makes me think again about the process of writing and to be excited by it, to find new ways myself, it encourages me, and if it does that, my hope is that it encourages the students. And if I

219

am honest, I enjoy the opportunity of reading my stories out loud, performing them.

In recent years, I have found myself performing more and more, giving concerts, with readings and music of my stories, stories such as *The Mozart Question*, *War Horse*, *Private Peaceful*, *The Best Christmas Present in the World* and *On Angel Wings*. Stories become alive for me when I read them out loud, and reading becomes performing. There are so many ways of telling tales, reading them, performing them, dramatizing them, filming them. Each is a new and vibrant way of storytelling, and I love to be involved. It is what my stories were written for: the telling as much as the reading. More, maybe.

It is rare for a writer to witness at first hand the effect of a story on an audience, for reading is usually done privately – unseen, unwitnessed. But telling it out to an audience is the great test, and – when it works – the great joy. When a story resonates, when that silence and stillness falls and we all live the story together, writer and teller and listener, then that's all the reward I need.

Some while ago now, I was asked to be writer in residence at a hotel in London, the Savoy Hotel on the Strand. It's rather grand, and huge, and very, very posh. Come and live in the hotel, they said, for three months, and give a talk or a reading or a concert from time to time. With my wife? I asked. Yes, they said. Free? I asked. Yes, they said. For the previous twenty-five years Clare and I had been living deep in the Devon countryside, totally immersed in our work on the farm, and we had just retired from our daily duties – just reached that age. Why not? we thought. We'll get to know London again. It'll be another way of living for a while. The last time we had spent any time in London was when I was a student. And I would be living just down the road from King's, my old college. We could go to the theatre, concerts, galleries, walk along the Thames. And it was the Savoy, for goodness' sake!

I never had any idea when we walked in there with our luggage that first day that I would find a story in this place. Mind you, my nose was probably twitching, my antennae out, ready to receive. We had an enormous room, a bed the size of Devon, and everyone was kindness itself. We were royally treated. But I very soon realized that the hotel, frequented over the decades by the powerful and the famous – Winston Churchill, Marilyn Monroe, millionaires and billionaires from all over the world, queen bees, king bees, honeybees all – was run by a small army of worker bees. The doormen, the receptionists, the bellboys, the porters, the cleaners, the cooks and waiters, waitresses, the managers – they were all there to look after the guests, to make them feel special. And they did. They came, I soon discovered, from all over the world – I counted over thirty countries. Some were students, studying full-time and working every hour they could find, to pay for their studies and to send money home. Others were full-time at the hotel, had been at the

Savoy for years, knew how it all worked. And all were well trained and highly professional. However, I discovered that they were not, in general, very well paid. Whereas the people they were looking after were among the richest in the world. This hotel was, I was thinking, a microcosm of the world outside, where the gap between the rich and poor had scarcely narrowed in a hundred years.

We lived in this bubble, enjoying all the pampering – up to a point – certainly enjoying arranging literary evenings, giving concerts and talks. I remember a teatime event for families when I interviewed the wonderful Judith Kerr (*The Tiger Who Came to Tea*, the Mog series, *When Hitler Stole Pink Rabbit*). She was of an age to remember how the world was in 1930s Berlin and London. It was a rare insight into those times. But interesting though these events were, and fun though it was to have your bed turned down for you each night, to have clean white towels fresh every day, we soon longed for home, for muddy wellies, and hayfields, and for swallows skimming over them! So back and forth we went, from the farm in Devon, a simple life of simple pleasures, to the Savoy, a sumptuous life of sumptuous pleasures. But very soon, I had the beginnings of a story in my head, a small but strong fire was burning there. A cat story. Here's why.

One day, the manager at the Savoy introduced me to what he called the mascot of the hotel, a rather beautiful and elegant sculpture of a black cat. He was called

The real Kaspar at
The Savoy Hotel, London

Kaspar. And he was kept on show in the hotel lobby. Had we not been introduced, I don't know whether Kaspar and I would ever have met. "You like stories, don't you?" the manager said. "I shall tell you Kaspar's story. And it's true, every word." Now, I especially like true stories, so I listened. "Well," he began, "it happened a long while ago, more than a hundred years ago now. A meeting was held here, of businessmen, in one of the rooms we have for such things. Thirteen men came to this meeting – the usual thing: lots of talk-talk, food, drink, cigars and more talk-talk. Right at the end of the meeting, one of the old businessmen looked around the table and suddenly said, 'Don't much like the look of this. Just realized, there's thirteen of us sitting here. Unlucky number.'"

"They all laughed at this, but it was a nervous laugh. Everyone knew you shouldn't walk under ladders, that magpies are unlucky and that you don't sit down at a table with thirteen people. Then another old duffer scoffed, 'What an utter load of old superstitious nonsense. Clap-trap. Cobblers. Tish-tosh.' And they all agreed and there was more nervous laughter. The meeting broke up and off they all went. The old duffer headed straight for Southampton, to catch the ship for South Africa. A few months later, after an uneventful sailing, he was in Johannesburg, just walking down the street, when some-one came up to him and shot him. When word got back to the Savoy Hotel about this terrible happening, they decided they had to do something about it. They made a rule that never again would they have a meeting around a table with just thirteen people there. They would insist that if there were going to be thirteen, they would always put out a fourteenth chair, and in the fourteenth chair they would sit a lucky black cat. Not a live one, of course, but one sculpted by a great Italian artist out of black ebony. So that's what was arranged. And that's why Kaspar's here."

He took me to see Kaspar. I stroked him, looked into his eyes. He seemed rather disdainful, superior – a prince of cats, I thought, and he knows it, not cuddly, but rather independent, his own master. He sat there so dignified, so self-assured, his tail curled like a question mark. "Why Kaspar?" I asked. "Who knows?" The manager shrugged. "Maybe that's for you to find out when you write your story about him." "Is that what I'm going to do?" I asked. "Probably," he replied. And he was right. I was.

But I had no idea what it would be about at all until one morning in the hotel when I went down to breakfast. I was on my own, I remember. Often, Clare takes a little longer in the morning than I do. I was coming down the wide staircase towards the breakfast room, taking my time, when I happened to look up. I think until that moment I had taken the opulence of the Savoy almost for granted. It is so overwhelming that otherwise you would spend all your time gawping at it. Everywhere there are glittering, sparkling chandeliers, wall paintings, lush, deep carpets, ornately framed pictures, huge gilded

225

mirrors. In the end, you stopped looking. It was just too much, too glitzy, too glamorous, and had begun to make me feel quite uncomfortable. I had by now discovered that when you go through the doors where the waiters and waitresses go, into the hidden working areas where the worker bees hurry back and forth, the hidden behind is rather gloomy and shabby and grim, a huge contrast to this world of extravagance.

Anyway, I was standing on those steps looking down into the magnificence of the breakfast room, when I was suddenly reminded of a black and white photograph I had seen of a dining room just like this, the same grandeur, the same over-the-top decor. It took me a few moments to remember where I had seen this photograph. Then I remembered. It was in a book I had read about the *Titanic*, the fastest, most luxurious ship the world had ever known, where the rich lived in first class in great opulence, while the poor and the crew lived in steerage below decks in quite a different world. This dining room at the Savoy was to me the dining room for the first-class passengers on the *Titanic*, and I was walking down into it. Ahead, I could see the passengers, the waiters bustling about, serving their every need, and out of the window beyond, the sun was shining on water – not seawater, of course, but the Thames. A bellboy passed me on the steps, with a cheery, "Good morning, sir."

As I sat there at my table moments later, I knew that bellboy would be the hero of my story, that this would be his story, his and Kaspar's. Somehow, some way, they would end up on the *Titanic*, they would both survive that terrible tragedy in which 1,500 died, rich and poor alike, and then I would find a way for Kaspar to come back to the Savoy, where he belonged. I began to dream my story. It took me a while, but I did it. And I loved doing it.

By the way, Kaspar is still there, in the lobby at the Savoy. You just ask the man in the top hat at the door if you can go in and meet Kaspar. He'll let you in. He's kind; they all are at the Savoy. You can stand there and stroke Kaspar, tell him you know his story, all about Johnny Trott, the bellboy, and the *Titanic*, all about how he came home again. He'd like that. And so would I.

KASPAR: PRINCE OF CATS

My fellow stokers ribbed me mercilessly from time to time, for I was the baby among them. I didn't mind. They ribbed the little Japanese man too till they discovered that, small though he was, he could shovel more coal than any of us. He was called Michiya, but we called him Little Mitch – and he was little, littler even than me. Maybe because we had been fellow stowaways, or maybe because we were both about the same size, he became quite a friend.

He spoke no English at all, so we conversed in gestures and smiles. We managed to make ourselves well enough understood. Like the rest of them I was black from head to toe after every shift. But Captain Smith was true to his word, we were all well enough looked after. We had plenty of hot water to wash ourselves clean, we had all the food we could eat and a warm bunk to sleep in. I didn't go up on deck that much. It was a long way up, and when I did have an hour or two off I found I was just too tired to do anything much except sleep. Down there in the bowels of the ship I didn't know if it was night or day – and I didn't much care either. It was just work, sleep, eat, work, sleep, eat. I was too tired even to dream.

When I did go up on deck I looked out on a moonlit sea, or a sunlit sea, that was always as flat as a pond and shining. I never saw another ship, just the wide horizons. Occasionally there were birds soaring over the decks, and once to everyone's great excitement we spotted dozens of leaping dolphins. I had never known such beauty. Every time I went up on deck though, I was drawn towards the First Class part of the ship. I'd stay there by the rail for a while, hoping against hope I might see Lizziebeth come walking by with Kaspar on his lead.

But I never saw them. I thought of them though as I shovelled and sweated, as I lay in my bunk in between shifts, as I looked over that glassy sea. I kept trying to summon up the courage to climb over the railings and find my way again back to their cabin. I longed to see the look of surprise on Lizziebeth's face when she saw I was on board. I knew how pleased she'd be to see me, that Kaspar would swish his tail and smile up at me. But about Lizziebeth's mother and father I couldn't be at all sure. The truth is that I still believed they would think badly of me for stowing away as I had.

I decided that it would be better to wait until we got to New York, and then I'd just walk up to them all and surprise them on the quayside. I'd tell them then and there that I'd taken Lizziebeth's advice and come to live in America, in the land of the free. They'd never need to know I'd stowed away.

I was half sleeping, half dreaming in my bunk, dreaming

that Kaspar was yowling at me, trying to wake me. We were in some kind of danger and he was trying to warn me. Then it happened. The ship suddenly shuddered and shook. I sat up. Right away it felt to me like some kind of a collision, and I could tell it had happened on the starboard side. A long silence followed. Then I heard a great rushing and roaring of escaping steam, like a death rattle. I knew something had gone terribly wrong, that the ship had been wounded. The engines had stopped.

Half a dozen of us got dressed at once and rushed up to the third deck, the boat deck. We all expected to see the ship we had collided with, because that was what we thought had happened. But we could see nothing, no ship, nothing but the stars and an empty sea all around. There was no one else on deck except us. It was as if no one else had felt it, as if it had all been a bad dream. No one else had woken, so it followed that nothing had happened. I was almost beginning to believe I had imagined the whole thing, when I saw Little Mitch come rushing along the deck towards us carrying something in both hands. It was a huge piece of ice shaped like a giant tooth, jagged and sharp. He was shouting the same thing over and over again, but I couldn't understand him, none of us could. Then one of the other stokers said it. "Iceberg! It's off an iceberg! We've only gone and hit a flaming iceberg!"

The Titanic

The *Titanic*, built in Belfast for the White Star Line, was the world's largest passenger ship at the time of her launch in 1912. Late on 14 April, five days into her maiden voyage from Southampton to New York, she struck an iceberg a glancing blow and went down two hours and forty minutes later. She only had enough lifeboats for one-third of her passengers. One thousand five hundred people drowned in the freezing cold North Atlantic.

Seventeen-year-old Jack Thayer was one of about forty lucky survivors who were plucked from the sea. The shouts from those thrown into the icy water swelled, he said, into "one long continuous wailing chant. This terrible cry lasted for twenty or thirty minutes, gradually dying away, as one after another could no longer withstand the cold and exposure..." According to the survivors, those in the lifeboats neglected their duty. Jack later complained: "The most heartrending part of the whole tragedy was the failure of those boats which were only partially loaded, to pick up the poor souls in the water. There they were, listening to the cries, and still they did not come back. If they had turned back several hundred more would have been saved."

A top-price ticket on this most luxurious of contemporary liners cost as much as a luxury car. A steerage ticket would have cost the average working man about a month's wages. Many of the emigrants in steerage would have spent all they had on the ticket. First-class passengers had access to a gymnasium, swimming pool, libraries, wireless telegraph, high-class restaurants and lavish cabins. The passengers included some of the wealthiest people in the world. Even steerage passengers had exceptional facilities for the time. Their cabins had running water, a washbasin and electricity, and there were three meals a day. (Other steamships required them to bring their own food.) Most steerage passengers were poor emigrants to the United States, mainly Irish, Swedes, Syrians and Finns.

There was a contemporary sense that somehow first-class passengers were more worth saving. This is reflected in the words of steerage passenger Anna Lundi, from Finland: "I can never understand why God would have spared a poor Finnish girl when all those rich people drowned." Critics of what happened as the *Titanic* was sinking ironically reworked the notion of "women and children first" as "first-class passengers first", because nearly two-thirds of first-class passengers survived, compared with a quarter of steerage passengers. Only one child drowned from the first and second classes, compared with fifty-five out of eighty steerage children. However, nearly half the steerage women survived, but only a third of first-class men.

The great majority of crew members were from the Southampton area, where one in four households lost a family member. At Northam School, near the docks, 120 out of 250 pupils lost their father. Teacher Annie Hopkins wrote in the school logbook: "A great many girls are absent this afternoon, owing to the sad news regarding the *Titanic*. Fathers and brothers are on the vessel and some of the little ones have been in tears all afternoon."

With no welfare state nor insurance, hundreds of families who had lost breadwinners faced desperate poverty. A relief fund was set up afterwards, to ease the financial pressures on them.

The disaster was greeted with worldwide shock at the scale of the loss of life, and outrage at the failures that had led to it. Subsequent inquiries revealed deficiencies in current maritime safety regulations, and found that the lack of lifeboats on deck was due to the owners' wrong belief that, in an emergency, the design of the *Titanic* would enable her to stay afloat long enough for her passengers and crew to be transferred safely to a rescue vessel. They had also wished to ensure unobstructed views for passengers on deck.

So was there a Kaspar on board? Certainly there was an extraordinary array of animals. Ella White had brought four French roosters and hens, another woman had thirty cockerels, and Elizabeth Nye a yellow canary. Luckily for Charles Moore's one hundred English foxhounds, a change of plan meant they were on another vessel. Three lapdogs survived. Elizabeth Rothschild had refused to board a lifeboat unless her dog was allowed to come, but Helen Bishop lamented abandoning her dog, remembering that he had held on to her dress with his teeth. "The loss of my little dog hurt me very much. He so wanted to accompany me."

There is no record of a surviving cat on the *Titanic*, but its cat mascot, Jenny, had given birth to kittens on the boat's trial run from Belfast to Southampton. After the tragedy, some locals claimed that a cat had disembarked at Southampton before the fateful journey. Up and down the gangplank she went, retrieving one kitten at a time, depositing each on the dock, until the whole family was off. She, and the kittens, then disappeared. Maybe Jenny had had a premonition.

The Mozart Question

THE DREAM

I have travelled a fair bit, for work and pleasure, and, like most of us, I have my favourite places to which I return whenever the opportunity arises. Some places I cannot do without for long – Scilly, Cornwall, rural France and especially Venice. I do not go on these travels consciously searching for stories, but I do know that I am making myself available should I come across an idea for a story that resonates with me, engages me, will not leave me alone. It is rare that happens in the space of twenty-four hours, but the events of one day in 1990 in Venice left me in no doubt that I would write *The Mozart Question*, that I had to write it, needed to write it, and do it at once.

In a street close to our little hotel in the Dorsoduro

part of Venice, near the Accademia Bridge, I discovered a barber's shop. Growing up, I had often seen in London those red and white striped poles above a barber's shop. Many of the barbers of my childhood were Italian. And here I was in the city of red and white poles, of gondolas tied up to them, the city from which so many of those Italian London barbers may well have come, and whose poles you can find now outside barbers' shops all around the world. Walking past this barber's shop in Venice, I thought, Go and have a haircut in a proper Venetian barber's – my hair was looking a bit scraggy anyway. So in I went.

I was greeted with a shy, silent smile and ushered to the chair. The place was tidy, immaculate, the barber too. There was no radio, just the two of us. And he stayed tactfully silent which was just as well, because, I'm ashamed to say, my Italian is strictly limited to *ciao*, *grazie* and *cappucino*. As he cut my hair, I found myself utterly entranced by his fingers as they worked the scissors. They were fast, deft, expert, rhythmic, almost as if he had a tune in his head that he was conducting with his scissors.

It reminded me after a while of that extraordinary film *The Great Dictator*, in which Charlie Chaplin plays a humble Jewish barber who has the misfortune to be mistaken for Adolf Hitler. There is a glorious scene in the film, where, to the accompaniment of Brahms' Hungarian Dance No. 5, he cuts and shaves and trims his customer with such dexterity, such skill, oblivious to everything else in the world except his craft and the music.

After twenty minutes or so, I walked out into the sunlit street, my hair trim and perfect and Italian, knowing I had witnessed a performance of supreme skill. Never once did he use a machine. He was simply a maestro with the scissors, a genius. (Every time I return to Venice I go back to the same place to have my hair cut. It is a ritual I look forward to. I have never been disappointed.)

That same afternoon, Clare and I decided to discover a place I think we had always avoided until now. Venice may be one of the most beautiful places on this Earth, but there is a great sadness hanging over it, because it is fading, crumbling, sinking, and maybe because it is a tourists' Mecca now, overcrowded, over-commercial, its great moment in history past. However splendid and magnificent the architecture, however lively the bustle and music and mime of the streets, it is a decaying place, threatened constantly by the invasion of the sea, by the ever-increasing pressure of tourism. It is a place that reflects the human condition, both achingly beautiful and deeply sorrowful.

So, not wishing perhaps to overload our spirits with sadness, we had over the years always resisted going to visit the area of Venice known as the Ghetto. We knew what had happened there in the Second World War, that of the 400 Jews taken away to the concentration camps, only very few had returned. We went in the end, I think, because we knew that we had to, that we should. This was, after all, the place that gave its name to Jewish ghettos all over Europe, the first ghetto.

You go in through an archway, over a bridge or two, past a synagogue, and, at last, into a small square, a well in the centre, apartment buildings all around, stark, plain. Here, the Jewish people of Venice had lived for hundreds of years, separated from the rest of the population, shut in at night, but left to get on with their lives. And it was here, in that square, that they had been gathered together in 1944 and taken away. There is a café there now, a few Jewish bookshops, and happily, the Ghetto of today is alive again with Jewish families. So, it is a place of horror and anguish, but of hope and renewal too.

That evening, we went to an opera in La Fenice opera house, Benjamin Britten's *The Turn of the Screw*, which was extraordinarily powerful but rather dark and sinister. As we were walking home to our hotel, we were talking

though not of Benjamin Britten, but of the Ghetto, which had left us so moved that afternoon. When we came round the corner into the square below the Accademia Bridge we heard the sound of a guitar playing, beautifully. There seemed at first to be no one about, but then we saw a small boy in his pyjamas – he was maybe five or six – sitting on his tricycle, leaning on the handlebars, his chin resting on his hands. That was when we saw the guitarist too, standing just a few yards away, under the lamp post. The boy had not seen us, and neither had the musician. We stopped in the shadows and listened and looked. The music was Spanish, eighteenth century, elegant, delicately and passionately played by a young man lost entirely in his music. The little boy sat there gazing up at him. He did not move. Neither did we. We were all rooted to the spot by the beauty of the music, the place, the moment. I thought then, This is the kind of moment that changes lives. Maybe, because of this moment, that boy in his pyjamas would love music for ever, might even want to play it for himself, or compose it, or sing it.

I wondered if he was the son of my barber, and wondered if possibly my barber might have been Jewish. I knew as I listened that I already had in my head a story set in the heaven

of Venice and in the hell of a concentration camp. I was aware already of the orchestras the Nazis had organized, how some inmates of the camps, many of them Jews, had been obliged to play for their oppressors, forced to sit there to play as the trains came in bringing new loads of prisoners, some to be selected for slave labour, some for the gas chambers. The music was to calm them, to make it all seem fine, that there was nothing to worry about. I thought then how it would be to have had to play in such an orchestra, to survive and then to try to live a normal life again afterwards. How would you feel when you heard again the music you had played? A lot of it was Mozart – marches, minuets, divertimentos. Would you ever want to hear it or play it again? Would you tell your children what had happened or simply keep quiet about it?

I began writing *The Mozart Question* almost at once, while I was there in Venice, while "the fire was in my head". I wanted to affirm the power of love and music, of the human spirit to survive, to triumph over fear and hatred.

THE MOZART QUESTION

"Then late one summer's evening I was lying half awake in my bed when I heard the sound of a violin. I thought Papa must have changed his mind and was playing again at last. But then I heard him and Mama talking in the kitchen below, and realized anyway that the music was coming from much further away.

"I listened at the window. I could hear it only intermittently over the sound of people talking and walking, over the throbbing engines of passing water buses, but I was quite sure now that it was coming from somewhere beyond the bridge. I had to find out. In my pyjamas I stole past the kitchen door, down the stairs and out into the street. It was a warm night, and quite dark. I ran up over the bridge and there, all on his own, standing by the lamp in the square, was an old man playing the violin, his violin case open at his feet.

"No one else was there. No one had stopped to listen. I squatted down as close as I dared. He was so wrapped up in his playing that he did not notice me at first. I could see now that he was much older even than Papa. Then he saw me crouching there watching him. He stopped playing. 'Hello,' he said. 'You're out late. What's your name?' He had kind eyes; I noticed that at once.

"'Paolo,' I told him. 'Paolo Levi. My papa plays the violin. He played in an orchestra once.'

"'So did I,' said the old man, 'all my life. But now I am what I always wanted to be, a soloist. I shall play you some Mozart. Do you like Mozart?'

"'I don't know,' I replied. I knew Mozart's name, of course, but I don't think I had ever listened to any of his music.

"'He wrote this piece when he was even younger than you. I should guess that you're about seven.'

"'Nine,' I said.

"'Well, Mozart wrote this when he was just six years old. He wrote it for the piano, but I can play it on the violin.'

"So he played Mozart, and I listened. As he played, others came and gathered round for a while before dropping a coin or two in his violin case and moving on. I didn't move on. I stayed. The music he played to me that night touched my soul. It was the night that changed my life for ever.

"Whenever I crossed the Accademia Bridge after that I always looked out for him. Whenever I heard him playing I went to listen. I never told Mama or Papa. I think it was the first secret I kept from them. But I did not feel guilty about it, not one bit. After all, hadn't they kept a secret from me?

Then one evening the old man – I had found out by now that his name was Benjamin Horowitz and that he was sixty-two years old – one evening he let me hold his violin, showed me how to hold it properly, how to draw the bow across the strings, how to make it sing. The moment I did that, I knew I had to be a violinist. I have never wanted to do or be anything else since.

"So Benjamin – Signor Horowitz I always called him then – became my first teacher. Now every time I ran over the bridge to see him he would show me a little more, how to tighten the bow just right, how to use the resin, how to hold the violin under my chin using no hands at all and what each string was called. That was when I told him about Papa's violin at home, and about how he didn't play it any more. 'He couldn't anyway,' I said, 'because it's a bit broken. I think it needs mending a bit. Two of the strings are missing, the A and the E, and there's hardly a hair left on the bow at all. But I could practise on it if it was mended, couldn't I?'

"'Bring it to my house sometime,' Benjamin said, 'and leave it with me. I'll see what I can do.'"

Nazi concentration camps

We are sometimes urged to "move on"; even to erase the memory of wars, the bombing of civilians, massacres or genocides. But many feel that in remembering lie the seeds of understanding, which can lead to forgiveness and reconciliation and focus the desire to avoid future conflicts. "Lest we forget" is a phrase from the First World War encouraging us to remember those who died in conflict.

The first Nazi concentration camps were erected in Germany in 1933, immediately after Hitler became chancellor. Initially, concentration camps housed forced labour, usually on back-breaking and dangerous building projects, including building the camps themselves. Even before they were developed as extermination camps, death rates were high, and prisoners felt they were being literally worked to death.

The first inmates of the camps were mainly political opponents. Later, the list of victims grew to include Jews, resistance fighters and "opponents of the state", Gypsies, homosexuals, Jehovah's Witnesses, criminals, the disabled, the mentally ill, and the "antisocial", such as beggars or vagrants. Under a Nazi secret plan, "Master Plan East", the elimination of people from Slavic countries such as Poland and Russia, whatever their racial make-up, was also planned.

Hitler and the Nazis believed that the genes of the people they had identified as undesirable polluted an idealized German Aryan "master race". Hitler blamed the Jews for Germany's loss of the First World War and in his book, *Mein Kampf*, he promised to "rid" Germany of all Jews. After he came to power in 1933, laws were soon passed to limit Jewish rights to work and to vote. Once the Second World War started, the Nazis began forcing all of the Jewish people into a small district in each city they captured. Called a "ghetto", the area was fenced in and guarded. It was very crowded, there was little food, water or medicine available. But it became much worse.

The Nazis developed the death camps as part of their plan for what they called the "Final Solution to the Jewish Question".

The people taken to these camps, from all over occupied Europe, were told they were relocating to a new and better place. But on arrival, anyone unable to work – children, the old, the weak, and any pregnant women, were isolated and immediately taken to specially designed buildings. Here, thinking they were about to have a shower, they were killed with poison gas. The rest were subjected to hard labour, and had a temporary reprieve. Millions died of starvation, or were later gassed.

Only one in ten Jews living in Germany and Poland at the beginning of the war survived the camps. About five million non-Jews were murdered.

Those prisoners who had skills useful to the Nazis, particularly musicians, might survive for longer. Fania Fénelon, the French pianist and singer, recalled how she, and other musicians, had clean clothes, daily showers and a reasonable food supply. "There were so many musicians in Terezin, there could have been two full symphony orchestras performing simultaneously daily. In addition, there were a number of chamber orchestras playing at various times." Not surprisingly, the musicians' "privileges" set them apart from the other prisoners and made them objects of jealousy and suspicion.

The price of survival for the performing musicians, however, was hideous. Musicians were often used for the apparently harmless role of entertaining the camp guards and officers, many of whom were music enthusiasts. But they also had to perform for hours at roll call, regardless of weather conditions. Musicians were also forced to meet the daily trains bringing the prisoners to the camps. The music continued as new arrivals were sorted. Camp survivor Sam Pivnik reported: "He [the guard] gestured to the right (for life) and to the left (for death)." In addition, there were regular selections of those too weak to work another day and musicians were required to play light-hearted or marching music for hours on end throughout, watching the selected trudge to the gas chambers. They had to play during executions, such as the hanging of prisoners who had attempted escape. The suicide rate amongst musicians in concentration camps was one of the highest of any group of prisoners.

Yet, in some ways, performers and camp inmates used music as a form of resistance. Performers organized the repertoire and included their own compositions, boosting morale for themselves and fellow inmates. Traditional or newly composed songs could be sung at any time and required little practice or preparation. Group-singing sessions produced a sense of companionship and belonging. The playing of traditional songs and tunes, or of new music, counteracted the SS's intention to crush the prisoners' physical and cultural existence. Arguably, music in the camps helped some inmates retain their sanity, identity and traditions.

Running Wild

Chapter One

A sudden change of heart

Will always wanted train journeys to go on forever, an
this one. He liked trains, the rattle and the rhythm of th
loved to press his forehead against the cold of the glas
single rain drop with his finger as it found its way dow
window. Sometimes he'd just be gazing out at the cou
rushing by, at cows and horses skittering away over th
clouds of starlings whirling in the wind, at a formation
flying high towards the evening sun.

But mostly, he'd be on the look out for wild animals,

Running Wild

THE DREAM

There are a handful of books I read when I was young that I now know sowed the early seeds of ideas, hopes and beliefs that have developed and stayed with me all my life. So important were these books to me, then and since, that, for a long while, I had not dared even to attempt to write a story that explored the same worlds, the same themes. It was as if these books were hallowed ground, so well written, so known, so familiar, so beloved that I deliberately steered well clear of them. These great iconic stories were for reading, for enjoying, for remembering, not for echoing in my own writing.

The Jungle Book by Rudyard Kipling was one such book, and Kipling one of my great author heroes. For decades of my writing life, I avoided jungles and wild children, and elephants. And yet, something was beginning over the years to niggle me. I had come to espouse, in my own life and in my writing, the principles and

251

philosophy behind Kipling's tale. As I grew up, I came to understand that *we*, the human species, are simply a part of the natural world about us, not superior to it, or separate from it. I am sure the naturalist David Attenborough also played a great part in developing my awareness of all this, and the poet Ted Hughes as well.

We are successful as a species, too successful, it seems to me, for our own good, and certainly too successful for the good of the planet. We are super-intelligent hunter-gatherers, who have come to dominate the world about us, and to feel as if we rule it. In so doing, we have come to look upon our fellow creatures as lesser creatures, to be exploited for food or entertainment, and to be exterminated if necessary, if that is in our interest, whenever they get in our way. We want to be top predator. We are mankind. We want to remake the world as we want it to be. We have the right and we have the power. And the more we assume the right, the more powerful and clever and exploitative we become of the world of nature, the more we come to feel separate from the world about us, rather than an integral part of it.

Our religions often support and confirm this arrogance, this assumption of superiority. God chose us – and he must be right after all – set us apart and above all the other animals. We were his chosen creatures. But *The Jungle Book* told me a different story; *The Elephant's Child* too. In both stories there is a deep love and respect for our fellow creatures. There is an assumption that we are simply one of the beasts, and should be learning to live in harmony with them, and with the wildness of nature too, living close to it, and learning to understand and respect the Earth and all its living creatures and plants. A wild boy could do this in *The Jungle Book*, had to do this. It was the only way to survive. He was one of the animals, wild as they were, living alongside them, facing their dangers, struggling to survive with them.

In this largely urban world we are ever increasingly removed from our connection with this world of nature. One way of restoring our connection to the wild, to the countryside – and, for most of us, this is all that is left of the wild – is to go there, not just to watch a TV programme about it, not just to look and take a photograph either, but to go away, to stay long enough to have some sense of belonging, to reconnect, to learn that the fish in the river, the herons and the otters, all the creatures that live there, are reliant upon us to keep the river clean for their survival, that the water is theirs as much as ours; that when we grow and harvest our corn and our hay, we should leave space for the ground birds to nest, for rodents and rabbits, for deer. Yes, we glean our food and sustenance from the countryside, but it is a bounty we must not take for granted, and one we must learn to share. To look up and see two buzzards up there floating on a thermal, hunting, feeding their young, is to begin to understand their needs, their struggle to survive. Drink the cows' milk, eat carrots, dig potatoes, and we understand how the Earth sustains us and how it will only go on doing so for as long as we sustain it. This has largely been the thinking behind Farms for City Children, the charity that Clare and I began forty years ago now. Over 120,000 city children have come to live for a week on the three farms we work on. Every visit for every child reinforces a new sense of belonging to nature, our reliance upon it and our responsibility to live in harmony with it.

Working on this project all these years alongside farmers and country people and teachers and children, I found it became more and more important to the writer in me to try to think of a way not to echo *The Jungle Book* but to tell my own story, a story now more urgently important and relevant than ever before. We are overcrowding the planet, we are overheating the Earth and its seas, we are overexploiting its resources, decimating the wildlife and plant life whenever it becomes inconvenient, whenever we feel it inhibits our progress. We have become consumed by greed.

I had discovered as I was thinking about all this, before I had ever decided to write it, that there are already a large number of wild-child stories, some legendary, many not fictional at all. There are well-documented stories from ancient and more modern times, from all over the world, about children lost or discarded, living wild with the animals. Most famous, of course, is the legendary story of Romulus and Remus, who were reared in the wild by a she-wolf and who grew up to be founders of

Rome. But there really were, not that long ago, children living among wild dogs in the streets of urban Russia, others discovered hiding in the forests of France in the eighteenth century, or deep in the rural heart of India. There is documentary evidence for many of these stories, photographs, even. Of course, invention may have exaggerated the truths behind them, but that is storytelling.

The more I read of these wild children, the more fascinated I became and the more I was tempted to dare to think of writing my own *Jungle Book*. If Kipling could do it, I could do it! But all these wild-child stories I knew, legendary or otherwise, had come from the past, were cocooned in the comfort of the past. I had to make a break with all that and create a wild child that lives now, not back in the days of Kipling and empire, not in the antique world of Tarzan. I wanted, somehow, to connect my story to the urban world of today. But try as I did, I could not find a way to do this. How in the world of today, with all our sophisticated communication technology, could a child ever become wild, truly out of touch? And how could a child of today ever get lost in a jungle and survive, credibly? The story stayed on hold in my mind, waiting for its moment. The moment came on the wave of the greatest natural disaster and tragedy of my lifetime.

It happened on Boxing Day 2004, when the most powerful tsunami in anyone's living memory struck the shores of Sri Lanka, Indonesia, India and Thailand. It left over 300,000 dead. It overwhelmed and destroyed wherever it struck, laying waste entire regions. For weeks and months, the newspapers and television were full of the devastation and grieving. The violence of it, the scale of misery the tsunami caused horrified the world and touched our hearts. Nations and people did not simply agonize, they did what they could to help, to save lives, to provide shelter and food and water, to give and support, wherever it was needed. It was never enough. We all knew that despite all these efforts, the suffering was appalling. And it was the depth of the suffering that made us all feel helpless and hopeless. It was in the midst of all this that I read one day in a newspaper the first positive story to come out of all this suffering. It lifted my spirits, and, ultimately, it was to do more than that. It was this story that enabled me to begin to write my wild-child story, and with an elephant too!

Here is the story I read, in brief. An English family was on holiday in Sri Lanka – if I remember rightly. On Boxing Day 2004, they were on the beach below their hotel, and one of the children, a boy, was going for an elephant ride, something he had been longing to do. He was already some distance from the family, the elephant led by a mahout, the boy riding up in the howdah, loving it all, when the elephant began to become agitated. She had sensed something was wrong. She became wilder and wilder, at last breaking away from the mahout and charging up the beach, away from the sea and into the jungle, the boy clinging on in his howdah. Higher and higher they went, leaving the beach and sea behind them. And by now, the danger the elephant had sensed was growing with every moment, but was still largely unnoticed.

The sea appeared to be retreating into itself. Strangely, weirdly, it was being sucked away, leaving vast expanses of sand covered with thousands of stranded flapping fish. The children, mainly from fishing families, could not believe their luck and rushed out to gather the fish. But then, too late, they looked up and saw the great wave rushing in. Children, tourists, everyone tried to make a run for it, but the speed and the power of the tsunami wave swept all before it away, people, houses, hotels, cars, animals. It tore down entire villages and forests. And all the while, the elephant and the boy on her back were making their way higher and higher, deeper and deeper into the jungle, at every step distancing themselves from the disaster that was engulfing everything and everyone behind them.

The story goes that after it was over, the family, who had survived, went looking for the boy, fearing the worst. After days of searching they heard about an elephant who had emerged from the jungle with an English boy up in the howdah, safe, saved. It was him! Their boy had survived! In gratitude for all the elephant had done, the family provided for her for the rest of her life. The story may be embellished in parts – who knows? It was in a newspaper after all! But there was truth at its heart. For those, like me, who read it, it was a shining light of hope in the midst of this terrible tragedy. And for the writer in me, the door into my wild-child story had opened. Now I knew how my wild child of today would find himself in the depths of the jungle, and with an elephant as a companion! And that jungle really was a place of orang-utans and Sumatran tigers, a jungle under threat, great swathes of the forest being slashed and burnt to make room for palm oil plantations for our toothpaste and our peanut butter. Here my wild child and his elephant had to learn to survive together with the other animals, indeed fight the good fight to save the jungle itself. But I knew I had more to understand, and more dreamtime to do before I could begin. This would be an epic story, and I had to get it right.

In my story-making, nothing is more important than my dreamtime. I know I have to be patient, to allow time for ideas or dreams (call them what you will) to weave themselves together in and around research, and to give time for happenstance to help a story on its way. I have learnt never to face the empty page until I am ready to tell my dream down onto it, and then to tell it as if I am confiding to my best, most trusted friend in the world, and to tell it as I see it, hear it and feel it. So with *Running Wild*, I told myself, learn about orang-utans, who might well be extinct in ten years, learn about Sumatran tigers, who will not last even that long, learn about the decimation of our tropical forests, learn about elephants, their unique intelligence, their supreme sensitivity – they too are threatened with exploitation and extinction. Throw off any cloak of "civilization", learn to be wild. Becoming wild was the hardest thing to do. But over the years, I have found my own way of making such leaps of imagination. I have become horse in *War Horse*, dog in *Born to Run*, and young again in almost all the stories I tell. Now I would be young and wild. To do it, I would have to know this whole new world of the jungle as my wild boy does, discover it with him, hope and fear with him in his struggle to survive. I would become wild boy. I would run wild.

RUNNING WILD

In a strange way I actually found myself missing the tiger. I kept hoping I would see him again. More than that, I was even longing for it. As I lay there one night in my sleeping nest, I kept remembering the tiger poster on the wall of the classroom back at school. I could see it so clearly, lit by the afternoon sun slanting in through the classroom window. That tiger used to gaze down at me with the very same look in his eyes as the tiger Oona and I had encountered on the jungle trail that day. There was a poem underneath the picture. We'd all had to learn it by heart for homework, but I could only ever manage to recite the first verse before drying up. I couldn't remember even that much now, but the first couple of lines did come back to me, and I spoke them out loud again and again, because I thought it sounded so much how the tiger had looked to me, as if the poet had been there and seen him with me. And anyway, I thought Oona would like to hear it.

'"Tyger Tyger burning bright, in the forests of the night.
What immortal hand or eye could frame thy fearful symmetry?"'

I got a deep rumble of appreciation from down below, and I knew she'd be smiling away down there in the darkness. I wished now that I had learned it better so that I could have recited the rest of it for her. As I went to sleep that night, I tried to see the words again as they were printed on the poster, but all I could visualize were snatches of lines, bits and pieces. However, the harder I tried, the more I was remembering. I hoped it was all there somewhere, deep in my memory, lost for the moment, but not entirely forgotten.

When we did see the tiger again, it turned out to be in no sense a repetition of the earlier stand-off. There was no hissing this time, no trumpeting. This time he came wandering on to the track in front of us, and looked back at us over his shoulder, as if to say: "Are you going my way? That's fine by me." I was tingling with apprehension and excitement, and I could feel that Oona remained wary too. She did not show it though. As she walked on she never broke the rhythm of her stride. We followed the tiger through the jungle for most of that morning.

After a while, I began to relax, more and more sure all the time that the tiger was not doing this because he wanted to eat me. It was simply because he liked the company. There could be no other explanation. He had the whole forest to wander in, and yet he had chosen to wander along with us. When Oona paused to eat from time to time, the tiger would lie down in the shadow of the trees nearby and clean himself, then yawn, stretch out and wait until Oona was ready to go on again.

So at ease did I become that day with our new travelling companion that I felt I might even try to talk to him. But then I didn't seem to know what I should say. I mean, what do you say to a tiger? It was so important to say the right thing, but I couldn't find the right words. So I decided in the end to recite the poem for him – the bits I could remember anyway – because I felt the words were full of wonder and respect, and I hoped he might pick up on that. Somehow – and to be honest, I have no idea how – when I began to recite the poem this time, every line, then every verse, all of it, just flowed from my memory, almost as if the poet was inside my head and speaking it out for me, maybe because he too knew this was the right moment for his poem to be heard, that this listener was the one he'd written it for, the listener who mattered to him more than any other. I remembered his name then, suddenly. Blake, William Blake. It said so on the poster, right at the bottom.

"Tyger Tyger burning bright, in the forests of the night.

What immortal hand or eye could frame thy fearful symmetry?"

As I spoke it, I so wanted the tiger to listen to me. I was encouraged by his ears, that were turning constantly, backwards, forwards, this way and that. I recited the poem again, projecting my voice this time, so that the tiger should be in no doubt that the poem had been written just for him, and that I was reciting it just for him too. I was so pleased with myself for remembering it. I recited the poem over and over again, to prove to myself that I really could do it, and to drum it into my brain so that I would never be able to forget it.

Just as I began it for the umpteenth time, the tiger stopped in his tracks, and turned to look up at me. At that moment I had no doubt whatsoever that he had been listening, no doubt that he knew these words were about him, and for him. His eyes burned into mine, just for a moment, and I felt there was no hunger there any more.

It wasn't mere curiosity either. It was a meeting of minds. Shortly after this, the tiger lifted one of his front paws, shook it as if he'd just stood on a thorn, then sprang lightly away into the shadows of the trees, and vanished.

Endangered animals

The tsunami on 26 December 2004 was one of the world's worst natural disasters. It affected five million people in fourteen countries, with 230,000 dying in the immediate flooding, and many succumbing to disease afterwards. One and a half million lost their homes. Indonesia was the worst hit, with waves travelling up to two kilometres inland.

A tsunami (from the Japanese word for "harbour wave") is a series of waves created when a large volume of water is rapidly displaced. They can be caused by earthquakes, volcanic eruptions or landslides. But they can also be caused by humans, through the detonation of a nuclear device at sea, for example. Because of the immense volumes of water and energy involved, tsunamis can be devastating, and it is not possible to prevent them. Early warning is rare, but it is the only protection. At least twenty-five tsunamis were recorded in the last century, many in the Asia-Pacific region.

Some believe that animals have a sixth sense, providing advance warning of such natural disasters. Sri Lankan media sources claimed that elephants moved inland when the tsunami struck in 2004, away from the approaching noise. At the Yala National Park three elephants were seen running away from the beach. On India's Cuddalore coast, where thousands of people perished, it was reported on the radio that buffaloes, goats and dogs were found unharmed. Flamingos had flown to higher ground beforehand. However, the consensus of scientific opinion is that no "sixth sense" is involved. For instance, Whit Gibbons, an ecologist at the University of Georgia, argues that "Many animals detect certain natural signals, such as the early tremblings of an earthquake, long before humans. This means they have opportunity to react before we can... As far as running inland to get away from a tsunami, I think any fast animal would probably do so because that's where the forests are... The woods [and higher ground] are the safest place for most animals. Completely natural and not at all mystical."

Sadly, animals in the area affected by the 2004 tsunami are at greater risk from humans than they are from natural disasters. Indonesia is home to many famous endangered animals - elephants, orang-utans and rhinos. Less well-known endangered species also living there are the clouded leopard, the sun bear and the Bornean gibbon. Now forests all over the region are being logged, burnt and cleared in order to make way for agricultural land. Half the world's tropical timber, used for paper and furniture manufacture, comes from this area.

Orang-utans are closely related to humans, sharing 97 per cent of our DNA, and are very intelligent. The word "orang-utan" is derived from the Malay words meaning "person of the forest". They are natives of Indonesia and Malaysia, and are currently found only in the rainforests of Borneo and Sumatra. "Great apes" as opposed to monkeys (monkeys usually have tails), they are arboreal, which means that they spend nearly all their time in the trees (where they build nests) and hardly ever come to the ground, unlike other apes such as chimpanzees, gorillas and humans. They have longer arms than other apes and their hair is reddish brown. Again, unlike gorillas and chimpanzees, orang-utans are not true knuckle-walkers and travel over the ground by shuffling on their palms with their fingers curved inwards. They are more solitary than other apes, with males and females only coming together to mate. Although orang-utans are generally passive towards humans, aggression towards other orang-utans is very common and they can be fiercely territorial.

Mothers stay with their babies until they reach the age of six or seven. But many baby orang-utans are taken from their mothers to be sold as pets, and the adults are hunted for meat. Females give birth to just one infant at a time every eight or nine years, making their populations very susceptible to even very low levels of hunting. The mother orang-utan is almost always killed to capture her infant. For every orang-utan orphan that is sold, six to eight orang-utans die in the process of capture and transport.

Over the last hundred years, numbers of orang-utans in the wild are thought to have dropped from over 300,000 to less than 6,600 in Sumatra, and 54,000 in Borneo. Unless dramatic action is taken, it is likely that the Sumatran orang-utans will be the first of the great apes to become extinct.

An Elephant in the Garden

THE DREAM

I will start with my fascination with elephants. Why this fascination? It began with a story, the first story I loved, and still my favourite story. It was the story I wanted to hear my mother read to us again and again, and was her favourite story too. She used to read to us every night before we went to sleep. My brother, Pieter, and I would crawl into the same bed up in our attic room, and snuggle down. I could not count the number of times she read us "The Elephant's Child", from Rudyard Kipling's *Just So Stories*. Everything in this story made me smile, the fun of it, the music in the words, the rhythm in the sentences, the gloriously inventive explanation of how the elephant got its trunk, and the deeply satisfying ending, in which this much put-upon elephant's child gets to use his newly acquired, newly stretched, proper elephant's trunk – elephants had just had little short snouts up until then – to spank his bullying relatives, who had always given him such a hard time because he would keep asking awkward questions.

It is precisely because this story was so precious to me that I could never bring myself even to attempt to write an elephant into one of my stories. I could never hope to write anything so good, so fine, so funny, so perfect. Great writers can inhibit sometimes as much as they can inspire. But I suppose, deep inside me, I must have clung to the notion that one day I might dare try it, if ever an idea occurred that seemed so right that I had to do it, that it was worth the risk. Then strangely, as if they had been waiting dormant all this time, two elephant ideas for stories came along in quick succession. For two years or more, elephants ruled my dreamtime and my story-making. First in *Running Wild*, and then in *An Elephant in the Garden*, a story very far removed in tone from the world of Kipling's *Just So Stories*, a story I thought I dreamt up out of nowhere, but, of course, no story comes from nowhere. There are times when the stuff of dreams and reality blur, become so confused that you are not sure where the one ends and the other begins.

Here's how *An Elephant in the Garden* began. We have been in the habit, Clare and I, of listening to the radio through the night-time, the BBC World Service. For us, it is a wonderful lullaby. The droning and burbling helps us to drop off to sleep, and when we wake, we sometimes find an interesting programme that helps us to forget we can't sleep, soothes anxiety and enables us, sooner or later, to fall asleep again. Clare sleeps deeply, dreams, I think, less than I do. I dream often, partly because I wake more often – and I'm told we dream most intensely just before we wake. I dream vividly, wake up sometimes, heart pounding with excitement or fear, engendered by some vivid dream. But – and here's the frustrating problem – I can rarely remember what my dreams are about. I can't tell you the number of times I have been dreaming a wonderful, extraordinary dream, and often within the dream, I am even aware it is a dream and promise myself I must dream it to the end to find out what happens. I tell myself in my dream that I must remember it when I wake up, get out of bed and write it down at once so I don't forget it. Then I wake up and, more often than not, it is already gone, flown away, for-gotten! Infuriating! But just occasionally, I do wake up and remember – I have even been known to get out of bed and write my dream down whilst the memory of it was still clear in my mind.

One morning, with the light of dawn breaking and the sound of birdsong outside the window, I woke up holding a dream in my head. And such a dream! I didn't get up and write it down; I just lay there, amazed at how clear and detailed the dream had been. I waited until Clare stirred. "You awake?" I asked. I had to tell her, had to tell someone. She mumbled something, not best pleased at being woken. "I just had the most amazing dream," I told her. She murmured something that indicated to me that she really wasn't interested at this hour of the morning, and couldn't it wait? She wanted to be left to go back to sleep. But I was already into my story.

"I don't know why," I said, "but I think it all happened in Belfast. There was this lady and she worked in a Belfast zoo, looked after the elephants. It was sometime during the Second World War. One day, she went off to work as usual. When she got there, she found the zoo director, her boss, was gathering everyone together for a meeting. 'Look,' he said, 'you're not going to like this, but we haven't got any choice. Orders. If the Germans come and bomb the city – which they will very likely, sooner or later, because of the port and the dockyards, I'm afraid we will have to be ready to destroy all the large animals. We can't have bombs falling on the zoo, breaking open the cages, setting wild animals free to roam the city. I'm sorry, but there it is. In the event of an air raid, they will all have to be shot at once.' Of course, everyone was very upset – most of all, the elephant lady, who loved her elephants dearly.

"Afterwards, she went up to the director and said, 'Look, sir, you know I have one young orphan elephant I have brought up myself for two years now. She's gentle as a lamb, everyone knows she is. We can't shoot her, sir.

272

We just can't. I'll look after her, see she doesn't get loose if a raid comes.'

'And how are you going to do that?' the director asked. 'You go home every evening. We all do.'

'I can take her home with me,' she replied. 'Keep her in my back garden. It's a walled garden, quite safe. She'll never be out of my sight, I promise.'

'You could do that?' he asked. He hummed and hawed, but, in the end, let her take the young elephant home. So that's what she did. Every night she'd walk the elephant back home through the streets and look after her in her back garden."

"I never had such a vivid dream before," I told Clare. "And what's more, I remember all of it, everything."

Clare turned over. "That's because it wasn't a dream," she mumbled. "Unless I dreamt exactly the same dream, which I didn't. It was on the radio. I heard it. Now, please can I get some sleep?"

I got up, went to my computer, typed in "Belfast Zoo WW2, Blitz, elephant". And at once, up came a black and white photograph from the *Belfast Telegraph*, of a lady and an elephant in a back garden. True. Impossible but true. No dream. But what a story, all the same. I knew at once I would tell the story of that elephant, and call it *An Elephant in the Garden*. But as the weeks passed, it occurred to me that I had written often about the Second World War, and usually, though not always, from a British perspective. Wasn't it about time I wrote a story set in

Germany? There was bombing there too and on a massive scale.

Dresden came to mind immediately, a city set on fire and utterly destroyed by Allied bombing in 1945, raids in which thousands upon thousands of people had died, horribly. I would set it in Dresden, but was there a zoo in

The real elephant from Belfast Zoo

Dresden? I did my research and discovered there was indeed a zoo in Dresden. More than that, I discovered the very same order had gone out to everyone in Dresden Zoo, that, should the American and British bombers come – and they expected it – then all the large animals – tigers, leopards, lions and elephants – were all to be shot before they could escape into the city.

I knew something about the bombing of Dresden, but now I was finding out more and more about it – which was a painful experience – and of the flight westwards, afterwards, of millions of people to escape the bombing and the Red Army invading from the east. The roads were crammed with desperate families, carrying all they could with them. I knew, as I did my research, that my family – two children and the mother who worked in Dresden Zoo as an elephant keeper – who had looked after the young elephant in their garden until the raids, would be part of this exodus of refugees, this huge migration across Germany. They too would be seeking safety, and would have the elephant with them.

My Uncle Pieter had been killed early in the war in the RAF. Had he lived longer, I thought, he might well have been on that Dresden raid – he was in Bomber Command. I brought him back to life in this story. He is shot down and looked after by this family, becomes part of the family, helps them in their escape.

I was fortunate to have an insight into how it was to be part of that flight westwards across Germany towards the end of the war. The grandmother of a friend of mine had left a written account, a typescript with photographs, of her family's perilous journey to the west. She was the widow of one of those German Army officers who had tried to assassinate Hitler in 1944 and bring an end to the war, a plot that had failed. Her husband had been arrested

and executed with all the other conspirators. She wrote
this account of her family's struggle to escape and survive
afterwards, a family history, written to tell her grandchildren about her late husband, their grandfather, and
about the family's flight across Germany to safety. It was
their journey that inspired the perilous escape of my
Dresden family, their elephant, and a shot-down RAF air-
man they befriend and who befriends them. So this is no
"Just So Story". It could not be more different, yet, without
my mother reading me *The Elephant's Child*, I doubt *An
Elephant in the Garden* would ever have been written.
This is a story with so many seeds – but my mother and
Kipling sowed the first one between them. And my mother
would have loved *An Elephant in the Garden*, I think,
because of this; but also because her brother, my Uncle
Pieter, plays such an important part in the story. They both
liked playing parts; they were both actors, after all.

AN ELEPHANT IN THE GARDEN

"It is the middle of the night," growled the old man. "What is it that you want?"

"Please. We need a doctor," Mutti told him. "My son, he is very sick. Please."

Then from further inside the house came another voice, a woman's voice. "Who is it, Hans? Is it more of them? Let them in."

The door opened wider, and we saw then a lady in a dressing gown, coming down a huge wide staircase, and then hurrying towards us across the hallway.

"She says they need a doctor, Countess," the old man said. They were both peering at us now, from behind the lamplight.

"We are from Dresden," Mutti told them.

"Am I seeing things?" the lady asked. "Or is that an elephant?"

"I can explain about that later," Mutti replied. "But my son is ill, seriously ill, and I have to find a doctor. Please. It is urgent."

The lady did not hesitate. She took Mutti by the arm and led her into the hallway. "Come in, come in," she said. "I shall send for the doctor from the village right away. And Hans, you will find a place for that animal in the stables."

I had no idea that night who these people were, and neither did I care. We would soon have a doctor for Karli, and we had found shelter for him too. That was all that mattered. And it would be warm too. I could even smell food. But I did not get to go in right away. Mutti asked me to take care of Marlene, and to make sure that she had something to eat and drink. So, led by Hans, the old man in the nightcap, who muttered angrily to himself the whole time, I took her round the side of the house, through a great archway and into a stable yard. I saw to it that she had all she needed, hay and water both, and left her to it. She seemed quite happy, happier certainly than the horses across the yard from her, who were becoming increasingly unsettled at the appearance of this strange intruder.

As we walked back towards the house – the place seemed immense to me, more like a castle than a house – Hans was still grumbling on, but less to himself and rather more to me, about how he could never get a good night's sleep anymore, how it was bad enough that the countess had opened her doors to all and sundry, but now she was turning the stable yard into a zoo. It was all too much, he said, too much.

It was not until he was leading me back into the house and up the grand staircase that I began to see for myself what he was complaining about. Everywhere I looked, every centimetre of floor space, was occupied. People were lying fast asleep, in the corridors, on the landings, and, I presumed, in every room. And those that were not asleep were sitting there on straw-filled sacks looking up at me blankly as I passed by. There was bewilderment on every face I saw. Hans took me up to the top of the house, to the attic, where I saw Karli lying stretched out on a mattress by a fire with Mutti kneeling over him, bathing his forehead. Peter was busy piling more wood on the fire.

"He has a fever, Elizabeth," Mutti said, looking up at me, her eyes full of tears. "He's burning up. Where is that doctor? Where is he?"

For the rest of the night Karli lay there tossing and turning, sometimes delirious, and all three of us took it in turns to try to cool him. None of us slept, we just sat there watching him, hoping the fever would leave him, longing for the doctor to come. When he did come at long last, the lady came with him, dressed now rather grandly, and all in black. The doctor examined him, and said that Karli should be kept warm at all costs, and that the more water we could get him to drink the better. The doctor gave us some medicine for Karli and told us that on no account was he to go out in the cold, or travel, until he was completely well again.

It was only now, once he had gone, that the lady in black introduced herself. "Everyone just calls me Countess," she said, shaking each of us rather formally by the hand. "We do not bother much with names here – it is safer that way. I think we have about seventy refugees now in the house – all sorts, mostly families from the east resting up for a few days. Everyone is passing through. It seems as if the whole world is in flight. We have soldiers on their way home on leave, or returning to their regiments at the front, some deserters no doubt, and we have a few vagrants too. I ask no questions. We have a hot meal only once a day, at mid-day, and then soup and bread in the evening. It is not much, but it is the best we can manage, I'm afraid. As you know, food is becoming very scarce everywhere now. You may stay as long as you like, certainly until the young boy is better, but I would not advise you to stay on much longer after that. The Russians are not so far away now, maybe a few weeks away, no more. The Americans are closer, by all accounts, but who knows who will get here first?"

Mutti thanked her from the bottom of her heart for all her kindness towards us.

The British bombing campaign

The city of Dresden in Germany suffered one of the most severe bombing campaigns of the Second World War. Fifteen square kilometres of the city centre were utterly destroyed.

In four raids, between 13 and 15 February 1945, almost 1,300 heavy bombers from the RAF and the US Army Air Forces dropped about 3,900 tonnes of high-explosive bombs and, on one night, 650,000 incendiary devices. An RAF crew reported smoke rising to a height of 4,572 metres.

The incessant bombing created a self-sustaining and devastating fire-storm that swept through the streets. Road surfaces melted, and people found that their feet burnt as they tried to escape. Few in the city centre survived.

One who did, Rudolph Eichner, wrote: "There were no warning sirens... The cellars of the hospital quickly became hopelessly overcrowded with people who could no longer find shelter in their own burning buildings. Apart from the fire risk, it was becoming increasingly impossible to breathe, because the air was being pulled out by the increasing strength of the blaze. We could not stand up, we were on all fours, crawling. The wind was full of sparks and carrying bits of blazing furniture, debris and burning bits of bodies."

Nobody knows exactly how many people died in Dresden during the bombing campaign, as it was crammed with up to half a million refugees. The figure lies between 25,000 and 100,000.

At the beginning of the Second World War, the bombing of military targets was expected, but the first bombing of London caused outrage, because it was accidental. Bombing London had been specifically prohibited by Hitler, not through humanitarian concern, but because Hitler believed that Britain might still agree peace terms. On 24 August 1940, Luftwaffe bombers, aiming for military targets near London, drifted off course. They dropped bombs on the centre of London. Several homes were destroyed and nine civilians killed. In retaliation, prime minister Winston Churchill ordered Berlin to be bombed the next evening, stunning the Germans by the attack on their capital. Berliners had been repeatedly assured by Luftwaffe chief, Hermann Göring, that this would never happen.

The notorious and shameful bombing of Dresden took place near the end of the war. By then, Germany was in full retreat. In an internal RAF memo from 1945, the strategy behind the bombing of Dresden was discussed: "Dresden is the largest unbombed city the enemy has got. In the midst of winter with refugees pouring westwards and troops to be rested, roofs are at a premium. The intentions of the attack are to hit the enemy where he will feel it most, behind an already partially collapsed front, to prevent the use of the city in the way of further advance, and incidentally to show the Russians when they arrive what Bomber Command can do."

The destruction of Dresden continues to appall the British national conscience. Some historians suggest that the Allies "descended to the enemy's level", and that it was militarily unnecessary as Germany was a "spent force" by this time. Indeed, after the raids, Churchill tried to distance himself, describing the policy of bombing cities as "mere acts of terror and wanton destruction". Others argue that Dresden was not simply a cultural centre, but was home to factories producing weapons and equipment. It had a rail base to send troops east to the war front with the Soviets.

Others felt that any action that helped to shorten the war was justified. Bomber Harris held such a view: "I do not personally regard the whole of the remaining cities of Germany as worth the bones of one British Grenadier." He stated openly: "The destruction of industrial sites always was some sort of bonus for us. Our real targets always were the inner cities." Such rationalization of killing and destruction is unfortunately something still familiar today in other wars around the world.

shadow

THE DREAM

I have often, maybe too often, written stories about wars and conflicts of the past. This is, I think, largely because of my own past, growing up as I did in the aftermath of the Second World War. The effects of war, the bomb-sites, the rationing, the sadness and the grieving, the pride and passion, the stories were all around me at home, in the war games we played in the streets and at school, in the comic books we read. Those things stayed with me, and as memory of childhood informs why and what I care and write about so much, I suppose it was inevitable that war would play a significant part in my story-making. But I have no actual memories of war, just the aftermath of it, the damage left.

Borrowed memories too often played their part in these stories. *Friend or Foe*, for instance, is loosely based on the experiences of my Aunt Bess, who, at the beginning of the Second World War was a teacher in a London junior school, and had to evacuate all the children in her school down to Cornwall, to escape the bombing. Other stories of that war have followed, over the years – among them, *The Amazing Story of Adolphus Tips*, *Billy the Kid*, *The Mozart Question*, *An Elephant in the Garden*, and many others. And the First World War – because I had grown up with the poems and the plays and the songs of the times, I suppose – also began to find its way into my books – again, largely inspired by the borrowed memories of those who had been there and lived through it.

But then, one day, in a school I was visiting, where they had studied my books in detail, I was asked why did I not write about the wars that were going on now? I am not sure how I replied. I hope it wasn't too trite, or too evasive. I suspect it might have been both, because, if truth be told, I was rather flummoxed, probably because this was a young reader challenging me to write out of what must have seemed to him to be my comfort zone. There was clearly implied criticism here, and I knew it was justified.

I reflected on this afterwards and it made me distinctly uncomfortable to do so. I had to acknowledge to myself that I had indeed always been writing about past conflicts, and had therefore, to a degree at least, employed the perspective of time and of history as a kind of comfort zone. Maybe this had inadvertently distanced me and the reader from the actuality and brutality and suffering of the wars of today. Like it or not, benefit of hindsight can so easily encourage an overly convenient and simplistic way of thinking about any war.

I realized that, if I was not careful, I could easily be falling into the trap of simply using war to make stories, stories of old wars, over-and-done-with wars, wars that we don't need to worry about too much. By not writing about wars of today, was I not implying to readers young and old that wars only happened in the past, that they were the important wars, that the world was not like that now? With so much conflict in the world, where was the integrity in that?

And this was not the first time I had been asked such a testing question. In Amman in Jordan some time before, I had been asked by a teenage Palestinian girl why I had never written about the conflict in Palestine and Israel, that surely this was at the heart of so many troubles in the world, the cause of so much suffering. I remember I said at the time that it was because I did not know enough about it. She said, and quite politely, that maybe I could find out. It soon became a question I could not ignore. It took me years to find a way to write a story about this conflict, years of dreamtime before I was able to write *The Kites Are Flying!*, a story of hope in the midst of despair. It was, and is, difficult sometimes to believe in hope, but the only hope for peace, in that seemingly unending conflict, was, I thought, in the children on either side. So I wrote about them, and about flying kites over the wall that divides the two communities.

Both the boy in the school in England and the girl in Amman had been right, in a way. It was too easy to dwell on the past, to take the comfortable route of writing about wars that were over and done. I would have to do what he challenged me to do, as I had with the girl in Amman. I would write about Afghanistan, where soldiers on all sides would be fighting and dying as I wrote. I would no longer have the hiding place of history, if that's what it had been.

I was a soldier, briefly, a long while ago, but never went to war. I had trained for it, though, so when reading newspaper reports of Afghanistan, or Iraq, I understood at least something of what these young men were going through. Like everyone else, I saw the coffins coming home, the grieving families, and was asking the questions of myself that so many were asking: "What was this war for?" "Why did we send our young men to fight and die in this place so far away?" "Is it even winnable?" "Haven't we sent armies there twice before to fight in hopeless campaigns?" The more questions I asked myself, the more urgent it seemed to be to write a story about this war, if nothing else so that I could begin to understand it better myself.

Somehow, sooner or later, I seem to tumble upon the heart of a story – by accident or design, I am never quite sure which. Probably both, the one provoking the other. With *Shadow*, I happened upon four different stories, true stories, that enabled me to begin the process of weaving my tale together. For me, the oxygen of truth is so often a great enabler.

Some images you never forget, even if you want to. The blowing-up by the Taliban of the great Buddha statues of Bamiyan in 2001, a World Heritage Site, shocked the world. It was not wanton destruction so much as a calculated attempt to desecrate a holy place, and expunge a culture, to annihilate a religion, to deracinate a people. So when, some years later, I was invited to watch a documentary film called *The Boy from Bamiyan* by Phil Grabsky, I remembered the name, recalled what had happened there. And here was an extraordinarily powerful film about a boy called Mir, who grows up in the caves of Bamiyan, lives among the rubble of the ruins of the place. It brought me close for the first time to the lives of the children of Afghanistan who have lived through all these years of war, years of terror or turbulence. So many of them have never known a world without war. Mir and his family stay and survive and rebuild despite all the hardships. Many, of course, do not. Many thousands of Afghan families have fled, have come to Britain seeking safety and refuge, seeking asylum.

Then, quite out of the blue, a newspaper story helped me along the way as I was dreaming up the story that was to become *Shadow*. There are very few stories about any war that make you smile, that lift your spirits. But I found one, or, rather, it found me. Actually some kind friend sent it to me because they thought I might like it. I did.

Here's the story. In 2008, in Afghanistan, a company of Australian and Afghan soldiers were on patrol with their sniffer dog, Sabi, a black Labrador. (These dogs were routinely used to sniff out roadside explosives.) They were ambushed by the Taliban and got into a fire-fight. When it was over, the soldiers looked around for Sabi. He had disappeared. They knew the Taliban especially targeted dogs like Sabi, who had saved countless lives by sniffing out roadside bombs hidden by the Taliban. So the soldiers feared the worst. They looked for Sabi every time they went out on patrol after that, but there was no sign of him, no sighting. Then, fourteen months later, an American soldier spotted a black Labrador wandering in the desert, not in the best condition, but alive and friendly. The story of Sabi's disappearance was well known, so it wasn't long before he was reunited with the Australian and Afghan soldiers he had known.

But, I thought, how on earth had Subi survived that long? Certainly not on his own. Someone must have fed him, looked after him. Dogs are not favoured pets among the Hazara people of that region, but might a young boy living in those caves of Bamiyan find in him a good companion? Maybe. And maybe his family, terrorized by the Taliban, decide to flee to Britain, to join an uncle already there. My story seemed to be telling itself by now. But one last piece of the jigsaw was needed before I could make my story whole. I didn't know what it would look like. I just knew it was necessary.

Then I heard something from a friend I could hardly believe to be true. Did I know, she said, that there is a detention centre in England (a prison, effectively) where asylum seekers who are due to be expelled, sent home – whichever you call it – are confined for weeks, sometimes months. And did I know that among them are many, many children? So therefore, in this country, our country, we are imprisoning children who have committed no crime, other than seeking asylum – which is not a crime. I could not believe it. But it was true. It is called Yarl's Wood, in Bedfordshire. Appalled, outraged, I knew now where my story would end up. I wasn't sure exactly how it would finish. I'm never sure how a story will end when I begin it. But I knew Yarl's Wood would play a shameful part in the denouement. Now I didn't just have the desire to tell my story, I had the compulsion I always need. I had the wool, the warp and the weft, and the design in my head. I had the loom too, my pen and my scribbling book. I was the weaver. I had all I needed. I could get on.

A year or so later, the book published, I found myself with the BBC television crew outside the gates of Yarl's Wood, making a documentary about the place and about all those asylum-seeking families and children locked up inside. We were not allowed in. We stood there, outside the high-wire fence, and I quoted from William Blake's "Auguries of Innocence": "A robin redbreast in a cage, Puts all heaven in a rage". I was in a rage too, as were so many others who had campaigned tirelessly for this abominable practice of imprisoning children to be stopped. And still the battle is not over.

One way I can help fight a battle that needs to be fought is to write about it, tell a story about it, raise awareness, to help bring about change. Rather greater writers have done this before me, from Charles Dickens in *A Christmas Carol*, in which he exposes the cruelty and poverty he had witnessed all around him in the streets of London; to Ted Hughes' *Iron Woman*, which is so strong in its condemnation of how we despoil and poison our environment. It is a fine tradition. These masters led where I have tried to follow, in *Shadow* and in *The Kites Are Flying!*, and in many other stories too.

SHADOW

The door of the container opened. The daylight blinded us. We could not see who it was at first.

It was not the police.

It turned out to be the fixer man, and his gang, the same people who had put us in there. They said we could get out if we wanted and stretch our legs, that we were waiting for some other people to join us.

We were in a kind of loading bay with lorries all around, but not many people. We should have run off there and then, but one of the fixer's gang always seemed to be watching us, so we didn't dare.

Only a few minutes later, it was too late.

The other refugees arrived, and we were all herded back into the same container, given some more blankets, a little fruit, and a bottle or two of water. They slammed the doors shut on us again and the fixer shouted at us, that no matter what, we mustn't call out, or we'd all be caught and taken to prison. We could hear the lorry being loaded up around us.

It was a while, I remember, before my eyes became

accustomed to the dark again, and I could see the others.

As the lorry drove off we sat there in silence for a while, just looking at one another. I counted twelve of us in all, mostly from Iran, and a family – mother, father and a little boy – from Pakistan, and beside us an old couple from Afghanistan, from Kabul.

It was Ahmed, the little boy from Pakistan, who got us talking. He came over to me to show me his toy train, because I was the only other kid there, because he knew he could trust me, I think – it was plastic and bright red, I remember, and he was very proud of it.

He knelt down to show me how it worked on the floor, telling everyone about how his grandpa worked on the trains in Pakistan. And, in secret, I showed him the silver-star badge Sergeant Brodie had given me. Ahmed loved looking at it. He was full of questions about it, about every-thing. He liked me, he said, because I had a name that sounded like his. It wasn't long before we were telling one another our stories. To begin with, Ahmed and me, we laughed a lot, and played about, and that cheered everyone up. But it didn't last. I think our laughter lasted about as long as the fruit and water.

I don't know where that lorry took us, nor how many days and nights we were locked up in the container. They didn't let us out, not once, not to go to the toilet even, noth-ing. And we didn't dare shout out. They brought us no more water, no more food. We were freezing by night, and stifling hot by day.

When I was awake, I just longed to be asleep, so I could forget what was happening, forget how much I was longing every moment for water and for food. Waking up was the worst. When we talked amongst each other now, it was usually to guess where we were, whether we were still in Iran, or in Turkey, or maybe in Italy. But none of this made any sense to me, because I had no idea where any of these places were.

Most of them, like Ahmed and his parents, said they were trying to get to England, like we were, but a few were going to Germany or Sweden. One or two had tried before, like the old couple from Kabul who were going to live with their son in England, they told us, but they had already been caught twice and sent back. They were never going to give up trying, they said.

But in the end the stories stopped altogether, and there was no more talking, just the sound of moaning and crying, and praying. We all prayed. For me the journey in that lorry was like travelling through a long dark tunnel, with no light at the end of it. And there was no air to breathe either, that was the worst of it. People were coughing and choking, and Ahmed was being sick too. But he still held on to his little red train.

The smell, I'll never forget the smell.

After that I think I must have lost consciousness, because I don't remember much more. When I woke up – it was probably days later, I don't know – the lorry had stopped. Maybe it was the shouting and the crying that woke me up, because that was all I could hear. Mother and the others were on their feet and banging on the side of the container, screaming to be let out.

By the time they came for us and dragged me out of there, I was only half alive.

But I was luckier than Little Ahmed.

When his father carried him out into the daylight, we could see for sure that he was dead. Ahmed's mother was wailing in her grief. It was like a cry of pain from deep inside her, a crying that I knew would never end for her. I never heard such a dreadful sound before, and I hope I never will again.

Later that same day, after they had buried him, his mother gave me his toy train to look after, because I had been like a brother to Ahmed, she said.

I've still got Ahmed's little red train, back home in Manchester. The police, when they came to take us away, wouldn't let me bring it with me. I forgot it and wanted to go back for it, and they wouldn't let me. There wasn't time, they said. It's on the windowsill in my bedroom.

I dream about Ahmed quite a bit, and often it's almost the same dream. He's with Shadow, and with Sergeant Brodie, and they're playing together outside the walls of a castle. It's night and the sky is a ceiling of painted stars, and he's throwing a ball for her.

Strange that, how in dreams people who never even knew one another, can meet up in places they could never have been to.

Animals in war

On the edge of Hyde Park, in London, is the Animals in War Memorial. Unveiled in 2004, it stands as a tribute to all the animals that served, suffered and died in the wars and conflicts of the twentieth century.

Not everyone agrees or supports the idea of a memorial or medals for animals. A *Guardian* reporter wrote: "It is a soppy parody of the medals handed out to actual human soldiers that says more about modern sentimentality than about anything a well-trained dog is capable of ... there are no good dogs, just good owners. Animals have no vices or virtues."

People who live closely and work respectfully with animals would dispute this. Maria Dickin, founder of the veterinary charity the PDSA, instituted the Dickin Medal in 1943. Its metal disc says: FOR GALLANTRY. WE ALSO SERVE. It recognizes "conspicuous gallantry or devotion to duty while serving or associated with any branch of the Armed Forces or Civil Defence Units".

Surprisingly, more pigeons have received this medal than dogs, cats or horses. This reflects their central role in war communications, often under bombardment. During the Second World War, the British used about 250,000 homing pigeons, working with agents behind enemy lines, and bringing back battle news from the Front. They served on aircraft, warships and even submarines, backing up other forms of communication. Another pigeon role was raising the alarm when an aircraft crashed or was forced to land.

A medal was given to American pigeon "G.I. Joe" after he saved the lives of a thousand soldiers and civilians in the village of Calvi Vecchia, Italy. American troops who were unaware that the village had been captured by the British 169th Infantry Brigade, radioed for the village to be bombed, but received the message delivered by G.I. Joe, just in time to prevent a major tragedy.

Only one cat has received the medal. In 1949, Simon was an effective rat-catcher (only doing, you might think, what came naturally) on the frigate HMS *Amethyst*, based in Hong Kong. The frigate was protecting British interests in the Yangtze river in China during the battles between the Chinese Communists and the Nationalists. Communist guns opened fire, causing many injuries and casualties. One of the first rounds tore through the *Amethyst*'s captain's cabin, seriously wounding Simon. But he recovered and was credited with keeping up the crew's morale. Following the ship's escape from the Yangtze, Simon became an instant celebrity, lauded in the Allied press.

More recently, some of the dogs who received Dickin Medals were, like the dog in *Shadow*, army sniffer dogs in Afghanistan. As a puppy, Treo, a black Labrador, was badly behaved and difficult to control. But intensive army training turned him into a successful military dog. On his first patrol, he found a stash of weapons hidden in a hut at the back of a mud-walled compound. In 2008, he found a number of improvised explosive devices (IEDs). They were particularly dangerous "daisy chain" devices, two or more bombs wired together to maximize casualties. Within weeks of Treo's arrival, the Royal Marines intercepted Taliban radio messages about "targeting the black dog".

His handler, Sergeant Heyhoe, described his close relationship with Treo: "You have to understand each other, recognize the slightest change in each other. The trick is to channel your fear, knowing that this will make both you and the dog concentrate better. Although he was a black dog in 50°C heat, I never doubted him." Treo saved many soldiers and civilians from death or serious injury. After the death of his roommate, Heyhoe returned to Britain, suffering from post-traumatic stress disorder. He believes Treo, who came with him, helped him through the dark days: "He's a proper dog who never gives kisses, but the times when I needed him, he'd sit beside me. He knew when I was suffering."

The first honorary Dickin Medal was announced in 2014, at the start of the centenary commemorations of the First World War. The horse was Warrior, who, like the fictional Joey in *War Horse*, served on the Western Front. He was chosen to represent the bravery and sacrifice that millions of animals displayed during the Great War. Warrior was subjected to machine gun attacks by air, survived falling shells at the Battle of the Somme, was buried under debris and got stuck in mud at Passchendaele, and was twice trapped under the burning beams of his stables. Warrior was dubbed "the horse they couldn't kill". The PDSA, at the award ceremony in the Imperial War Museum, said Warrior was a "true survivor" and his story "epitomizes the vital roles played by millions of animals".

Whatever you think of medals for animals, a fitting memorial stands in Port Elisabeth, South Africa. A kneeling soldier is giving water to his horse. The words inscribed below say: THE GREAT-NESS OF A NATION CONSISTS NOT SO MUCH IN THE NUMBER OF ITS PEOPLE OR THE EXTENT OF ITS TERRI-TORY AS IN THE EXTENT AND JUSTICE OF ITS COMPASSION.

Little Manfred

THE DREAM

Frequently, my stories have their earliest beginnings in things: objects, artefacts, ordinary everyday things, or some amazing discovery in a museum perhaps, or a wonderful sculpture I have come across, a gruesome, hideous object I would rather not look at twice, or a painting I cannot forget. Each has a secret story locked away inside it. All I have to do as a dream-maker, a story-maker, is to unlock it. I often feel that these strange meetings between me and these things are somehow meant to be – no different from meetings with people in this respect – that fate has brought us together. Silly, I know, but somehow this belief helps motivate me to dream on, to begin to make my story. *Little Manfred* began because of a meeting I had with a toy dog. But that meeting only happened in the first place because it was known I had been inspired in such ways to tell my stories before. I think I had better explain.

A few years ago, I came on holiday to Scilly (I'm actually writing this on Scilly, on the island of Bryher), and met the farmer and his wife who grow the vegetables here. In a very matter of fact way, they told me, "Thought you might be interested, Michael. We were ploughing the potato field a while ago, when the back wheel of the tractor got itself stuck down a hole. We managed to drive it out, then went back to have a look. It wasn't just a little hole; it was a tomb. We peered inside, and there was a rusty old sword lying at the bottom. We lifted it out, brought it home. It's in the greenhouse. You want to see it?"

There it was laid out on a newspaper in amongst the ripening tomatoes. "Experts had a look," they told me. "They reckon it's over two thousand years old. It's going off to a museum to be dated accurately and restored."

The Scilly islands are full of cists and tomb sites. I have seen dozens, hundreds, climbed down into many, but this was a newly discovered tomb, and discovered by a tractor wheel, and, until then, undisturbed for all this time! I gazed down at the sword, reached out and touched it. One word came into my mind: "Excalibur" – King Arthur's sword. There's a legend he is still out here on Scilly, probably under an island, one of the Eastern Isles, called "Little Arthur", waiting to come back when he is needed. Alfred, Lord Tennyson, the great poet, knew the legend. He came here before he wrote his Arthurian poems. It's a legend you want to believe. A few months of dreamtime later, I was writing my story. I called it *The Sleeping Sword*.

Then there's the ancient Irish torc, of twisted gold, that I found in a museum in Dublin, discovered by a boy in a bog in Galway, that in the end became the talisman for the children in *Twist of Gold*. There's the key in *Alone on a Wide Wide Sea*, the only clue in a girl's search for her long-lost family. And *War Horse* may owe in part its beginnings to the reminiscences of three old men in my village, but the original notion came from four pictures we had discovered in an old family tea chest, frames broken, glass broken, pictures in gouache of horses and soldiers in that war, of horses charging up a hill into wire, some already caught in it.

The Imperial War Museum used these pictures in an exhibition of children's books about war. And, as a result, I think it later invited me to write a story about any exhibit in their museum. To be honest, I wasn't at all sure at first that I wanted to do it. From what I remembered of this museum, there were a lot of missiles and planes and guns, and I had already been to war often enough in my stories. I said as much to them. They were very helpful, explaining they had smaller, more domestic, perhaps more interesting and unusual things to show me if I would like to come up and visit the museum. I went with Michael Foreman, who I hoped would illustrate whatever story I might come up with. He had to be as enthusiastic about the idea of the story as me. That was very important.

I could hardly believe it when I saw it first on the table in front of us – a small toy dog, a dachshund, beautifully crafted, painted nut-brown with black paws. There were four red wheels and a string with which to pull it. Hardly a weapon of war, I thought. What on earth was a toy dog doing in this museum of warfare? Then they told me the story, which I will now tell you.

It seems that after the Second World War was over, there were hundreds of thousands of German prisoners of war here, who did not go home at once, but were kept on in Britain, in prisoner-of-war camps all over the country. They were used to help clear up war damage and often to work on farms. Many did not go home for over a year. Some found themselves living with farming families, in village communities. One such host family were the Dukes from Crockenhill in Kent. Just before their German guest/POW left for home, he made this little dachshund dog out of disused apple boxes, and a toy bear as well for the children of the family, as a parting gift to thank them for their kindness and hospitality. He was called Walter Klemenz. Once he got home, he sent them a fond letter. Clearly, he had been made to feel very much at home while he was with them. The family gave both the toys and the letter to the museum, because they felt it was important for us to know and understand that there could be goodwill and kindness between old enemies, even after such a terrible war.

Looking at the little dog on the table in front of us,

reading Walter's letter sent from Germany back to his "family" in England, both Michael Foreman and I knew we wanted to tell this story, a story of the beginnings of reconciliation. The little brown dog was a powerful symbol of hope for the future. I had grown up like most boys playing war games in the playground, in the bombsites. Michael had too. The enemy, the "baddies", were always the Germans. The comics we read were full of British soldiers, who were the "goodies" and always handsome, and always won. It took a long while for all this anger and hatred and prejudice to die away. Time helped, as had that Duke family in Kent, as had Walter Klemenz, who had made the little dachshund toy. They were the pathfinders of peace.

Michael Foreman, who is a serious football fan, reminded me, as we were discussing how our story would go, that the first German the British people came to respect, admire and like after that war was a great footballer called Bert Trautmann. Everyone knew Bert Trautmann – even I did, and I was not a football fan. He had been a German paratrooper during the war, but later became a brave goalkeeper who played for Manchester City from 1949 to 1964. He had broken his neck in a cup final, but had gone on playing. He had won the admiration of everyone. There *were* good Germans, and they played football rather well too.

Michael also reminded me that in 1966, German supporters had come over in their thousands for the final of the World Cup at Wembley, and that, for the most part, there was great camaraderie between them. Yes, everyone wanted their own side to win. But this was a game between friendly peoples, not old enemies any more. Although it would have been the first time that many of those Germans had been to England, some of them, I thought, some must have fought in the war, and some must even have been prisoners of war. Write about one of those, maybe a fictional Walter Klemenz coming back for the first time, after all those years, to England. Maybe he would want to visit the farm where he had worked, the family that had been his family for a while, for whom he made the little dachshund dog.

So Michael drew the dog and I dreamt up the tale, growing the story of reconciliation out of the horror and tragedy of the sinking of two great battleships, HMS *Hood* of the Royal Navy and the *Admiral Graf Spee* of the German Navy, out of the lives of sailors from both sides, whose lives became woven together by war, and who, years later, because of that little toy dog, became the best of friends.

LITTLE MANFRED

"But it wasn't long before they were treating us as if we were a part of the family. They let us eat with them at their table; we even went to church with them on Sundays. We worked with them, looking after the horses, ploughing, harvesting, spreading muck on the fields, fetching water, digging ditches, picking stones off the fields, whatever it was that needed doing. I was always a little slower than the others, because I had to walk with a stick, after my injury. But I was a hard worker. And on the days we were not needed on the farm, we were sent to work with the other prisoners down on the beaches, clearing the wire and the mines. There were mines all round the coast, you see. They had been put there, years before, to stop an invasion from the sea. But of course in the end there never was an invasion. Then after the war was over, we prisoners of war, we had to help clear it all away, to make the beaches safe again.

"In the evenings, Manfred would often sit and read a story to Grace – I remember this very well. I did it sometimes myself, if Manfred was still out feeding the animals after dark. But I knew always that Grace liked it better when Manfred was there. His English was much better than mine, although after two years of living there, I could speak it quite well.

"At Christmas, Manfred and I sang to them some German carols – that was Mrs Williams's idea. Manfred taught Grace to sing *'Stille Nacht'*, *'Silent Night'*, in German. And, in the end, the villagers were kind – for most of the time, anyway. There were one or two who crossed the street to the other side, so they did not have to speak to us, but we had to expect that. In this war many had suffered greatly, had great griefs and sadnesses to bear; and where there is sadness, there is often anger. I think perhaps that the anger lasts longer even than the sadness. For Manfred, Grace became almost like a daughter, the daughter he was parted from. I never saw him happier than when he was with her.

"Then at last came the good news that Manfred and I were soon to be going home. This was when Manfred decided he would make something special for Grace, a gift from us both to leave behind. Manfred loved to make things, out of wood usually. He had always been clever with his hands. Anyway, he found some bits of wood in the barn – this wood, I remember, came from apple crates in the barn – and out of this wood he carved a little dog, a dachshund like the one he and Jutta and little Inga had at home. He made wheels for it too. I painted it – a brown body, of course, with a little black nose, eyes, ears, and a green

310

chassis too. And the wheels, I painted bright red."

"Little Manfred!" said Alex. "You painted Little Manfred?"

"Manfred made him, and I painted him," Walter told him proudly. "We made Little Manfred together. I tied on a piece of string too, so Grace could pull him along. This was all done in secret, in the bedroom we shared together, because we wanted it to be a surprise for her. Manfred said it would be like a 'dog of peace'. I have always remembered those words. We were very pleased with him, and hid him away under my bed so that we could give him to Grace on the day we left."

Prisoners of war

In February 1939, the largest battleship afloat was launched: the *Bismarck*. Weighing in at more than 50,000 tonnes fully loaded, she was the pride of the German fleet.

On 19 May 1941, along with other ships and U-boats (German submarines), the *Bismarck* set out from the Baltic Sea for the Atlantic Ocean. Their mission was to intercept and destroy Allied ships carrying food and essential raw materials. The *Bismarck* was spotted between Greenland and Iceland by HMS *Norfolk*, Britain's newest battleship. Together with HMS *Hood*, HMS *Norfolk* altered course to intercept her. On 24 May, in a brief action, HMS *Hood* was blown up and sunk. Out of her crew of 1,418, only three men survived.

The *Bismarck* had been damaged in the battle, but managed to get away, and made for German-occupied France for repairs. She was tracked down and attacked by Swordfish aircraft, an outdated and slow biplane torpedo bomber. A torpedo jammed her rudder and steering gear, leaving her unable to manoeuvre. Pounded by British battleships and destroyers, she was finally sunk on the morning of 27 May.

Her end is still a matter of dispute. Was she deliberately sunk by her crew, as survivors claimed? Or was she sunk by torpedoes from HMS *Dorsetshire*? Either way, in the words of Admiral Tovey, who had led the hunt against her: "*Bismarck* had put up a most gallant fight against impossible odds, worthy of the old days of the Imperial German Navy, and she went down with her colours flying."

Of her 2,200 crew, only 116 survived. Some were picked up by HMS *Dorsetshire*, but a warning went out that there were U-boats in the area, and the British ships left, abandoning the rest of the survivors to the sea.

Those rescued, like Walter in *Little Manfred*, were brought to the United Kingdom as prisoners of war. Some prisoners of war were held in Britain, though many were sent to Canada, to reduce the cost of feeding them and because a German invasion was thought to be imminent. The last thing Britain wanted was prisoners helping the invading Germans. At the beginning of the war, there were only two prisoner-of-war camps but by the end there were 600 camps, housing nearly 500,000 prisoners.

The camps varied greatly from site to site. Some were in existing premises, such as disused factories, hotels, colleges or stately homes. Most, though, were constructed from corrugated tin and wood. These structures were known as Nissen huts and some can still be seen today in rural parts of Scotland and Wales.

The first major influx of prisoners of war, in July 1941, were Italians captured in the Middle East. German prisoners flooded into Britain from the summer of 1944 following the D-Day landings in France. These prisoners were interrogated to assess their loyalty to the Nazi regime. They would be graded by a colour patch of white, grey or black. Those considered "hardcore" Nazis wore a black patch. For Nazis this would sometimes mean a camp in the wilds of Scotland, where they would be put to agricultural work on farms.

In the camps, there were lectures, concerts, gardening and handicrafts. Sport was popular, with football, boxing and wrestling being the main activities, and chess and playing cards were common pastimes. There were opportunities for education as well in some camps, with lessons in English, shorthand, mechanics, physics and forestry. Making toys for the local children was another feature of life as a POW. Work was optional but most chose to do it as it passed the time more quickly. Prisoners received the same amount of daily rations as British servicemen – more than the civilian population received.

At the end of the war, the prisoners who decided to stay in Britain became known as "DPs" or "displaced persons". The most famous of these was former

Luftwaffe paratrooper Bernhard "Bert" Trautmann, who played 545 matches for Manchester City between 1949 and 1964. In 2004, he was awarded an honorary OBE for his promotion, through football, of Anglo-German understanding.

The little dog in
The Imperial War Museum

Out of
the Ashes

THE DREAM

Spring 2001

I remember we were on holiday in St Ives in Cornwall when we first heard about it on the news. There had been an outbreak of foot-and-mouth disease up in the North somewhere. A long way away, we thought. It won't affect us on the farm in Devon. We'll be fine. At the time we lived and worked on a farm, so we felt considerable sympathy and solidarity for those farmers up in the North whose animals were already being slaughtered to prevent the spread of the disease. They could not move their animals to market; they could not even leave the farm or have visitors; they were prisoners on their own farms. Their lives and businesses were in turmoil. But it was up North, we kept telling ourselves, hundreds of miles from

Devon. Nothing to worry about. This disease couldn't affect farmers around us in Iddesleigh. Could it? For that to happen, infected animals would have to come down to the South-West, and there was a ban on all movement of farm animals. It couldn't happen. Could it? We would stay in Cornwall, finish our holiday.

But within just a few days, we heard of the first case of foot-and-mouth in Devon, and not five miles from our village. We rushed back home. There were piles of straw soaked in disinfectant, stinking of it, at the end of the lane, at every farm gate. The siege was on. There was tension on every face. People spoke about nothing else except this threat that everyone knew could spell disaster for so many farmers and animals. And, for us, for all of us who worked at Farms for City Children, we knew it could spell disaster too. Already, the government was discouraging all unnecessary visits to the countryside, to farms, in particular. And the disease was being spotted now in hotspots all over the country, in areas to which infected animals had been transported before that first case in the North Country had been discovered. Our part of Devon was one of the hottest spots of all.

Despite all the precautions, the disease was taking hold, spreading from farm to farm, village to village. And wherever it was found, the mass killings of all cloven-hoofed animals took place and the fires began to burn. Closer and closer it came. You had only to look out of the window to see the smoke drifting down the Ockment

Valley. Until now, we had always thought of our place in deepest Devonshire as a paradise in the heart of England, a paradise of trees and fields and rivers and valleys and hills, a place of buzzards and herons and swallows and larks, of deer and foxes and badgers, unchanged for a thousand years, farmed for a thousand years. And now paradise was becoming hell before our eyes. Dead sheep and cows lay piled up in the fields. The stench of death and smoke was everywhere. This was how I had always imagined the plague might be, how living in a war zone might feel. Our lives were not in danger, of course, but our livelihoods were, our whole way of life was.

For some twenty years before the outbreak of foot-and-mouth we had worked alongside our farmer partners, the Ward family, at Farms for City Children. Like all the other farmers in the parish, I knew how much they cared for their animals, how much pride they had in their farms and their way of being. Standing with them, leaning on a farm gate, as I had so often done, and watching their cows and sheep grazing, I had sensed how deeply they felt about their stock, how close and complex is the relationship between a farmer and his farm and his animals, what pleasure it gives farmers to see their herds and flocks healthy and thriving, to see a field of barley growing tall and golden in the sun. Now they went out every day with dread in their hearts to see their stock, looking for those telltale signs of foot-and-mouth disease: limping, listlessness, lesions on tongues and hooves. Gone were the

319

smiles, the merry quips, the cheery chat. They waited, we waited, for the inevitable. Neighbouring farms all around were struck down one by one. It was only a matter of time, we thought. There were ever more fires, more smoke – and ever more stories too of farmers falling into depression under the strain of it all.

It was during this time of terrible tension that I read a story in a local newspaper about a farmer's daughter in a village near by. Those dreaded telltale signs of the disease had been discovered on her farm. The vets had come and confirmed the family's worst fears. It was foot-and-mouth. All the animals would have to be slaughtered, every sheep and lamb, every cow and calf on the farm. They were distraught. But the farmer's daughter had a plan. She had been bringing up an orphan lamb, her pet lamb, on the bottle. There was no way she was going to allow the lamb to be killed. So, on the morning when the vets came to do the killing, she hid her lamb away upstairs in her bedroom cupboard, without anyone knowing, and turned up the CD player so that the bleating of the lamb would not be heard. Her plan so nearly worked. What she hadn't realized, though, was that the vets had already counted all the animals on the farm when they first came, and now, on this second visit they discovered that one lamb was missing.

Her mother suspected at once what her daughter might have done – she knew how passionately fond of the lamb she was. The game was up, the lamb was discovered in the bedroom cupboard and put down with all the others. It was a story of such dreadful, powerful sadness, a story I could not forget.

In the end, the Ward family was lucky. The precautions taken to halt the spread of the disease seemed to have worked, but they had lived through terrible times for months on end. And for months on end, nearly a year, Farms for City Children had to close its doors to the children. It was a while before we were once again allowed to have our visitors from the cities on the farm, and during this time, the charity was forced to make a lot of people redundant. They was no money to pay them. This unemployment happened all over the countryside, the collateral damage caused by the disease. It had been a time of great anxiety and misery for all of us. But the Wards' farm had survived and so, in the end, did Farms for City Children, with the help of very many helpers and supporters who believed in what we were doing and wanted to enable the city children to keep coming down to the farm, to live in the countryside for a week, to work as farmers. They, like us, could see how much good it was doing for the lives of those children, how important it was.

Just after the outbreak was over and we were all getting back to some kind of normality, I received a large envelope in the post – opened it and out flew a bat, right up into my face. It came from an editor friend of mine, Marion Lloyd, at Macmillan. There was a letter with this bat, asking me if I would write a horror story – bats, vampires, monsters, ghosts, that sort of story. I'm still not sure why she asked me, because I really don't write stories like that. To be honest, I can't take horror stories seriously. I've never been keen on fantasy of any kind – I don't know why. Maybe I really do lack imagination – that is, after all, what my teacher told me often enough at my junior school at St Matthias on the Warwick Road in London. Anyway, I was about to ring her up to say no to her horror story idea, when I thought again. Hang on, I said to myself. Haven't I just lived through the greatest horror story of my life, not a fantasy horror, but a horror right there outside my window? Haven't I seen it with my own eyes, felt it in my heart, breathed it in almost?

I decided I would tell the story of that girl, that farmer's daughter, tell the story of the foot-and-mouth epidemic through the eyes and voice of a child caught up in the middle of it. I would tell it in diary form – I had done this before in *The Wreck of the Zanzibar*. It helped me to become her as I was writing it, to feel it as she must have felt it, as so many farmers' children must have witnessed it. I wrote the story by hand, as I always do, which works wonderfully well for me, especially when I am writing a story as a diary. And maybe because I had just lived through the crisis of foot-and-mouth myself, I wrote it fast, inside a week. I saw it all so clearly in my mind's eye, no further research needed, very little dreamtime. I took the exercise book up to London, my hastily scribbled story filling every page of it. At the publisher's, I suggested reading it to Marion aloud. She called in everyone from the office and I began. I could tell as I was reading it that they were quickly lost in the story and all were as moved by listening to it as I had been writing it.

Within weeks, Michael Foreman had done the most wonderful and heartbreaking drawings for the book, and my granddaughter Lea had proved to be the perfect face for the cover – behind the photograph of her, the countryside in flames. No book I have ever written has been produced faster. Even to this day, I cannot read it, though. It takes me back to a time of such suffering that I would rather not go there. But all the same, I am glad I wrote it. It may be a hard book to endure, but for most people who read it, the experience of such suffering is remote. Most people are urban by background and culture and very separated now from how people live on farms and in the countryside. It is from books, from stories, that we can learn about the lives of others. We learn empathy and understanding and that is important, I think.

OUT OF THE ASHES

Tuesday, March 13th

I'll never be able to think of this date without thinking of the Angels of Death. So much has happened and all of it so fast and so final. Today began yesterday. Last night after I'd finished writing my diary, I made a decision. I was lying in my bed at Auntie Liz's and thinking about Little Josh, and home and Mum and Dad. I just decided I had to go home, that I had caused this, that I had to be there with them.

I waited till everyone was in bed and asleep. I left a letter on my pillow explaining everything to Auntie Liz, telling her I was going home. Then I got dressed, packed my things, and crept downstairs. I ran out of the village, up through the graveyard and on to the footpath – no one would see me if I went that way. I thought I'd find the way home easily – I'd done it hundreds of times before – but never in the dark. As it turned out, it was a good thing that I lost my way. The footpath should have brought me out on to the road right

324

opposite our gate, but instead I came out on the road further up. I looked back down the road towards our farm gate and there was a police car parked right across the gateway, and a policeman standing by the car smoking a cigarette. I waited until he got back in the car, then sprinted across the road and up through Front Field and home.

The lights were still on in the kitchen. Mum and Dad were sitting there at the table and talking over a cup of tea. I just walked in and told them everything. I told them that it was me who'd brought back the foot-and-mouth after I'd been riding on Mr Bailey's farm. I told them I was staying home no matter what. I don't know how much they understood of what I said because I was crying so much. But they understood enough. Dad held my hands and told me it was no one's fault, not mine, not anyone's. The foot and mouth disease could have come on the wind, in the smoke, on bird droppings, car tyres – a hundred different ways, he said. And Mum said I shouldn't have run away like I did, but I knew they were both really pleased I had and neither of them blamed me at all. I could tell that from the way they hugged me. It was a strange thing to be suddenly happy in the middle of all this, but I was.

Today began again this morning. I was up early and went off to feed Little Josh, while Dad did the milking. Mum let all the ewes and lambs out into Front Field. We stood and watched them as they spread out over the field, the ewes at once busy at their grazing, the lambs springing and skipping, loving their sudden freedom, their last freedom. Neither of us said a word. We didn't need to because we were both thinking the same thoughts. Little Josh wouldn't stay with the others. He followed me home into the kitchen. So I fed him. But even when I'd fed him he wanted to stay by me.

We saw the men in white – the slaughterers and the vets – walking up the farm lane as we finished our breakfast. Dad got up, pulled on his overalls, and went out without a word. Mum cried when he'd gone. I put my arms around her and tried to comfort her, but I didn't cry. I didn't cry because my mind was on other things and it was racing. I was looking down at Little Josh lying at my feet, and I was thinking. I was thinking about how I was going to hide him away, so that the men in white would never find him. I didn't know where I would hide him, but I knew it had to be done. And it had to be soon, very soon. There wasn't much time.

My chance came when Mum got up from the table and said she just couldn't sit there and let Dad do it on his own, that she had to go with him. The moment she'd gone, I scooped Josh up into my arms and ran upstairs. I cleared out everything I could from the bottom of my cupboard and laid down some newspaper. I sat on my bed and fed him again until he couldn't drink another drop. I told him that he must be quiet, that he must go to sleep and keep quiet. He seemed happy enough – until I lifted him in and shut the cupboard door on him. Then he started, bleating on and on, like he'd never stop. It was muffled, but I could still hear him, and if I could hear him, so could they. So I put on my

CD just loud enough to drown out his bleating and left him there. All I had to do now was to be sure that I kept my CD going.

Later, more slaughtermen in white arrived – "Angels of Death", Mum called them. She came in and told me the shooting would begin very soon, that I mustn't on any account go outside from now on. She didn't have to tell me. Nothing and no one could have made me go out and watch what they'd be doing. Just thinking of it was more than I could bear. I stayed in my room behind closed curtains, cradled Little Josh on my lap, put on my earphones and turned up my CD so loud that I couldn't hear the shooting, so that I couldn't feel or know anything except the thunder of the music in my head.

But then I had to change the CD. I took off my earphones without thinking. That was when I first heard the shooting, not loud, not near, but the crack of every shot told me that this was really happening. They were killing out there, killing Dad's family of animals.

Suddenly I thought of Ruby. She'd be frightened out of her mind at all the shooting. I put Little Josh back in the cupboard, turned up the CD, ran downstairs, and out across the yard to her stable.

Ruby was in a real state by the time I got there, all lathered up and terrified. I went in with her, closed the top of the stable door and hugged her, smoothing her, calming her all I could. After a while when the shooting stopped, she relaxed a little and rested her head on my shoulder. Even

then I could hear her heart pounding as if she'd been galloping.

Then I opened the door. I wish I hadn't. Dad was there. Mum was there, her arm round his shoulder. The men in white were there. There was blood on their overalls, blood on their boots. One of them was holding a clipboard and he was the one doing the talking. "There's no mistake, Mr

Morley," he was saying. "I've checked this list a dozen times now and we've counted the bodies. We're one lamb missing, one ram lamb, a Suffolk."

It's not their fault, I know, but if Mum and Dad hadn't seen me in the stable at that moment, if they hadn't looked at me like they did, no one would ever have guessed. Even Bobs was looking at me. Mum knew what I'd done the moment she caught my eye. She came over and explained that I had to give Little Josh up, had to say where he was, that every cloven-hoofed animal on the farm had to be killed. There couldn't be any exceptions. I buried my face in Ruby's neck. I was sobbing too much to say anything. I knew it was over, that it was hopeless, that sooner or later they would find him. So I told them I'd fetch him out myself. And that's what I did. I carried him out. He didn't struggle, just bleated a little as I handed him over. The man in white who took him off me had a face. It was Brad and his eyes were full of tears. "It'll be very quick," he said. "He won't know anything. He won't feel anything." And he carried him away around the back of the shed. A few moments later there was a shot. I felt it like a knife in my heart.

This evening the farm is still, is silent. The fields are empty, and it's raining.

Foot-and-mouth disease

Foot-and-mouth disease (FMD) is a highly infectious disease that affects cattle, sheep, goats, pigs and deer. It is fatal in about 5 per cent of cases. Animals suffer high fever for two or three days, after which they develop blisters in the mouth and on the feet. These may break open, causing lameness. FMD is spread by predators, and through contact with contaminated farming equipment, vehicles, clothing and feed.

On Monday 19 February 2001, FMD was detected in pigs in an abattoir in Essex. No one at that point realized that the outbreak stemmed from pigs eating infected animal feed in Northumbria. It was already incubating in more than fifty locations, in fifteen counties, from Devon to Dumfries and Galloway. The European Commission immediately banned all British milk, meat and livestock exports until the disease had been contained. Farming communities were thrown into turmoil and financial hardship. Tourism slumped. Rural Britain was in crisis.

Methods of controlling FMD include vaccination and stopping the sale of animals and meat. Keeping animals on the farms and banning markets is another control. Sometimes infected and at-risk animals are slaughtered.

Since the 1950s, it has been accepted that killing infected animals is a crude and primitive way of trying to clear up the disease. After an earlier outbreak in 1967, the official Ministry of Agriculture report addressed the human costs of killing the animals: "We recognize the mental anguish it may cause ... the shattering disaster, not computable in terms of money, that it may bring to a farmer who has to see the work of a lifetime destroyed in a day." According to some, the decision to kill herds is often based more on money and politics, rather than good science. Nevertheless, in March 2001, the same radical and controversial policy of wholesale slaughter was announced, including a three-kilometre "killing zone" around any outbreak. This ignored the fears expressed by the Chief Veterinary Officer that this policy might not be practical, or even legal.

Some of the personal experiences of having stock killed were especially grim. A mistake in a map grid reference, where a nearby farm was mistakenly thought to have FMD, caused the deaths of Philip Herd's livestock and even of his children's pets. Ange Chudley returned home to find men rounding up the family's animals for slaughter: "The farm was lambing at the time – the newborns had to go straight to slaughter. I was devastated. Every time you shut your eyes you just see dead animals." More than 3,000 of their animals were destroyed. Later, the neighbour's farm was found to have been uninfected.

Although farmers who had animals slaughtered received financial compensation, Eurwyn Edwards, director of a Welsh agricultural college, commented: "Farmers may have taken twenty or thirty years to build up their dairy herd. It's not only the animals they lost – but their produce for months afterwards." Nobody costed out the value of a lifetime's work and the massive personal impact on families losing their living and their future hopes. Many people suffered great stress and mental illnesses due to the terrible devastation in their lives and communities.

By the end of October 2001, more than 2,000 premises had been declared infected, and up to ten million animals had been slaughtered. The outbreak had been one of the worst the UK had ever seen. Many human lives, communities and livelihoods were irremediably damaged. There was a widespread lack of confidence in the Ministry of Agriculture and in the government's response to such crises. In Devon alone, more than 1,500 jobs were lost, and business bankruptcies rose by 50 per cent. The cost to farming nationally was £3 billion, and over £250 million was lost to the tourist industry.

Children's memories of that gruesome time still resonate with pain and confusion. Leigh Warne and sister Suzanne (twelve and fourteen at the time) remember: "It was the smell of the pyres you couldn't get away from." They were on their best behaviour as their parents tried to get through the crisis. "We had a scare - a sheep was found foaming at the mouth. You could see the fear in Mum and Dad. They were so quiet."

It was a false alarm.

Listen to
the Moon

THE DREAM

Listen to the Moon began, in a way, a very long time ago, in 1950. Clare, my wife, was a small girl of eight then, living in a large rambling house called Silverbeck, very near to where London Airport is now. She had chicken-pox. In those days, children who caught chickenpox or measles or scarlet fever were often isolated, to prevent other children from catching it. (I remember spending two weeks in my boarding-school sanatorium myself, in bed with the measles. Good fun it was. No lessons!)

Anyway, Clare was at home with her chickenpox. She was kept in a guest room down a corridor, away from everyone else, not allowed to play with her sisters. Her meals were brought to her, but otherwise, the days were long and tedious, and she soon became bored. In the

335

room, there was an old chest of drawers, and one day, because there was nothing else to do, and she'd already read lots of books and done lots of drawings by then, she thought she would see if there was anything interesting hidden away in it. There were socks, lots of them, and shirts and pillows – all her father's. She rummaged through, and suddenly came across something at the bottom of the drawer. A large medal, not shining silver or brass, but a rather dull grim brown. She picked it up. It was made of a heavy metal of some kind, and cold to the touch. It wasn't at all like other medals. No king's head, no laurel leaves, no ribbon. Instead, there was a strange image on it, in relief, which was difficult at first to make out. And there were letters and words too that she couldn't really understand. But the image was beginning to make sense to her. It was of a great ship sinking beneath the waves. There were people drowning in the sea; and on the deck of the ship, she could clearly make out shells and guns. She turned it over in her hand. On the back, the image was even more horrifying. A queue of people were lining up to buy tickets, obviously for the voyage on the ship. But the man selling them the tickets was a skeleton, his head a skull. Upset, afraid, Clare put it back in the drawer, and didn't look at it again. It was too sad, too gruesome. But she did not forget it.

Years later, quite some time after we were married, her father died, and she discovered he had left her this very chest of drawers. Opening the drawers, she discovered that all the clothes were gone, but the medal was still there. She remembered it instantly and showed it to me. LUSITANIA, the letters read, and then there were some words in German I did not understand. I knew there had been a huge ship, a passenger liner, of this name sunk in the First World War. But that was all I knew. The images on the medal haunted me, just as they had haunted Clare when she was little.

Over the years, entirely because of this medal, I began to piece together the story of the sinking of the *Lusitania*. The more I found out about it, the more the thought of all

Clare's Lusitania medal

those innocent families who lost their lives – over a thousand of them – and the suddenness of the sinking horrified me. This great ship, struck by one torpedo from a German submarine, went down in just eighteen minutes after a huge explosion. The *Titanic* had taken over three hours to sink. I happened to go many years later to a book festival in Kinsale on the south coast of Ireland, close to where the *Lusitania* had gone down in May 1915, just twelve miles out to sea. Many of those who perished are buried here, and there is a memorial to them. It was from Kinsale, I heard, that many dozens of boats put out to sea to try to rescue survivors, and, sadly, to pick up the bodies of the dead. The terrible story of the sinking of the *Lusitania* became vivid for me all over again.

I began, after this next visit, to read more extensively about the subject, kept taking out this medal, holding it, looking at it. I was beginning to believe I might write one day about this tragedy, but I knew it was still all too distant from me, too lost in the statistics of the losses, in the propaganda war between the British and the Germans that followed the sinking. It was the passengers who drowned and the survivors that interested me, not so much the politics of it. Yet the politics and the propaganda had to be part of the story I was beginning to think I might tell.

The medal, I knew by now, was part of the propaganda war. It had been brought out by the Germans to defend their part in the sinking. They had, it's quite true, issued a warning before the *Lusitania* sailed, had published it in newspapers in New York, making it clear that they had good cause to attack the ship because they knew that as well as the 2,000 passengers and crew on board, she would also be carrying weapons and armaments. The British denied it. The passengers must have been worried, of course, but at the time it was dismissed as German propaganda. Each side was doing all they could to demonize the other – this always happens before wars, in wars and after wars.

The controversy over the sinking of this great and beautiful ship is still alive a hundred years later, I discovered. Over a hundred Americans perished in the sinking, and America was neutral in the war at the time. They were enraged. The world was enraged. This horrible tragedy might well have helped bring the Americans into the war two years later, an intervention that ultimately brought the war to an end, to defeat for Germany. But it wasn't the controversy itself that I wanted to write about. I wanted to know about the passengers, about why they were on the ship, about their stories.

Then, by happenstance, I came across the remarkable story of how, three hours after the ship went down, one of the rescue boats from Kinsale, out searching for survivors, had come across the grand piano from the dining room of the ship floating on the ocean, and on it a survivor. I could not discover who this was, nor actually whether it was a survivor or a body. But it was the image of this unknown passenger lying there on the piano that I could not get out of my head. Now my dream could begin. My survivor would be a girl from New York crossing the Atlantic with her mother to see her father, a Canadian soldier, lying wounded in hospital in England. Whoever she had been, I would rescue her, tell her story.

And into this dream, and this always happens in my story-making, other stories wove themselves in, other places. I had read that, at the time, it had been often reported that German submarines would not sink passenger ships without warning. It was quite common practice for a submarine to surface, to warn the ship that she was about to be sunk by torpedo, but then to leave time for passengers and crew to leave the ship safely. There were even stories of enemy submarines, after a ship had been sunk, towing lifeboats full of surviving sailors nearer to the safety of the shore. There were still, it seems, even in the middle of this terrible war of attrition, instances of great humanity.

Then, looking at a map one day of the seas off the south coast of Ireland, I noticed that the nearest landfall in England was the Isles of Scilly. Well, I know the Isles of Scilly really well, every island almost, and some of them are uninhabited. One, St Helen's, has just one building still standing, clearly visible from the sea. It could be easily mistaken for an inhabited island. But it isn't. The building was put up two hundred years ago as a place of quarantine. Sick passengers with infectious diseases would be dropped off there, to recover, or often die, before the ship docked on the mainland – this to avoid the spread of disease. I've been in that roofless pest house, walked the island, eaten the blackberries, climbed the rocks, found the well. Someone could survive there for weeks, months even, undiscovered. I might have to research how it was to be a passenger on the *Lusitania*, sailing from New York to Liverpool that May, how life was on board a German U-boat, but the Scilly Isles I knew well, and I'd been longing to set a story there again.

As I get older, I understand more and more how essential memory is to our lives, to our sense of who we are, who we once were. It can be in old age that we begin to lose our memory – that is, after all, quite common – or it can be some grief or trauma that shuts ourselves off from our past. I wanted to explore this, to find out more about the healing of the mind, the rewiring of lost memory. Is memory once lost, lost for ever, or is there hope of recovery? And if so, in what circumstances is this truly likely to happen? So, tell the story, I thought, in such a way that the reader knows the past of the survivor of the *Lusitania*, the child found on that piano floating on the ocean, but she herself does not. The horror of the sinking has traumatized her, frozen her memory of all that happened, all she has seen and indeed who she is. My whole story would be her search to remember, to find herself again.

But she will need help in this. So who might there be to offer this help? Reading the history of Scilly at the time

341

of the First World War, I came across the story of a doctor on St Mary's, a man universally loved and respected because of his care for his patients at such a difficult time. This doctor would have his part to play in my story, so would a fisherman's family on Bryher, so would the school at Tresco. So would a horse. I knew how well horses can heal, how strong trust and affection can be between horse and rider. I have witnessed it. I have written about it in other stories.

Thinking around the subject, deep in my dreamtime, before I ever put pen to paper, I happened to be listening to a CD of a favourite piece of music: Mozart's "Andante Grazioso". I was thinking: Piano, piano, floating on the sea, a lifesaver for my survivor, but perhaps not only in the way I had first imagined. What if she played the piano? What, I wondered, might be her favourite piece to play on the piano? This! What would she want to hear and play over and over again, what would stay in her memory when all else seems to have been lost? Mozart's "Andante Grazioso", without any doubt.

That was it! I would have this supremely beautiful piece of music in her head, have it permeate her story, become essential to the healing of her memory, to her finding of herself, the key to the unfolding of her entire story.

LISTEN TO THE MOON

As Alfie stepped tentatively through the doorway into the ruins of the Pest House, the whimpering stopped. There was no sign of anyone inside, nothing but bracken and brambles. At the far end of the building, in under the chimney, there was a fireplace, covered in dried bracken, a thick carpet of it, almost as if someone had been making a bed.

A sudden bird flew up out of a niche in the wall, an explosion of fluttering that set Alfie's heart pounding. He pushed his way through the thick undergrowth that had long since made the ruins their own, brambles tearing at his shirt and trousers as he passed. Jim held back at the doorway. "No one here, Alfie," he whispered. "You can see there isn't."

But Alfie was pointing into the corner of the fireplace, and waving his hand at his father to be quiet.

"Don't you worry none," Alfie said, treading softly as he went, and slowly. "We'll have you out of here and home before you know it. We got our boat. Won't hurt you none, promise. S'all right, honest. You can come out now."

He had seen a face, a bone-white face, peering through the bracken, a child, a girl, hollow-cheeked, and with dark lank hair down to her shoulders. She was cowering there in the corner of the building, her fist in her mouth, her eyes staring up at him, wide with terror. She had a grey blanket round her shoulders. Her face was tear-stained, and she was shaking uncontrollably.

Alfie crouched down where he was, keeping his distance – he did not want to alarm her. He did not recognize her. If she had been from the islands, he would have known her for certain – he knew all the children on Scilly, everyone did, whichever island they came from. "Hello?" he said. "You got a name then, have you?" She shrank from him, breathing hard, coughing again now, and shivering under her blanket. "I'm Alfie. You needn't be afeared of me, girl." She was staring at Jim now, breathing hard. "That's Father. He won't hurt you any more'n I will. You hungry, are you? You been here long? You got a terrible cough on you. Where d'you come from then? How d'you get here, girl?" She said nothing, simply crouched there, frozen in her fear, her eyes darting wildly from Jim to Alfie, from Alfie to Jim. Alfie reached out slowly, and touched her blanket. "It's wet through," he said.

Her bare feet were covered in sand and mud, and what little he could see of her dress was nothing but tatters and rags. There were empty limpet shells scattered all about her feet, and a few broken eggshells, gulls' eggs they were. "We got mackerel for tea back home," he went on. "Mother does it beautiful, rolled in egg and oats, and we got bread-and-butter pudding for afters too. You'll like it. We got our boat down on the beach. You want to come with us?" He inched his way towards her, holding out his hand. "Can you walk, girl?"

She sprang up then like a frightened fawn, leapt past him and was stumbling through the bracken towards the doorway. She must have tripped because she suddenly disappeared into the undergrowth. Jim found her moments later, lying face down, unconscious. He turned her over. There were scratches and cuts all over her legs. One ankle was swollen and bruised. She wasn't breathing. Alfie was there on his knees beside her.

"Is she dead, Father?" he breathed. "Is she dead?" Jim felt her neck. He could feel no pulse. With panic rising in his chest, he remembered then how Alfie had fallen once down on to rocks when he was little, how he'd run all the way home with Alfie in his arms, quite sure he must be dead. He remembered how calm Mary had been, how she had taken charge at once, laid Alfie out on the kitchen table, put her ear to his mouth and felt his breath on her skin. He did the same now, put his ear to the girl's mouth, felt the warm breath, and knew there was life in her yet. He had to get her home fast. Mary would know what to do with her.

"You get to the boat, Alfie," he said. "Quick. I'll bring her."

He picked her up, and ran out of the Pest House, along the path to the dunes. She was light and limp and damp in his arms. He could feel she was little more than skin and bones. By the time he got there, Alfie had the boat in the water. He was standing in the shallows, holding it. "You get in, son," Jim said. "You look after her. I'll row." They wrapped her in Jim's coat, and laid her down with her head on Alfie's lap. "Hold her close," Jim told him. "We got to keep her warm as best we can." He pushed off then, leaping into the boat and gathering the oars almost in one movement.

Jim rowed like a man possessed out into the swell of the open ocean past the lighthouse on Round Island, and at long last into the calm of Tresco Channel. Every few moments as he rowed, he'd glance down at the girl as she lay there in Alfie's arms, her head bleeding, her eyes closed. Jim could see no life in her. She was sleeping as if she would never wake.

Alfie talked to her all the time; he hardly stopped. Holding her tight to him as the boat reared and rolled through the waves, he kept calling to her, willing her to wake up and open her eyes, telling her it wouldn't be long now, that she'd be all right. And sometimes Jim would join in too, whenever he could find the breath to do so, begging her to live, pleading with her, yelling at her even. "Wake up, girl! For Chrissake, wake up! Don't you dare go and die on us, you hear. Don't you dare!"

The Lusitania

In the early part of the First World War, most people in the United States were convinced that Europe's war was not their fight. President Wilson did not believe that America's interests were threatened by a European war – as long as trade was allowed to continue unhindered.

In May 1915, 20 kilometres off the coast of Ireland, a German U-boat sank the British liner, the *Lusitania*. There were 128 Americans among the 1,198 casualties. With the benefit of hindsight, the attack may be seen as one of Germany's biggest mistakes of the war, because, afterwards, American attitudes to involvement slowly changed. President Wilson repeatedly warned that the US would not tolerate unrestricted submarine warfare and demanded an end to attacks on passenger ships. Germany complied for a time.

Germany needed to prevent goods from America being imported by Britain, while also placating the US, keeping it neutral and out of the war. Britain wanted equipment and money from the States, and, ideally, Britain wanted the US to join the fight against Germany. Following the sinking of the *Lusitania*, a propaganda war ensued for the hearts and minds of the US people and government.

The Germans argued that they had given fair warning that ships travelling to Britain were in danger. On 1 May a small notice, placed by the German Embassy, appeared on the shipping page of the *New York Times*, directly under the announcement of the sailing of the *Lusitania*. The notice warned that Germany and Britain were at war and that a war zone existed around the British Isles. British ships were "liable to destruction", and people sailing in them "do so at their own risk".

Previously, U-boat captains had often surfaced and allowed crews and passengers of unarmed boats to take to lifeboats before the vessel was sunk. What the British public were not told was that the British Admiralty had recently issued orders directing merchant ships to escape from U-boats when possible, but "if a submarine comes up suddenly close ahead of you with obvious hostile intention, steer straight for her at your utmost speed..." Armed steamers were instructed to open fire on a submarine, even if it had not yet fired, which therefore meant U-boats would be less likely to surface and give warning before attacking. After the sinking, the British press made much of the fact that the *Lusitania* was torpedoed without warning.

Of course, the British press put the blame firmly on the Germans. The *Liverpool Courier* wrote: "The disaster to the *Lusitania*, in which helpless non-combatants were foully murdered, has affected Liverpool in particular. By one coward blow hundreds of homes in the city have been bereft." There were riots in Liverpool and other British cities. Germans and their businesses were attacked.

The Germans blamed the British for taking passengers on board ship when it was "known" there were 5,400 crates of ammunition in the hold of the *Lusitania*. The claim that the *Lusitania* might have been carrying shells and cartridges was not made known to the British public at the time. After the single torpedo struck, there was a further explosion, which many believe was caused by other illicit munitions cargo (military equipment), such as guncotton or aluminium powder.

The captain of the U-boat was awarded a medal by the German Kaiser (the Emperor). This further inflamed passions in Britain and the US, as did an (untrue) rumour that German schoolchildren had been awarded a day's holiday to celebrate the sinking.

Some see the incident as a turning point in the rules of war. Britain and the US certainly used the tragedy as a hugely successful propaganda campaign. When the US eventually declared war on Germany in April 1917, recruitment posters urged: REMEMBER THE *LUSITANIA*! A poster showed a mother submerged in blue-green water with a baby clasped in her arms, above the single blood-red word: ENLIST. The British also had a recruitment poster: TAKE UP THE SWORD OF JUSTICE – AVENGE THE *LUSITANIA*.

Successive British governments denied that there were munitions on board. But in 1982, the British government warned divers that there had been explosives on board. An estimated four million bullets were found in the wreck, but no evidence of other munitions. What else was on board we may never know. The British government still keeps secret some of the documents from the incident, including some of the signals passed between the Admiralty and the *Lusitania*. Such records as are available are often missing critical pages, so the idea of a conspiracy, or cover-up, will continue. The *Lusitania* herself is unlikely to give up any more of her secrets. She will soon disappear as time, tide and rust take their final toll.

My Father Is a Polar Bear

THE DREAM

Consciously or subconsciously, I roam around in all my stories, and often by name too. Autobiography creeps in somehow, often uninvited. It just happens, and I am not aware of it until after I have written it. There are, I know, far too many Michaels in my books. Sometimes I have very deliberately placed myself and my name there at the heart of the action (as in the novel *Kensuke's Kingdom*, and my short stories, *Half a Man* and *Meeting Cézanne*). Maybe this reveals a lack of imagination; but my thinking is that, for me, it is all the better to be there inside my tale, if I am going to write it, if I am going to believe in the story as I am telling it. It seems to work.

There are times when I simply use incidents and episodes of my youth as part of the story, as I did, for

353

instance, as Michael who runs away from boarding school in *The Butterfly Lion*, or in my short story *My One and Only Great Escape*, as the boy in *The War of Jenkins' Ear* (all three of them me, at the same school, my prep school in Sussex). It is not uncommon to find a boy or a girl central to one of my stories who feels isolated in the world, with a father who is absent or remote, a figure of authority, sometimes overly rigid, to be revered and feared. It is mother and child closeness that I knew as a child, with a father figure always more distant, geographically and emotionally, and this is reflected in books such as *Why the Whales Came* or *The Wreck of the Zanzibar*. There is often a longing for an absent father to be there, for a faraway father's love, as in *The Amazing Story of Adolphus Tips* or *Billy the Kid*.

It is no accident either that in so many of my stories the child finds himself or herself completely alone in the world, without parents altogether, having to manage, to survive: in *Kensuke's Kingdom*, in *Running Wild*, in *Alone on a Wide, Wide Sea*, in *King of the Cloud Forests*. Many children, myself included, do feel this overwhelming sense of isolation sometimes, even when surrounded by family and friends. Of course, it is not unusual for children in children's books to find themselves alone, separated from their parents. Orphan heroes are common enough in stories. It is a convention often used. Alice has no parent holding her hand in *Alice's Adventures in Wonderland*, nor has Paddington in his adventures.

Parents are nowhere to be seen, or they are a long way away, in Peru! Jim Hawkins in *Treasure Island* is not encumbered by the presence of parents out on his great adventure. He does not need them. He does not even miss them. Any story about a child alone in the world gives that child the freedom to discover and explore, to run wild, and it gives freedom also to the writer to create a hero or heroine, entirely uninhibited by parents, away from both their love and their control, a story in which anything can happen, in which parents cannot interfere.

Sometimes, though, I have kept even closer in the telling of my stories to the historical and actual happenings of my youth, allowing my childhood to be the story, not simply the dreamtime for it, but to be the story itself, and so close to the truth of my memory that it is hardly fiction at all, but rather autobiographical truth – embellished, certainly, fictionalized, yes, but not to distort the truth, rather to tease out a different kind of truth. Memory, as we know, is notoriously fickle and unreliable, especially when it comes to childhood memories. I have discovered from time to time, from the evidence of others who were there, that the factual history of my childhood does not necessarily coincide with my memory. Memory can exaggerate truth, or deny it altogether. But for the making of stories this does not matter.

Two of my favourite stories are so connected to my memory, so personal, that they almost wrote themselves. No research was needed, very little dreamtime, scarcely any leap of imagination or invention. They grew almost in their entirety out of the places and people I grew up with, that made me who I am – the writer I am too, come to that.

I have a photo at home – I am looking at it now – of the wedding of my mother and father in 1940. They are standing outside the porch of the church at Radlett in Hertfordshire, the happy couple side by side, my mother radiant, my father slightly sheepish, and looking rather uncomfortable in his wartime corporal's uniform, and, alongside them, not looking quite so happy, their parents – my grandparents – and various aunts and uncles. An ordinary enough family photo, but not for me. All during my childhood – indeed, for most of my young adult life – I did not know this photograph at all, and that was because this marriage was a marriage never mentioned, a marriage that had never happened. A taboo marriage.

The circumstances were common enough in wartime Britain. Mother and two children isolated, left vulnerable at home, the father abroad away at the war, the strain of separation, the stress of war, weighing heavily. And then a new man appears in the mother's life, dashing, attentive, passionate, insistent; and when the father comes home at the end of the war, he discovers his place has been taken. He tries for some kind of a reconciliation, but it is too late. There is a divorce. And divorce in those days was considered shameful, not to be spoken of, to be kept hidden.

My new stepfather, Jack Morpurgo, gave my brother Pieter and me his surname, and there followed two new children born to my mother. We were all of us Morpurgos now to the outside world. But as we grew up, Pieter and I knew we weren't, that we were different. We learnt also not to ask questions about this. As for my father, he decided, when I was three and Pieter a little older, that as we did not know him at all – he had been away at the war for all but a few weeks of our infancy – he would not stay around playing the occasional father role. Better, he thought, given the circumstances, to absent himself totally, saying only that he wished his surname, Bridge, to be always part of our name (I am Michael Andrew Bridge Morpurgo), and that if we ever wanted to see him later on, when we were grown up, then he would always be overjoyed to see us. None of this arrangement was, of course, known to us throughout our childhood.

So we grew up as Morpurgos in our new family, the divorce hidden and unspoken, with a new father. Our father, our real father, was never spoken of, was air-brushed out. He became a phantom father. Of course, within the wider family, the divorce was thought to be shameful and scurrilous – my mother suffered from this all her life – but very few outside the family knew about it, or, if they did, they were quiet about it. The family's dark secret was kept. My real father's name, Tony Van Bridge, was never spoken. We knew, Pieter and I, that he was an actor (as our mother had been), and that he had

357

emigrated to Canada. That was about all.

Pieter and I talked of him from time to time, and resented the pretence of being one family to the rest of the world. But we went along with it. It seemed very important to our mother that we should. About Tony, about her first marriage, she remained silent. Then, at an Easter gathering of family and friends one year (I was about eighteen at the time, I think), we were all sitting down at teatime to watch a television play on the BBC, of *Great Expectations* – in black and white in those days, of course. Television was relatively new to the family. When we watched, which was not that often, we generally watched together, all of us there. My stepfather was keen on Dickens, keen we should all be keen on Dickens too, so that was why we were watching.

The opening scene is well enough known. Young Pip is making his way home through the graveyard, in the half-dark. He is terrified of every rustling leaf, of the whine and whistle of the wind, of the owl hooting, almost running now to get out of the graveyard. Then, up from behind a gravestone rears the hideous figure of Magwitch, an escaped convict, who grabs him. Even though we were waiting for it, knew it was coming, it was a moment of horror for all of us sitting there watching.

Suddenly, my mother grasps my arm. "Oh my God," she breathes. "That's your father, that's Tony!" Well, no one was paying any attention any more to what happened to young Pip on the television. All eyes were on my mother, and on me and my brother. The unspoken had been spoken. All those years of pretence were undone in one single moment. Tony was in the room. Our father was in the room.

If I am honest, I recall very little of what happened next, but, of course, the genie was out of the bottle and could not be put back. It took a while, and some awkward discussions, before our mother could be persuaded to contact Tony in Canada and arrange a meeting. So, in the end, we did get together, one of those dreadful teatimes when the tension crackled and the teacups rattled and the teaspoons clinked, and no one knew quite what to say. But after that first tentative meeting, Tony came over every few years to visit us, and, finally, we went to see him in Canada. He was an easy man, gentle and kind, unassuming and rather sad sometimes in his demeanour. He had found a wonderful life on the stage, becoming very known and well thought of in Canada, at Stratford, Ontario and at the Shaw Festival in Niagara. I last saw him when he was in his eighties. He was still acting. His whole life was in acting. His company had become his family and he had become their mentor, their grandpa. So, when we went to see him we were treated very much as one of the family, which we were, of course. He had married again, but his second wife had died tragically. And then he married for a third time in his seventies, but it did not last. I think, though he never said it, that he never stopped loving my mother. When he died, a few years ago now, his wishes were that his ashes should be divided, half to be sprinkled on a beach in Bermuda, where he and his second wife had walked a lot together, and half to be laid in the earth in our garden in Devon with my mother's ashes. It was a love that never died.

From time to time, during his life, and since he died, we would come across, or be sent, reviews of his plays. Then, after his death, and quite by chance, when visiting a friend's house, I happened upon a huge pile of magazines – hundreds of copies of *Theatre World*. I picked up the one on the top, dated 1949, and was flipping through. The pages fell open at a spread that was immediately interesting to me. There was a photograph of two polar bears in costume, both about to eat a child. I read underneath that this was from a production at the Young Vic of Hans Christian Andersen's *The Snow Queen*. Then I read the actor's name. The polar bear on the left, the fiercest-looking one, was Tony Van Bridge. Me dad! So my father was a convict, AND a polar bear. What genes I have inside me!

Just tell it down, I thought. Let it tumble out of you. The whole story has been waiting long enough inside you. Call it *My Father Is a Polar Bear* rather than *My Father Is a Convict*. He'd like polar bear better.

Almost entirely autobiographical too was *Homecoming*, originally called *Singing for Mrs Pettigrew*. But this story is more about place and people, about the childhood home I loved. Why we moved as a family to Bradwell-on-Sea, a seaside village on the coast of Essex, I don't really know. It was a rather grand, but crumbling Georgian house, called New Hall, right in the middle of the village. My brother Pieter and I shared an attic at the top of the house – slightly

'One man in his time plays many parts' –
my father, the actor, Tony Van Bridge

separate from the rest of the family – but we liked it. It was our world. We used to go on long cycle rides exploring, past the US Air Force base, down the road to St Peter Ad Muram, St Peter's-on-the-Wall, one of the oldest Saxon chapels in Britain. We had fights with local children who resented us because we went away to school and spoke differently, and lived in a big house. We went camping, once in the garden of a strange lady who lived on her own in a railway carriage by the sea. I loved the marshes, the sea wall, and the wind, and the long and happy hours spent roaming free. I loved the wilderness of this garden, cricket on the front lawn, table tennis in the spidery barn. There were good times, despite that old family secret, and I felt for the first time in my life that I belonged in a close community. We knew everyone and everyone knew us.

But then the community fractured, shattered all around us. There was news that the government wanted to build an atomic power station just outside the village. There were those who were for it, those who were not. My family was against it. There was fierce and public argument. Tempers frayed. We lost the argument. The plans to build went ahead. We moved out. Go there now and you will see a huge concrete wart dominating the landscape. The power station devastated a community, warmed the seawater so that the oyster beds died. It never operated at full capacity, did not produce much local employment, nor the cheap electricity promised, and was finally shut down decades ago. It remains, of course, a relic of idiotic planning, of environmental destruction, soon, I am told, to be rebuilt and renewed, this time as a new nuclear power station. Poor Bradwell.

I've been back a time or two to see the place, visited St Peter's again, tramped the seawall, felt the wind on my face, remembered. If you walk past the village houses on the way to St Peter's, as I did on my last visit, you will pass a bungalow. It's called New Clear View. Honestly! And everywhere you go, there is a view of the monster, the monster that drove us out of our home all those years ago.

MY FATHER IS A POLAR BEAR

Downstairs, the whole family were gathered in the sitting room: my mother, Douglas, Terry and my two sisters (half-sisters really, but of course no one ever called them that), Aunt Betty, now married, with twin daughters, my cousins, who were truly awful – I promise you. We were decorating the tree, or rather the twins were fighting over every single dingly-dangly glitter ball, every strand of tinsel. I was trying to fix up the Christmas tree lights which, of course, wouldn't work – again – whilst Aunty Betty was doing her best to avert a war by bribing the dreadful cousins away from the tree with a Mars bar each. It took a while, but in the end she got both of them up onto her lap, and soon they were stuffing themselves contentedly with Mars bars. Blessed peace.

This was the very first Christmas we had had the television. Given half a chance we'd have had it on all the time. But, wisely enough I suppose, Douglas had rationed us to just one programme a day over Christmas. He didn't want the Christmas celebrations interfered with by "that thing in the corner", as he called it. By common consent, we had chosen the Christmas Eve film on the BBC at five o'clock.

Five o'clock was a very long time coming that day, and when at last Douglas got up and turned on the television, it seemed to take for ever to warm up. Then, there it was on the screen: *Great Expectations* by Charles Dickens. The half-mended lights were at once discarded, the decorating abandoned, as we all settled down to watch in rapt anticipation. Maybe you know the moment: Young Pip is making his way through the graveyard at dusk, mist swirling around him, an owl screeching, gravestones rearing out of the gloom, branches like ghoulish fingers whipping at him as he passes, reaching out to snatch him. He moves through the graveyard timorously, tentatively, like a frightened fawn. Every snap of a twig, every barking fox, every *aarking* heron, sends shivers into our very souls.

Suddenly, a face! A hideous face, a monstrous face, looms up from behind a gravestone. Magwitch, the escaped convict, ancient, craggy and crooked, with long white hair and a straggly beard. A wild man with wild eyes, the eyes of a wolf.

The cousins screamed in unison, long and loud, which broke the tension for all of us and made us laugh. All except my mother.

"Oh my God," she breathed, grasping my arm. "That's your father! It is. It's him. It's Peter."

All the years of pretence, the whole long conspiracy of silence, were undone in that one moment. The drama on the television paled into sudden insignificance. The hush in the room was palpable.

Douglas coughed. "I think I'll fetch some more logs," he said. And my two half-sisters went out with him, in solidarity I think. So did Aunty Betty and the twins; and that left my mother, Terry and me alone together.

I could not take my eyes off the screen. After a while I said to Terry, "He doesn't look much like a pixie to me."

"Doesn't look much like a polar bear either," Terry replied. At Magwitch's every appearance I tried to see through his make-up (I just hoped it *was* make-up!) to discover how my father really looked. It was impossible. My polar bear father, my pixie father, had become my convict father.

Until the credits came up at the end my mother never said a word. Then all she said was, "Well, the potatoes won't peel themselves, and I've got the Brussels sprouts to do as well." Christmas was a very subdued affair that year, I can tell you.

They say you can't put a genie back in the bottle. Not true. No one in the family ever spoke of the incident afterwards – except Terry and me, of course. Everyone behaved as if it had never happened. Enough was enough. Terry and I decided it was time to broach the whole forbidden subject with our mother, in private. We waited until the furore of Christmas was over, and caught her alone in the kitchen one evening. We asked her point-blank to tell us about him, our "first" father, our "missing" father.

"I don't want to talk about him," she said. She wouldn't even look at us. "All I know is that he lives somewhere in Canada now. It was another life. I was another person then. It's not important." We tried to press her, but that was all she would tell us.

Michael's family

Michael's real father, Tony, was not really a polar bear, of course. But the secrecy surrounding his existence hid him from view as effectively as the polar bear costume in the story.

In the late 1930s, divorce was very rare. Then the upheaval of the Second World War brought about changes of attitude throughout Britain, and views on marriage and divorce were part of this change. The enforced separations of war had torn families apart and there had been a startling outbreak of unhappiness, adultery and collapsing marriages. The idea that marriage was a stabilizing force in society was shaken.

In October 1943, when Michael was born, the Archbishops of Canterbury and York had spoken out against "moral laxity", reminding Christians that promiscuity and adultery were sins that destroyed homes and visited "years of suffering" on children. By 1949, a poll found that 57 per cent "more or less approved" of divorce as a regrettable necessity.

Michael's mother, Kippe, was a churchgoer. The refusal of the local bishop to allow her to take communion after her divorce added to her sense of guilt. None of Kippe's family attended her second marriage to Jack in 1947. The newly married couple must have felt very isolated.

All those involved came from a generation who thought it disgraceful to "wash dirty linen in public". This was a time when people were very aware of what other people would think. Divorce was something to be ashamed of, never to be discussed with the children and to be hidden if possible.

By the 1970s there were thousands of divorces a year in England and Wales. And today divorce is widespread and socially accepted, as are living together and having children outside marriage.

Parenting roles have also changed drastically since when Michael was a child. Fathers and step-fathers used to be seen as the source of stability, discipline, and often as the family's main bread-winner. They were role models for hard work and good behaviour. For the war generation, fathers were not expected to be as close to their children. Few fathers attended their children's births.

Much of the secrecy about Michael's birth father was due to the desire of Jack and Kippe Morpurgo for Jack to be viewed as the "real" father of the family, but there were also the social factors. The disgrace of divorce was empha-sized within the extended family when Kippe's father, the Belgian poet and writer, Emile Cammaerts, published a treatise on marriage.

Adultery was a "sin"; second marriages were a "sham", and put a child's soul in danger. Emile and his wife Tita were children of broken marriages and both had an almost pathological horror of divorce.

The Cammaerts and the Morpurgo families had more similarities than they realized in the other secrets they kept. Emile Cammaerts had been an ardent Belgian Nationalist and atheist, and had spent time in an anarchist commune. He converted to Christianity and took on many of the outward trappings of the English establishment. Jack Morpurgo, in his autobiography, claimed that his father "like his ancestors for several generations, was Cockney-born". His father was, in fact, Dutch, and, like Jack's mother, from Amsterdam. Like Kippe's father, he too took on the mantle of the bowler-hatted English city gent, joined the Anglican church and did all he could to help his son become an "insider" in English society.

It seems that Jack Morpurgo was taught to hide the past until secrecy became habitual. The huge secret was that the family was Jewish; Jack's parents had been married in a synagogue. Those cousins and distant relations who stayed behind in Amsterdam mostly perished in the concentration camps of the Second World War, but they were never referred to. The next generation was unaware of their Jewish origins, long after the prevalent anti-Semitism of Jack's youth had waned. Worldwide, many Jews did everything they could to conceal Jewish origins in the early years of the twentieth century.

Maybe Tony became just another secret in a family used to keeping secrets. Michael says that he "was never spoken of, was airbrushed out. He became a phantom father".

<u>My father is a polar bear</u>

(or)

(A very subdued affair)

Tracking down a polar bear shouldn't be that difficult. You just follow the pawprints – easy enough for any competent Innuit. My father is a polar bear, ~~so therefore, you might think, he should have been easy enough to track down. But he wasn't. You might think too, that if my father was a polar bear, then logically I'd have to be a polar bear myself. But I'm not. Honestly I'm not.~~ Now if you had a father who was a polar bear, you'd be curious, wouldn't you? You'd go looking for him. That's what I did, I went looking for him, and I'm telling you he wasn't at all easy to find. But then I'm no Innuit, I suppose.

In a way I was lucky, because I always had two fathers. ~~One was a polar bear, one wasn't.)~~ I had a father who <u>was</u> there – I called him Douglas; and one who wasn't ~~there and he was~~ the one I'd never even met – the polar

1

me, everyone in the house

it saved a lot of awkward

about it anyway. Having

e, troubled me deeply.

lar bear, I was even-

you up to date a

w be useful here.

later found out,

d World War.

?) While my

th a dashing

ppens a lot

cuated to

and my

g in those days, I

ing to walk and talk and do my business in the right

Acknowledgements

Photo credits: p. 12 © Ali Bannister; p. 90 © Brian Robert Marshall. This work is licensed under the Creative Commons Attribution-Share Alike 2.0 Generic Licence. To view a copy of this licence, visit http://creativecommons.org/licenses/by-sa/2.0/ or send a letter to Creative Commons, 171 Second Street, Suite 300, San Francisco, California, 94105, USA; p. 145 Chelsea pensioners © 2015 McDowall Photography; p. 167 Photo by Dan Kitwood/Getty Images; p. 223 courtesy of The Savoy Hotel; p. 274 courtesy of Belfast Zoo; p. 315 © Imperial War Museums (EPH 6354); p. 351 © Imperial War Museums (Art.IWM PST 13654)

Extracts taken from the following books by Michael Morpurgo:

War Horse, first published 1982 by Kaye and Ward Ltd
Why the Whales Came, first published 1985 by William Heinemann Ltd
The Wreck of the Zanzibar, first published 1995 by William Heinemann Ltd
My Friend Walter, first published 1988 by William Heinemann Ltd
Waiting for Anya, first published 1990 by William Heinemann Ltd
The Dancing Bear, first published 1994 by HarperCollins Publishers Ltd
The Butterfly Lion, first published 1996 by HarperCollins Publishers Ltd
Kensuke's Kingdom, first published 1999 by William Heinemann Ltd
Billy the Kid, first published 2000 by Pavilion Books Ltd
Private Peaceful, first published 2003 by HarperCollins Publishers Ltd
The Amazing Story of Adolphus Tips, first published 2005 by HarperCollins Publishers Ltd
I Believe in Unicorns, first published 2004 as a short story in *The Times*; longer version published 2005 by Walker Books Ltd
Alone on a Wide Wide Sea, first published 2006 by HarperCollins Publishers Ltd
Kaspar: Prince of Cats, first published 2008 by HarperCollins Publishers Ltd
The Mozart Question, first published 2006 in *Singing for Mrs Pettigrew: A Storymaker's Journey* by Walker Books Ltd; published 2007 by Walker Books Ltd
Running Wild, first published 2009 by HarperCollins Publishers Ltd
An Elephant in the Garden, first published 2010 by HarperCollins Publishers Ltd
Shadow, first published 2010 by HarperCollins Publishers Ltd
Little Manfred, first published 2011 by HarperCollins Publishers Ltd
Out of the Ashes, first published 2001 by Macmillan's Children's Books Ltd
Listen to the Moon, first published 2014 by HarperCollins Publishers Ltd
My Father Is a Polar Bear, first published 2000 in *From Hereabout Hill* by Egmont UK Ltd; published 2015 by Walker Books Ltd

With thanks to Seven Stories for materials from the Morpurgo archive.